MW01536443

THEY CALLED ME

"The Ugly American Girl"

By Ellen Patnaude

a memoir

Dedication

This book is dedicated to Mireya.
Simply put, without her, I would not have survived.

It is also dedicated to my children, that they may know the story one day of how I became the person that raised them.

All names, except that of the author, have been changed to protect the innocent and the guilty.

Prologue

I was up at 7 a.m., my usual time to rise. It gave me a solid two hours around the apartment before I had to leave for work in the genetics lab at the hospital in downtown Detroit.

I liked this time of morning. Though I had never really considered myself a morning person, I enjoyed listening to National Public Radio's morning news programs as I made coffee, showered, dressed and prepared for my day.

Mark was never up at this hour; he didn't have anywhere to go.

I walked into the small kitchen where the sun was just beginning to stream through the large window opposite the doorway. Last night's dinner dishes were still in the sink, leftovers still in the pan on the stove. The rule was that if I cooked, which I did most of the time, Mark was supposed to clean up. But I knew if I left for work without doing it, everything would still be there when I got home.

I pushed up the sleeves of my long-sleeved t-shirt and sighed as I carried the pan from the stove to the garbage can. *Nothing like a waste of good food*, I thought, dumping out the leftover enchiladas and refried beans I had prepared the night before.

Hard as I tried, I couldn't keep the old familiar irritation from creeping into my bones, draping over my early morning mood like a wet, moldy blanket. I had half a mind to march into the bedroom and demand that Mark get up to take care of this mess but knew it wouldn't change anything. I had tried before. So I started the coffee pot and set to scrubbing.

After a shower had washed the smell of it and the resentment out of my system, I went into the bedroom to dress for work. I stood in front of the closet, carefully considering what to wear that day as I did every day. I pulled out a few things, looked at them, changed my mind, and continued searching.

"Hey, do you think you could turn the damn radio down?" came a groggy and grumpy voice from the bed. "Some of us are trying to sleep."

"Well, some of us shouldn't leave dirty dishes behind for others to clean up and still manage to stay up half the night", I replied, not bothering to turn around. "And what productive things are on your list today, sir?"

I settled on my comfortable black pants, a cream colored long sweater and a deep red flowing vest – one of my favorite outfits. It made me feel sexy even though I had struggled with one major problem since college: I was 40 pounds overweight.

"It's too early in the morning for you to be nagging at me", Mark answered, burying his head under his pillow. I knew he hoped I would just leave soon.

I dressed quickly as I glanced at the clock; I would be late if I didn't hurry. "You know, Mark, my mom's friend that works at the high school did tell you that you could get a job in a heartbeat if you were willing to teach in the city of Detroit. Why don't you call her?"

As he began his long list of excuses for not wanting to teach full time, I tuned him out. I had heard it all before and could have recited it back to him. I finished putting on my shoes and walked out of the bedroom.

"Hey, you aren't even listening to me!" he said with indignation.

"Why bother? It's like listening to a broken record", I countered, my own anger finally creeping into my voice. "But as long as I'm the only one bringing in a paycheck around here, how about you get off your lazy ass and clean up after yourself once in a while!"

I was yelling now, the spats of the past two weeks piling up on me.

"We need groceries, laundry has to be done, and this apartment needs to be cleaned and picked up! I'm not your maid or your mother, so stop treating me like it!" I walked out the door, lighting another cigarette as I went.

The day went slowly at work. My favorite co-workers seemed to all be missing on the same day. Some were sick, others out with their kids who were sick, one was on vacation.

I tried not to think about the fight with Mark while I peered through my microscope, but it was nearly impossible. We seemed to be fighting all the time these days, a cyclical argument that never got resolved. I wanted him to either get a job or do more around the apartment, and he seemed to want to just work small, short-term part-time jobs at his leisure and live like a pig.

We had only been married six months and I wasn't sure how much longer this could last. We were supposed to be going down to a rural town in Nicaragua, Central America to live and work for two years. They wanted us to go just three months after we got married, but I felt strongly that we needed more time to get ourselves together. Mark agreed in theory, but did not live like we still had another year to go in the States.

When I had called Esther, who was in charge of the partnership program we were supposed to be going to work for in Nicaragua, to tell her that we needed to postpone it for a year to get our feet under us, she had not reacted well at all. She seemed much more interested in getting us down there than in worrying about our mental or marital readiness.

I had asked Mark to make the call, knowing that I was not Esther's favorite person (and vice versa, for that matter), but, in the end, I had called. He was taking too long, and I was afraid he would let Esther talk him into going sooner. I wasn't convinced he wanted to wait another year as we had agreed.

Mark kept telling me that everything would be fine once we moved to Nicaragua. His argument was that we would both be working in jobs we wanted to do, which would eliminate this strain of me working in one I hated and him not working at all. He continued that since going to Nicaragua was what we really wanted to do, we just had to hang on until we could go, and everything would be better.

I sighed as I changed the slides in my microscope. I wanted badly to believe him. But what would happen when we came home? Or would we stay there forever? I didn't know. Regardless, we had to survive the next year together or never get the chance to find out.

I wiped the tear off my cheek that had escaped unnoticed until it fell on my paperwork. I looked up at the clock, saw that it was finally time to go, packed up my things and left the lab.

As my key turned in the lock at home, I called up the stairs for Mark. There was no reply. I could faintly hear music coming from our second-story flat as I trudged up. As I reached the top steps, I could also smell something cooking.

I opened the door to find Mark standing at the stove stirring something in a pot. He was wearing shorts and a t-shirt, even though it was winter outside, and he was barefoot, as usual. He turned as I came into the kitchen and flashed me a big grin.

"Hi!" he said cheerfully. He turned back to his pot on the stove, stirring methodically. "I have to keep stirring this so it won't burn."

"What are you making?" I asked, pleased he was thoughtful enough to do the cooking for once.

"I decided to make spaghetti for dinner, so I thought I would make sauce from scratch. I thought it would be healthier and better than those cans and jars off the shelf." He sounded genuinely proud of himself.

"Did you get a recipe somewhere?" I asked, trying not to get concerned as I looked into the pot of mostly whole tomatoes. My feeling of pleasure from a moment ago began to fade as I looked around the kitchen and saw evidence only of his tomatoes.

"No! I figured, how hard could it be? I just bought tomatoes from the store and figured I'd start there. I mean, what else is in tomato sauce anyway besides the tomatoes?"

He continued stirring but seemed to take on a slightly defensive posture, and his brow crinkled. "The trouble is I thought this would take about 45 minutes, and I've now been cooking these down for over four hours and they don't seem to be turning into sauce."

I was trying not to let my anger boil like the tomatoes. I found no humor in the situation; only one more thing for me to clean up. "Well, I've never made sauce from scratch, but I would assume there's more than just tomatoes in it. And four hours?? You've been doing this for four hours?"

I was incredulous. There was no hiding my anger now. "Is this the sum total of how you've spent your day?"

Mark had the grace to look a bit sheepish as I stormed out of the room to his pathetic, "Well... I went shopping for them first..."

A loud argument ensued which went as many had before, and many would again. I felt like the entire burden for financially supporting us weighed on me, as well as the responsibility of keeping us in clean clothes, a clean apartment and with prepared food on the table.

Mark sat silently most of the time, letting my tirade rain down on him as he sulked like a child being scolded. I was like a prosecuting attorney and he was the accused on the stand without a defense attorney to protect him.

In the end, I made macaroni and cheese from a box, and we sat silently in front of the TV eating our dinner. I went out to the back porch to smoke and read a book after dinner while Mark retreated to the office in the second bedroom to surf the Internet. I went to bed first, as was most often the case, and he stayed up until 2:30 in the morning.

He did not do the dishes.

In the morning, it began again.

Chapter 1

The plane banked to the right, revealing through the window a sprawling urban landscape at dusk. Even at ten thousand feet there were no clouds to block the view. I peered down into the twilight. My stomach was churning -- this was Managua. I took a deep breath, blowing it out slowly.

It was impossible to make out the city's center. There were no skyscrapers or even a cluster of buildings to identify it; only small, squat dwellings as far as the eye could see. I could make out a few landmarks I had seen on two previous trips. I could almost see one iconic monument. At the top of one of its highest hills loomed the three-story silhouette of Augusto Sandino, the one-time revolutionary leader that watched over the city.

In another direction sat something massive, white and shaped like a pyramid. It was one of the very few multi-story buildings that had survived a terrible earthquake back in 1973 - the Intercontinental Hotel built by the Japanese. As my eyes continued to scan, I tried to picture what the city must have looked like before the destruction. It saddened me that the city had never been restored.

Then there was the extravagant Catholic Cathedral, the new building that had displaced the homes of hundreds of poor families. One of the major funders of the project was American Tom Monahan, founder of Dominoes Pizza and a Detroit-area business tycoon. Yes, from my hometown. I remembered visiting the Cathedral on our first trip two years before and turning away in disgust as I tried to wrap my head around what our tour guide told us. He said that hundreds of squatter families had built a tent city on the site over the years. It wasn't much, but it was everything that these families had. When the powerful and "benevolent" Catholic Church built the Cathedral, the families had been kicked off the land with nowhere to go, their tent city torn down. The most maddening part was looking at a low-lying stone wall that encircled three-quarters of the Cathedral – it served no discernible function but had been constructed with enough stones to rebuild a lot of houses.

Sizeable mountains framed the panoramic view including two large ones I thought might be volcanoes. I considered turning to my husband to ask him, but thought better of it. Instead I again took a deep breath and rubbed a hand across my still-churning stomach. The closer we got to landing, the more intense my anxiety.

The flight attendant came on the intercom. *"Bienvenidos a Nicaragua, damas y caballeros. Son las ocho y media y la temperatura es a trenta y un grados."*

What?! I didn't understand what she was saying. I glanced over at my husband.

"Vamos a aterisar en unos momentos, entonces favor alistar todos sus papeles para pasar por imigración lo mas rápido posible."

With that, people around us started moving in their seats, gathering their stuff and generally giving me the feeling we were about to land. I found myself mimicking their movements without really understanding what was going on.

"*Gracias por volar con Continental y otra vez, bienvenidos a Nicaragua.*"

I caught the "*gracias*" part and paused, waiting for the translation into English. When it didn't come after a moment, I looked expectantly again over to my husband, my anxiety rising again. "What did ..."?

"Welcome to Nicaragua, ladies and gentlemen. The local time is 8:30 p.m. and the temperature outside is 87 degrees."

I relaxed slightly as the translation began.

"We will be landing in just a few moments, so please have all of your documents ready to make your passage through Immigration as efficient as possible. Thank you for choosing to fly with Continental today, and once again, welcome to Nicaragua."

"Yes!" I exclaimed. "I love it here already just for the weather!"

"Yeah, great", Mark replied, his voice heavy with sarcasm. "That should make getting through Customs and Immigration with no air conditioning a real blast." He was handsome when he flashed his quick smile, but that didn't seem to come my way as much these days. He had recently cut off his long, sandy-blond curly hair in preparation for this time abroad and now had a short buzz cut that made his hair look much darker brown and made him look almost mean with the scowl he now wore on his face.

I turned away to look back out the window, determined not to let him ruin what I was sure was going to be a new beginning to our young and fragile marriage. I struggled to gather up my things in the tight space, the familiar feelings of discomfort, shame and disgust in my own overweight body washing over me. Jostling along with the other passengers of the packed flight, Mark and I made our way slowly towards the exit. The blast of hot air as the cabin door opened onto the tarmac almost knocked me off my feet. It was like a physical wave of hot, steaming mist and I was instantly sweating through my oversized t-shirt. The baggy jeans I wore clung to my legs making it difficult to walk.

It was mid-February and while I remembered the heat from previous visits, the change from the ice storm we'd left behind in Detroit caught me off guard. It added to my increasing feeling of being off balance.

Once down the stairs and on solid ground, I turned to look at the mountains behind me. "Which one is that one again, honey?" I asked Mark as he came up behind me.

"Keep moving, would you?" he replied with a note of irritation in his voice. The one bag he had slung over his broad shoulder seemed to weigh nothing, and he didn't even look as if he noticed the heat. Though he was also dressed in a t-shirt and jeans, his clothing fit his slender body much more comfortably than mine. "Let's not let the entire plane beat us to the Immigration line. Don't you remember what it's like getting into this country?"

I bit my tongue against the smart retort building in my throat and picked up my three bags to follow him.

Chapter 2

Once inside the sweatbox of a terminal, things were chaotic and moving too quickly for me to keep up. I tried to remain calm and stay close to Mark as people swirled around me, chattering away in rapid Spanish that I did not understand.

There were guards or police, I wasn't sure which, posted every few feet it seemed. They were dressed in Army fatigues and all had what looked to me like M-16s and AK-47s slung casually over their shoulders. They did not smile. The looks on their faces were ones of concentration as they continuously scanned the crowds of people. I tried not to visibly cringe as I wondered if the safety latches on the firearms were in place.

I remembered from my two brief visits in as many years that this was just the Nicaraguan version of airport security, but it didn't make the cold fear I felt walking past them any easier to deal with. On top of the hot sweat dripping down between my breasts and running down the back of my soaked t-shirt, I broke out in a fresh cold sweat as one of the guards watched us walk past with a frigid look in his eye.

The line for Immigration was a mile long, it seemed, and Mark was already annoyed and sulking silently. He didn't even appear to notice the guards and their guns. I felt like a deer caught in headlights as I just tried to stick close to him. Like the guards, I was continuously scanning the crowds of people. I felt almost naked standing there. Even having been to the country twice before, I still felt totally unfamiliar with the entry process. And this time, it was just Mark and myself – no group. I looked up at Mark's face to see if I could read any of the feelings I had reflected there. He was scowling and had a look of concentration. He did not seem to notice that I was still there. It made me feel even more vulnerable. I resisted the urge to kick him, more to get his attention than anything.

The voices swirling around us inside the terminal were reaching a volume level that was maddening and yet seemed to just keep getting louder. There was a large glass wall separating the inside of the terminal, where we stood in line, from the outside world. Throngs of people pressed up against the glass waiting eagerly for family and friends to get through the clearance process.

As I watched, the mass of people seemed to be in perpetual motion, jostling and adjusting as people shoved to get a glimpse of our newly arrived flight. Shouts of recognition and joy and urgency were flying over and around us non-stop. I couldn't catch even a word or phrase of Spanish that was recognizable to me as people talked to each other around us, continuing to get louder and louder with each passing moment.

I started to feel a little dizzy and claustrophobic standing in the midst of it all. I reached for Mark's hand to try and anchor myself. As I brushed up against him, he instinctively pulled his hand away, looking down at it with his scowl deepening to see who had tried to take our passports and papers out of it. Before he could say anything, I grabbed instead onto his arm. He looked at me and must have read the fear on my face.

"A little noisy, huh?" he practically shouted, to be heard over the chaos. I just nodded dumbly, continuing to scan the room. He patted my hand.

As we stood waiting our turn, I looked around, willing myself to remain calm against the rising tide of fear washing over me, and tried to imagine the day when I might understand what the people around us were saying. I felt a little more secure with my hand in Mark's arm.

I remembered my experience of feeling similarly disoriented as I arrived in Paris, France a few years back to live a semester abroad during college. I hadn't understood anyone then, either. But this was different. Very different. The people around me were almost all a few inches shorter than me and Mark, and several shades darker in skin tone, making me feel like we stuck out like a couple of lost American tourists instead of the mission volunteers we were. I felt there was an important distinction to be made and was afraid people around us would get the wrong impression. The tourists were there to ogle the Nicaraguans, often with disgust, before heading to the beautiful beaches and resorts built on the backs of their hard labor. Or worse, they were do-gooders there to do things for the Nicaraguans instead of increasing the capacity of the natives to do for themselves. It was a mentality that both Mark and I despised. It was one of the few things we seemed to agree on these days.

The volume level in the room maintained an unbelievable intensity with dozens of conversations going on all at once between excited passengers arriving, Immigration officers and passengers, and family members shouting to their loved ones from just beyond the Immigration desks into the open-air baggage claim area.

The heat was stifling, the humidity continuing to hit me like a wall of suffocating air. I regretted wearing this pair of baggy jeans in order to have the maximum packing space in my small trunk. Not only had they turned into heavy, soaking wet weights on my legs but, as I looked around the crowd at all the smartly dressed women in their tight skirts, fashionable pants and flowing tops, I felt deeply unattractive. It was a familiar feeling.

Finally it was our turn with the Immigration officer. At Mark's instruction, I remained quiet during the exchange, understanding nothing that was being said and desperately wanting to.

"What did he say?" I asked as I struggled to keep up with Mark's brisk pace as he walked towards the baggage claim area.

"Welcome to Nicaragua", he said, once again turning sarcastic.

"You don't have to be such an asshole, you know," I snapped at him before I could stop myself. "I don't understand what people are saying. You do. I thought you were going to help me out on this one until I learn some Spanish", I continued, getting angrier as I spoke and feeling that tight bitter feeling in my throat that had become so familiar during our exchanges over the past year and a half.

Mark ignored me and kept walking the short distance to the baggage claim. "Let's just get our stuff and get out of here", he said, sounding tired.

As we watched the carousel go around, eventually both of our trunks and suitcases arrived. As I stood with my three carry-on bags and his one, Mark hauled everything off the belt. One of the wheels my father had put on the bottom of my trunk had come off, but as I piled my other suitcases and bags on top of it, I found it would still kind of roll along if I was careful and went slowly. Mark's trunk had come out unscathed by the journey, and his one carry-on bag and one suitcase fit easily on top of it. He made no offer to assist me and I was too proud and angry to ask him for help at that point.

As I huffed along, angry and beginning to feel overcome by the heat, Mark suddenly said, "Oh, good, look, there's Ana waiting for us!" he said, turning back to me. He saw me struggling to keep up and instantly his smile faded. He was slightly too well-bred to say it, but I knew he was thinking I had packed way too much stuff.

I tried not to let the flush of embarrassment I felt at his silent reprimand keep me from smiling brightly at Ana as we approached the small woman.

"¡Bienvenidos a Nicaragua!" Ana said happily as she embraced

first Mark, then me. She went on to say several things that I did not understand at all, and when she finished talking, Mark said, "¡Bueno!" and began to follow her without a word to me. Ana took a couple of my bags from me, but left me the trunk, which was becoming increasingly unmanageable. I struggled to catch up with them and said, "Please tell me what she said!"

"She said that the partners out in Santo Domingo are very excited to see us, but that we'll be spending a few days here in Managua getting oriented before we go out there", his tone slightly impatient.

"Great! I'm excited to get started, too. Can you tell her that for me?" I just wanted to be part of the conversation.

As Mark translated to Ana, I hoisted my trunk and other bags into the big Suburban and climbed into the back seat. Some of the trepidation that I had felt on the plane began to return as we navigated the narrow and darkened streets of Managua.

Chapter 3

We arrived at a small house with a narrow front yard, gated by a low, rickety wooden fence badly in need of a fresh paint job. It was pitch-black outside and only a dim light seeping from deeper inside lighted the entrance. I had ridden in silence listening to Ana and Mark chatter on about God knows what. Now, sitting in front of the house, I was hoping this wasn't where we were going to stay. There didn't appear to be enough room inside for more than two people to sleep.

"Here we are!" said Mark gaily, as he swung his long legs out of the car. At seeing me hanging back looking uncertain, he just shook his head and walked to the back of the truck to get his bags.

At the sound of our car doors, a couple emerged from the house. They looked to me to be in their early 40's and were smiling broadly. I didn't understand most of the introductions and exchanges that took place, but was grateful for the man, Ricardo, as he took my bags from me and muscled them into the house. The woman, Sandra, seemed to sense that I felt uneasy and took my arm to guide me inside.

Once there, I realized that the house was much, much larger than it appeared on the outside. It was easily four times as deep as it was wide. There was a spacious living room that was furnished with a sofa and a few plastic chairs, which opened into a kitchen and dining room area that had a large table and several chairs. However, that was where the roof ended leaving the outside edge of the room open to an enclosed courtyard. Down the left-hand side of the room was a short pathway that led to three rooms with closed doors, and I could see another at the end of the path. Taking my hand, Sandra led me down the path following Ricardo to the first room. It was fairly large with a full size bed and an armoire on one side and a sitting area with a little sofa and a lamp on the other. Ricardo piled up our suitcases and trunks on the floor, chatting the whole time with Mark in rapid Spanish. I felt as if I was in a daze and was grateful for Sandra's warm hand, which I gripped like an anchor. Then both Ricardo and Sandra turned to me and said, "Good night" in English, and stepped out of the room closing the door behind them.

As I heard their voices and footsteps fading down the path, I turned and looked at Mark who was busy moving my suitcase off of his trunk.

"Oh, my God, I didn't understand anything that just happened! What is this place? Who are these people??"

"Ricardo and Sandra", said Mark, not bothering to hide the

impatience in his voice. He opened his trunk and began looking through it for something.

"I mean, who are they to us?" I asked with exasperation. "I got their names, you idiot! Are we staying here?" I felt close to tears from the sheer frustration.

"No, we're just resting for a few minutes before they move us to the Grand Hotel of Managua", Mark said sarcastically. He stopped searching in his suitcase and turned to look at me. Upon seeing the genuine distress on my face, he softened a little. "We're going to stay here for a few days during our orientation with Ana", he said more gently. "Then we'll go out to Santo Domingo. They've hosted a number of Americans here before, so Ana figured they would be able to help us get acclimatized a little."

Mark's gentler tone did not help my composure. I felt all of the tension, fear, and anxiety that had been building since we left Detroit that morning wash over me as I covered my face with my hands and dissolved into tears.

Mark hesitated, and then moved across the room to gather me into his embrace. He wrapped his arms around me and put his cheek on top of my head.

"It's okay, baby; everything's gonna be okay", he said softly. "You're just tired. It's been a long day."

"Fuck you!" I lashed out at him, breaking away. "All you've done all day is be irritated with me, and now you want to comfort me? Go away!" I hissed at him, trying to keep my voice low. I turned away from him and collapsed into the small sofa. "You promised you were going to help me understand what was going on around me and all you've done is be a condescending asshole!"

Mark just looked at me and sighed, shaking his head. He turned away again and resumed his search for whatever he was looking for in his suitcase. I watched his back, breathing heavily, waiting for him to respond.

I realized that he wasn't going to speak to me, which just infuriated me further. I grabbed my shoulder bag off the floor and took out a new journal notebook, determined to stay up until he was asleep. As he changed his clothes and climbed into bed, I poured out my anger into the waiting, silent pages.

Chapter 4

Over the next few days, I became even more aware of what a different world we now inhabited as compared to the conveniences back home in Detroit. Even things that I had always considered pretty basic conveniences were either difficult to obtain or absent altogether. Mark spent most of two days trying to get Internet access established that we would be able to use to communicate with friends and family back in the states. We went together to a couple of banks to try and open an account with a check from our home bank in Detroit. Both Internet access and banking were denied to us. I began to worry that once we reached the isolation of Santo Domingo where we were to live for the next two years; we would face even more difficult obstacles than in the capitol.

While Mark was off trying to make his computer work, I was left to sit around Ricardo and Sandra's house waiting for him. I watched as the young woman they had working for them washed laundry by hand in a large, concrete wash tub with a washboard built into it, and watched as the seemingly mild-mannered Sandra harshly scolded the young woman when she didn't realize I was there. I watched their young daughter Liliana play with younger and older cousins and friends who came by as part of a never-ending parade of visitors who wanted to have a look at this pair of gringos. I watched and listened to everything going on around me without understanding much of anything that was said. As much as Mark irritated me these days, I had to admit (at least to myself) that I felt much more optimistic about this adventure when he was with me. When I was by myself surrounded by Nicaraguans, I felt very, very alone.

Our orientation with Ana really consisted of just a couple of hours in the Managua office of NECOG, the organization that we were partnered with locally. I really didn't know what the letters stood for, but I knew the gist of it was an evangelical council of churches. Basically, it was all of the non-Catholics. I had never had much positive experience with any denomination except for the National Protestant Church of America (NPCA) that had sent us to represent their partnership with the NECOG chapter in Santo Domingo.

In fact, I hadn't really had much experience period with any other faith tradition. My dad went to Mass every week without exception, but he never really taught me anything about the Catholic Church. My mom was of Jewish heritage, but had never practiced that faith herself, and had not passed it onto me either. Lacking any real faith formation myself, I felt very inadequate and ignorant in the presence of people who claimed a tradition.

I had been powerfully moved by the three-week intensive orientation retreat Mark and I had been part of in New Mexico before leaving. I hadn't wanted it to end. Now *that* was a set of people who seemed authentic and normal! They didn't make me feel inferior for my lack of formal knowledge of religion or my quiet, secret doubts about the whole Jesus thing. As I waited for Mark to return from his various outings, I found myself thinking about several of the other mission volunteers from that retreat and wondering how they were adjusting to their own situations. I somehow doubted that any of them were feeling quite as alone and overwhelmed as I was – they just seemed far more confident than that.

The other people working for NECOG in the Managua office at least were pretty normal. There was an older couple who had served in Latin America for the NPCA for decades; a younger couple who had just returned from a visit home to the States; and a handful of young Nicaraguans who had all studied in the States at some point. They made me feel more comfortable, but were never around for very long. It seemed everyone was busy and had a purpose – somewhere to go or something to do.

Everyone except me.

Chapter 5

Soon came the day for Mark and I to make the journey out to Santo Domingo. As we piled our luggage and trunks into Ana's truck once again to make our way to the airport, I tried to keep myself relaxed. My body had adjusted better to the heat by now, but as we started the drive to the airport where we were to take a small 12-seater plane to Santo Domingo, I broke out into a fresh sweat. Would the plane make it? Who would be there to meet us on the other side? Where were we going to live? Would I ever learn to understand and communicate with the people around me?

My head was swimming as we pulled up in front of the National Flight Terminal of the airport. It was an afterthought of an addition onto the main International Terminal and did not inspire confidence. Ana and Mark bounced out of the truck as I sat there contemplating the building for a moment.

"Come on! We're going to be late!" shouted Mark, raising his voice over the din of other voices, traffic, planes and other activity that now swirled around us.

He grabbed his luggage out of the truck, then began hauling mine out, too, looking as if he begrudged my clotheshorse tendencies as he struggled to lift my trunk. I felt like I was in a daze, while he was practically bursting with excitement to get out to Santo Domingo and get started on our work.

I climbed slowly out of the truck. I turned to Mark and said in a small voice, "Are you sure this is a good idea?"

"What are you worrying about?" Mark replied. "People take this flight every day. It's gonna be fine! I'll hold your hand. Just come on!" He was already wheeling our luggage toward the terminal.

"The flight wasn't all I was asking about", I muttered under my breath as I began to follow him into the small terminal.

The flight was worse than any of the scariest roller coaster rides I had ever been on. I clung to Mark as the small, over-burdened plane pitched and rolled in the air. Leaving Managua wasn't so bad – there weren't many mountains or obstacles near enough for the plane to navigate at close range. But as we got out over the enormous Lake Nicaragua, a storm hit. The sky blackened and rain beat down on the little 12-seater plane so hard that I was sure we were going down. The other seven passengers didn't seem to even notice, passing the time reading newspapers or sleeping, which only added to the feeling of surreal-ness I was experiencing. Soon the storm subsided and I could see clearer skies ahead of us. *I hope this is a good sign*, I thought fiercely to myself.

The plane began its descent into what I guessed was Santo Domingo; there weren't any flight attendants on board to ask. After a few moments of circling, one of the two pilots up front came on the intercom and mumbled something. Mark then told me it was just to say that we were indeed arriving in Santo Domingo. I still couldn't bring myself to really look out the window and watch. Mark told me that people were chasing cows and a few horses off of the runway below, which didn't do much to help me relax.

Soon we were on the ground and Juan Carlos, the Director of NECOG in Santo Domingo, was coming toward us, a big smile on his dark face. I had met him on the previous two delegation trips I'd been on, and I was relieved to see him – at last a familiar face! I willingly stepped into his open arms to accept his embrace.

There were a few others there, too, I noticed, stepping back so that Mark could greet Juan Carlos, our new boss, as well. Juanita, Juan Carlos's wife, I hugged next; the boy we'd seen on our first delegation trip, Gregorio, now looking much older than he had three years earlier; and a couple of other men I didn't recognize but who all nodded to me as they began taking the luggage off of the plane and putting it into Juan Carlos's waiting pick up truck. I guessed that they were also with NECOG, like Juan Carlos, Juanita and Gregorio.

When they were done, introductions were made all around, but my head was spinning too much to catch names or relevance. Within a few minutes we were all piled into the pick-up truck and heading down the road into the town. The air was just as hot as it had been in Managua, but somehow less stifling. I guessed it was due to the fact that the town seemed to be located in something of a valley, and there were no concrete streets, let alone concrete buildings, around to reflect more heat. All of the roads were dirt, made of the red clay common to the region and crushed rock that hadn't quite made it to "gravel" status.

I stared back at the kids in the street who stopped what they were doing to gawk at us. I smiled brightly and even waved to some of them, but they just continued to gawk. I remembered from the first trip there how much the extreme and concentrated poverty had affected me, particularly the hungry children. It was the one thing about this mission service that had made me hesitate. Would I be able to witness it without really doing much about it? That was what I perceived our contract with the church and NECOG to be about – go, walk with the people; do the specific job you are there to do, and remember that God was there before you arrived. I wasn't sure how that exactly was supposed to make me feel comforted, other than encouraging me to have the "grace" to accept the reality of their situations.

All thoughts vanished from my head as we pulled up in front of the NECOG office. It still wasn't much to look at, but it had definitely been expanded since our last visit. Instead of one building, there were now two. As Juan Carlos led us inside, I saw that the newer one had a long, narrow front room used as a reception area where a stout woman was sitting at a desk looking at us with a beautiful motherly smile. Juan Carlos introduced her as Alejandra.

The floor was dark brick-red ceramic tile as was nearly every other finished floor I had seen in Nicaragua. There was a newer computer sitting on the receptionist's desk, along with calculators and piles of paper work. Her desk itself was quite ornately carved. Further back were two more desks of a similar style with a man at each one. They looked up and nodded. One, introduced as Eduardo, smiled broadly, and the other kept a watchful, somber look on his face. His name was Lennon. I tried to suppress my smile, wondering if he knew anything about his namesake.

The door at the far end of the room led to a little roofless area where there was a huge concrete sink with a washboard built into it, like the one that I had seen at our guesthouse in Managua. There were two doors on the wall behind the sink, one of which led to a closet and the other led to a toilet. I was astonished and thrilled to see the toilet. On our previous visit to Santo Domingo, I had not seen any toilets. I did not think indoor plumbing had made it this far out into the countryside yet. I would never have admitted it to anyone other than Mark, but I loathed latrines. I was secretly hoping that there would be a toilet at our house and seeing one at NECOG's office fueled my hope.

The door in front of us led into a rear office, and after going up three steps to the door, we all filed inside. The room was air conditioned – another first for me in Santo Domingo. The door didn't open all the way because of the massive table and chairs set up in the middle of the room. Behind that was a desk, and the back wall, which was covered, floor to ceiling, with an open shelving system that was mostly empty. Before I could get my hopes up that this would be our office, Juan Carlos said in slow, deliberate Spanish with a huge grin on his face, *"Mi oficina!"*

Everyone filed out again – I really wasn't sure why this whole group of people was parading around the fairly cramped quarters with us in the first place – into the heat. Across what was now a driveway where the pick up truck had parked was the former main NECOG office. Inside the small room were two older desks, each with a plastic yard chair behind it, and a sign on the wall that none could mistake – *"¡Bienvenidos a Santo Domingo Marco y Hellen!"* – welcoming us to our new office. *Well,* I thought, suppressing a small sigh, *at least it's somewhat private.*

Chapter 6

Waiting out a downpour that lasted about five minutes, after which the sun returned full force, we once again piled into the truck and drove a few blocks to the only two-story house I had seen in town. It was attached on one side to a lower one-story house next to it. The space between them seemed to be some kind of pass through, although not quite big enough for a vehicle. The lower half of the house was made of cinder block, which was a very common type of construction for housing, painted light blue. The top row of cinder blocks was made with a star shape in the center to let light and air through. Where that row ended, the upper part of the house began, which was made of weather beaten wood, grayish in color. The front door was made of wood as well, with a "screen" door that was a black metal gate. There were no screens anywhere.

The front room was empty except for a very steep and rickety-looking staircase up to the second floor. The floors were tiled with dark red squares, as in the NECOG office. A doorway led into the back room of the main floor, which was meant to be a kitchen, bathroom, laundry room and dining room all in one but was empty right then. In one back corner was a three-quarter wall that held a shower. In the other back corner was the back door, which led out to the hard-packed dirt yard. There were a number of trees, which shaded the yard, as well as a handful of chickens clucking and grazing. It seemed to be sort of a common, shared yard. There were lines of barbed wire running everywhere. At first I was worried this was part of some kind of prison or camp, but then a woman walked over to one of the lines and started throwing wet laundry over it. The barbed wire was apparently clothesline – no clothespins necessary.

And straight ahead was the dreaded latrine. As Mark translated, Juan Carlos told us with pride that it had a brand new "throne" in it made of concrete. Reading the disappointment on my face, he quickly added that this could be a temporary situation until a toilet could be built....at our expense. As my face fell further, Juan Carlos laughed robustly. I thought I heard a twinge of cruelty as well.

Back in the house, everyone tramped up to the second floor. I almost lost my balance a couple of times as I navigated the narrow stairwell and battled my fear of heights. It opened up into a large, well-lit room with a smaller room at the back that had a door on it for privacy. At the front of the room was another black metal grate that was the only window covering of any kind.

"I'm not going up and down those damn stairs all the time!" Again the familiar wave of panic. "It's not safe! I'll fall and break my neck!"

"Relax", Mark said. "You'll get used to it. It's not that bad." He paused and looked around for a moment, then leaned towards me slightly and said, "Frankly, having a second story will keep us safer from burglary."

I rolled my eyes. The Nicaraguans chattered around me and gestured to the front window. Mark began to laugh.

"That's where our bed is going to come through!" he laughed. "This should be interesting to watch. Grab the camera!"

The Nicaraguans easily scurried down the stairs with Mark following. I hesitated, looking down at my husband's retreating shoulders. *This is more like a steep ladder than stairs*, I thought. As Mark turned to look back up at me with pity, my resolve suddenly hardened. I turned around and climbed down, treating it like a ladder. I reached the bottom and looked around triumphantly. "Take that, Mark. I'm not a sissy." I turned just in time to see him walking out the front door, not noticing my small victory.

2/20-21/97

Dear Mom & Dad -

Greetings from our first house, here in Santo Domingo! We arrived yesterday, after an eventful plane ride from Managua. We were in a small 12-seater plane, and we came through a couple rough showers that I honestly thought we would crash in. (I've decided I prefer land travel.) Luckily for us, there were only seven people on the plane, so we were able to bring all of our luggage with us.

We are pretty well situated here in our house. The bed is comfortable, although with this mosquito net, our space is limited. Our chairs and table have not yet arrived, but they have been sprayed and are drying at the furniture "store", which is more an open-air carpenter shop. Dad, I think you'd really enjoy seeing all the hand-made stuff; it seems well made to us. Anyway, we should get those yet today or in the morning.

We have purchased a few things, but are running out of

money and have to go to Managua for more for the time being. We will investigate a suggestion made by one of the Americans from NECOG in Managua to write a check to the bank here (we haven't found it as of yet) for $500 (or whatever), and in six weeks it should clear and we can get our money that way. Luckily, there is a celebration of 25 years of NECOG in Managua on the 27th that we are all going to (via land - smiley face), so we'll get more $$ then.

Anyway, we bought four plates (china because they were the cheapest), four plastic cups, a large plastic bowl, a sharp knife, a pitcher (plastic), a tub for water with a lid (large enough to hold enough water for days when there isn't any), a few small mirrors, and some nails. Juanita and Juan Carlos have loaned us a stove (gas) that is just 3 burners with no oven, but we can cook just about everything without one. (Today is Thursday, and we already have a list going of Saturday projects! One of them is seeing about constructing our solar oven.) Someone also loaned us three chairs that will probably stay until we get more.

Today we had a meeting with the Pastoral Committee, which basically runs NECOG. We got job descriptions different from what we thought, but in a good way, I think. Not only will Mark teach English to the teachers, but he will help with community relations between two *campesino* (peasant) banks that NECOG runs, mostly PR kind of work. He will also teach about the computer to staff, and one more thing we can't remember right now.

I will be organizing the reforestation project, giving seminars on ecology (I need a book on the ecology of Central America!!), working with a new program that is teaching the 50 street kids here to read and write, working with women who are abused, sick, etc., and working with the promotion of gender equality. (Whew!) All the non-biology stuff is through the Women's Pastoral Committee, and I get the idea I'm basically a consultant/organizer in all of my roles. We will certainly be busy! Also, NECOG here has remodeled, and we will have an office room of our own! There is an armed night watchman so the computer will be very safe there. There's a phone line, too, so we will not need one of our own, to save $$.

I must say, this is all very exciting! It looks like my learning of Spanish will be on-the-job, but I'm still planning to take at least a couple of weeks to just work on stuff in the office. We move into our office in a couple of weeks, so I'm not sure how much they expect us to do until then. Hopefully, not much. We need to prepare ourselves a little bit, especially me!

In the morning tomorrow, we are riding out to a pretty distant colony with Juan Carlos. He has to see someone there. I plan to photograph the landscape around us, as well as take some more pictures here in town.

I sure do miss you all a lot. I think of all of you at various times every day. I'm excited to get started working. My Spanish is improving, and after the very reassuring welcome we received today, I feel much better about being here. They (the pastors) said that they know it's hard for us to be so far from family, so they will be as much of a family to us as they can .

Anyway, all is well. I'm tired, so I'm going to bed now. We both love you, especially me, very much. We'll "talk" soon via e-mail.

Lots of love,

Ellen

Chapter 7

I managed to avoid using our latrine for a few days. I became very disciplined about using the bathroom at the NECOG office. Even though I wasn't really working there yet, I found ample reasons to stop by several times each day. I was so intimidated by the outhouse that I didn't really care if the staff had caught on to me. But I knew it wasn't practical to keep on doing it – the weekend was coming and I would have no reason to go to NECOG. I decided it was time to face this demon head on.

I waited for Mark to come home that afternoon and informed him it was time for me to visit our latrine. He knew I was terrified of it and tried not to laugh as I very somberly asked him to accompany me to the outhouse.

I threw the door open and gingerly peered inside. All that was there was a concrete toilet seat – nothing fancy. But I saw a cockroach skitter across the floor, up onto the seat and down into the pit.

"Gross!!!" I exclaimed. "There is definitely no way I am ever sitting on that seat! What if a cockroach crawls up my butt? Or worse?!?" I was already backing away from the latrine.

"Look, city girl," Mark said with a laugh he was no longer able to contain. "We're going to be here for two whole years. I have serious concerns for your digestive health if you are planning to avoid our bathroom for that entire time! Now let's have a look. It can't be that bad. I've used it plenty of times already."

"Yeah, well, country boy, you can relieve yourself standing up more than half the time!" I countered, a smile creeping onto my face as well. "Some of us don't have that option without serious consequences!" I was beginning to see the humor in the situation, but it didn't make me any more willing to sit down with that cockroach lurking somewhere below. I walked over to the "throne" again and peered down inside. I saw thousands of black, beady eyes staring back at me, covering the inside surface of the cylinder all the way down to the pit at the bottom.

I jumped back and screamed. "That's it! I knew it! I knew they'd be there waiting to attack me! No way I'm using that pot! I'll just go in a plastic bowl and you can just empty it like a good husband would!" We were both laughing by now, but mine was laced with hysteria.

"Dream on, baby!" He was laughing so hard there were tears coming out of his eyes. Once he caught his breath, he said, "Come on.

Let's go ask someone what we can do to get them out of there."

Walking towards the NECOG office, we found the young teenaged boy that worked as a gopher for Juan Carlos coming down the street. He listened patiently to Mark explain the situation with me trying to urgently emphasize my distress through exaggerated gestures. If the boy shared our humor at the situation, he didn't let on. Instead, he suggested that we get a can of "Bygon" from the local mini-super market. When we found it, we read the contents – it seemed to be the equivalent of Raid.

We returned to the house where the latrine door was still standing open. Some of our neighbors were now curiously peeking out of their rear windows and doorways watching these strange gringos to see what comical thing we would do next. Mark handed me the can.

"You do it. You're the one with the squatting phobia."

I cautiously approached the throne, shook the can one more time, and began emptying its contents down into the hole. Immediately thousands and thousands of cockroaches began streaming out of the hole, over the sides of the throne and in all directions to escape the toxic chemicals. I let out a squeal and stepped back, trying to get clear of them all. I watched in some kind of awe as they all began their death throes on the ground. My awe quickly turned to horror as I noticed the chickens that ranged in the open back yard area from all the neighbors began eating the dying cockroaches! I thought we should try and stop them, but Mark pointed out that they would just come back later and eat them anyway. I vowed that I would not eat chicken again.

A few hours later, I went back outside to check on the status of the latrine. There were dead and dying cockroaches covering almost every surface of the latrine floor and seat of the throne. I groaned and picked up a broom to sweep them away. I pushed the pile towards a garbage pit, not able to bring myself to throw them back down the latrine for fear they would somehow revive and come back to haunt me. I thought to myself as I swept, *I'm still not using this damn latrine any more than I absolutely have to.*

Dear Diary,

Having been worried about the first stage of culture shock (Enchantment) that was described to us during our orientation with NPCA before coming to Nicaragua, I still find myself being wary of things. I think I'm looking at things fairly realistically. I feel like if anything, I'm not enchanted <u>enough</u>! In any case, I'm excited and happy to be here. I just don't think everyone here is automatically a good person, as I did on my first couple of trips here.

I'm feeling a lot of emotional ups and downs. One day I'll feel totally optimistic about our new adventures here, and later the same day or the next day, something will happen (usually something embarrassingly minor) and I'll sink into a funk. It's exhausting! So much transition and change all at once.

Once we reached Santo Domingo, I just felt so abandoned, like we are all alone. I mean, I know in theory we aren't; I think Juan Carlos and the others are fairly happy that we're here, but I am definitely experiencing waves of homesickness. And the stupidest things make me cry! Like yesterday, I had been feeling homesick and had been a little teary. Well, we went over to the NECOG offices and I thought that one of the girls asked if I had been crying, which promptly made me start crying again! Obviously I did not understand anything she said, so after a very uncomfortable eternity, Mark translated that she had actually just asked if I had gotten some sun on my face! It was so humiliating I couldn't do anything but hide my face in my hands and flee. Ugh.

Chapter 8

This will be a good day – I refuse to spend it homesick, I thought as I hummed to myself. Today was my birthday – I turned 24 years old – and I was up early feeling optimistic about life. I put on my calf-length, full-skirted denim jumper to feel a little pretty. It wasn't in the tight-fitting style I was beginning to notice was popular around town, but just wearing a dress made me feel more feminine. I put my shoulder-length dark brown hair up in a ponytail to keep it off my neck. The heat wasn't bothering me so much after a couple of weeks in it, but I had a full day of unpacking and organizing the house planned.

After lunch, Juan Carlos's wife Juanita and Alejandra from the NECOG office came walking towards our house. I went to greet them, muttering, "This should be interesting", under my breath. They smiled broadly at me and wished me happy birthday in Spanish. Then Juanita began gesturing to the radio and pantomiming listening, speaking in rapid Spanish the whole time. By the third try, I gathered that they wanted me to listen to the radio for some reason. Alejandra had turned it on and tuned in a station I could hear blaring loudly from every radio on the street. I guessed that it might be the local station. The two women smiled at me again and left as suddenly as they had arrived.

I shook my head and continued unpacking a box of books. Mark had been gone most of the day somewhere. I wondered if he even remembered that it was my birthday.

Suddenly I heard my name on the radio! It was surrounded by a lot of Spanish that I didn't understand, but I heard my name clearly as the radio announcer had to slow down to pronounce it carefully. He got the Spanish version of my first name – Elena – but stumbled over our last name. I was delighted! I felt a rush of gratitude that they had known it was my birthday that was quickly followed by a tidal wave of homesickness. I clenched my fists and gritted my teeth, determined not to cry. A few tears escaped as I blinked rapidly.

I had just regained my composure and returned to the task at hand when a tentative knock came at the door. I peeked around the corner into the front room and saw Juan Carlos's eldest daughter standing there. She waved shyly and motioned that she wanted to come in. I waved her inside.

Through pantomime and a few scattered words, I understood that the teenager wanted me to go somewhere with her. Shrugging my shoulders in agreement, I put on my sandals and locked the door behind us. As we began walking down the little street towards the main square, I caught a glimpse of Juanita and Alejandra coming around the other corner. The teenager quickly grabbed my hand and pulled me along in the opposite direction.

Ah-hah, I smiled. *They are trying to surprise me.* As we walked towards the center of town, I pretended I did not think anything was strange about the situation, and held up my end of the broken conversation. Neither of us understood the other very well, so there was a lot of smiling and laughing. The more I thought of the absurdity of the situation, the more I laughed. It felt good.

We arrived at the Eskimo shop – the local ice cream parlor – and the teenager got what she ordered so quickly I realized the order must have been pre-placed. With two half-gallons of ice cream in hand, we began to walk in a roundabout route back to our house.

When we finally arrived, the front door was still closed as I had left it, but I was tall enough to see through the openings in the cinder blocks and could see the people gathered inside. The door opened as I reached for it, revealing about a dozen people inside. Mark was in the far corner grinning broadly. They all clearly thought they had caught me completely by surprise.

There were several awkward moments as we all stood listening to a recording of "Happy Birthday" in Spanish, but no one sang! However, everyone seemed very well intentioned and eager just to make me feel good. Everyone was there – Mark, Juan Carlos and his whole family, Lennon, Eduardo, Alejandra, and other NECOG staff. There was even a little birthday cake on the table. It was in the shape of a heart. As Juanita went to cut it, she asked Mark to translate something for her.

"They want you to know that this is your cake. Here in Nicaragua the custom is that the birthday person must decide to share their cake – it's not a foregone conclusion like at home. Juanita wants to know if you willingly share this cake with them. Also, since it is in the shape of a heart, she's hoping it is a sign that you are willing to also share your heart with them. Hokey, I know, but play along, will you?"

Actually, I had to swallow hard to keep from welling up with tears at the gesture. I didn't think it was hokey at all – rather a very raw and unpretentious way for Juanita to extend herself. Of course Mark, not having any emotional bones in his body, was something I was used to so I wasn't surprised at his editorial comment. I bit back a retort, not wanting the others to think it was in response to what Juanita had said. Instead, I simply turned towards Juanita and smiled my gratitude and permission to cut and serve the cake to all. I wanted to walk over to Mark and smash a piece of cake into his face, but I didn't think our guests would understand.

After cake, there were a few presents passed to me. There were beautiful handcrafted items among them, and then from Mark – a t-shirt. *Has anyone told him that I'm his wife??? A t-shirt???* I was embarrassed and furious. He made some lame excuse about it being the only thing available around here that he thought I would like. I knew it was the thought that counted. What bothered me was the lame way in which he presented the whole thing – like he was fulfilling his obligation to buy me *something* instead of his wanting to give something special to me. How typical. I tried not to look angry. I stole glances at the others in the room, trying to read their reactions. The women all busied themselves cleaning up and the men chatted among themselves. I watched the scene out of the corner of my eye, gathering up the gifts. I felt very much like an outsider at that moment, and still felt angry with Mark.

"Hey, Mark, thank everyone for me, would you? Tell them I thought all of *their* gifts were very thoughtful." I didn't care anymore if I sounded nasty.

Just then, someone came to the door and called the night watchman from NECOG over. He in turn spoke to Juan Carlos and then ran quickly out the door. Juan Carlos looked very somber as he addressed the room, which had grown quiet. I didn't understand him as he spoke, but I recognized the somber nature of his tone – something serious had happened. Our small spat forgotten, Mark crossed the room and spoke to me with a tremor in his voice.

"The night watchman's 12-year old daughter has just died, I think", he said softly. "Juan Carlos said we should all go over to his house for the wake."

"You mean tomorrow?" I asked with concern.

"No, right now. Apparently they do the wake right away here. It's only a few blocks away."

Everyone filed out of the small house and walked the few blocks to the house where the night watchman and his family lived. I saw a small form completely covered by a sheet resting on a rough wooden table. The table was sitting on the hard-packed dirt floor under an overhang of the roof – sort of a porch. The area was lit only by candlelight. About 15 people had already gathered and were speaking in hushed tones. No one appeared to be crying – just very somber, faces set in hard lines.

From others that had come with them, Mark managed to find out that the form on the table was the little girl. She had died only about 20 minutes prior to our arrival. The cause - meningitis.

The night watchman appeared from inside the house with another man. His face was set in grim lines. He walked over to his daughter's body. He placed one hand at the top of her head and the other against the bottoms of her feet. It looked to me like he was taking a measurement of some kind. As I looked on in horror, he turned to the man next to him and mumbled something, then the two of them walked away, like he had just given the measurements of a piece of furniture instead of his little girl's body. I felt desperately sad and anxious in a way that I couldn't explain. It brought home for me once again that we were in a strange land.

3/2/97

Dear Mom and Dad,

Well, it sure was good to talk to you! The connections out here just aren't very good. Seeing/Hearing how poor our phone voice connection was, maybe you can understand a bit better why the computer won't accept it. It needs to be able to clearly understand the other computer and if it can't, it won't function.

Picking oranges, mandarins and grapefruit today was really fun. We went to a close by settlement called Rio d'Oro (Gold River) to a farm of sorts that Juan Carlos and Juanita's friends own. The fruit here is unbelievably sweet! We'll make juice tomorrow.

Tonight we didn't feel like cooking, so we went to one of the many comedores (restaurants, or cafes, really) and had two plates (one each) of fried potatoes, beef strips, salad (made with cabbage) and rice, as well as two pops for me and two beers for Mark, all for about $5.50! Viva Nicaragua!

Tomorrow Mark will be gone all day observing classes. The teachers speak broken English, at best, and have very old teaching methods, so he has his work cut out for him! I'll be going to NECOG to try and get an idea of when Juan

Carlos wants me to start actually working on something. Also, Juanita starts training the teachers for the street kids tomorrow, so I'll just sit in on that. I'm also supposed to have another cooking lesson with their eldest daughter, so it will be a full day, I'm sure.

In spite of the small tragedies I tell you about, it's really GORGEOUS here, the people are incredibly nice, and we love it. Our house is our haven, and we are totally secure here . Please try and feel as good about this as we do.

Love you lots and lots,

Ellen

Chapter 9

My brow was furrowed in deep concentration as I pored over the leaflets in Spanish on deforestation. I cursed mildly under my breath as I once again reached for my English-Spanish dictionary. I was trying to get through one complete sentence without having to use the damned thing; it wasn't going so well. Being fluent in French was helping me somewhat, but having studied basic Spanish for only two semesters in college was not.

Juan Carlos's large frame suddenly filled the doorway. He motioned for me to come with him, smiling with a bit of mischief in his eyes. I warily followed him back to the main NECOG office where Lennon was waiting by his desk. Through some broken Spanish and a lot of gesturing, I managed to understand that I was to go with Lennon to visit one of the colonies where I would be working on reforestation efforts. Lennon traveled by motorcycle. I was apparently supposed to go on the back of his bike with him.

"Oh, no, I don't think so", I stammered, shaking my head as I backed myself towards the door. "I really don't think that's a good idea." I had no experience on motorcycles of any kind, even small ones like this one, and I had no interest in gaining any.

They got from my body language what I was saying, and all began to laugh good-naturedly. Making encouraging gestures and speaking rapidly at me, they gently pulled me towards the door where Lennon's bike was waiting. He got on and started it up, and turned to look at me again, obviously waiting for me to get on. He smiled at me. However, I was acutely aware of how he'd just called me "fat" the day before. The smile seemed to convey more amusement than friendliness.

I approached the small motorcycle and Lennon held out his hand to me, which I took while I swung one leg over the small seat behind him. My face was completely flushed from embarrassment at how much I weighed. I felt enormous next to Lennon's slender frame and was seriously worried that my added weight would not be sustained by the small bike. I willed myself to stop sweating.

As we began moving, I instinctively grabbed Lennon's waist to hold on, then immediately let go as if I had touched a hot iron. Then I grabbed on again quickly not knowing what else to hold on to to keep from falling off! My sweating and flushing increased as my heart rate climbed. I laughed nervously at the absurd picture I was sure we made as we rode down the street. Lennon chuckled back at me and patted my hand at his waist. I hoped that meant it was okay to put them there.

It was exhilarating to be on the back of Lennon's motorcycle as we went through town. Since the road was made of crushed rock, we didn't go very fast so as not to split open a tire on a sharp piece of the road. I tried to appear as casual and at ease as possible so that my giddiness wouldn't show, especially to Lennon.

Soon we left the town of Santo Domingo and were traveling past farms and open fields out towards one of the colonies. I was very nervous – it was the first time I had been away from Santo Domingo without Mark. I was having very mixed feelings and a confusing emotional response to riding in such an intimate space with Lennon. I tried to just relax and enjoy the beautiful scenery flowing by.

The poverty was extreme and obvious all around us. Almost as a taunting contrast, the landscape was lush green with trees and plants everywhere. The homes that were visible along the road periodically were little more than shacks, all with dirt floors and porches. The front doors on most of them stood wide open and women were briskly sweeping. Most homes had either a few chickens or a pig or two milling around in the front yard. Lots of children and very few men were in sight.

Soon we arrived in what I assumed was the *colonia*. The houses were closer together and there were more of them, as well as one of the blue and white buildings I had seen before that was a school. We rode slowly through the town, going off the road and through the vegetation (it really couldn't be called "grass") up to someone's house. As Lennon called out a greeting, a man came outside to greet us. I swung my leg over the bike to dismount and realized that my rear-end was asleep. I managed to step clear of the bike before bending down to pretend to retie my new boots while discreetly stretching out my aching muscles.

The man walking towards us had a very dark complexion and a broad, white smile. He was tall and lanky with an amused look in his eyes as he exchanged greetings with Lennon. It was obvious that they knew each other well. He kept his eyes on me, clearly waiting for me to regain my feet before formally greeting me. I tried to stand up and realized to my horror that I couldn't! My muscles were tighter than I had realized and crouching down had locked them up. The smile froze on my face, my hand halfway up to shake the stranger's, as I tried to think quickly what the hell to do to avoid falling hard onto my butt in the dirt.

I knew everyone in the vicinity with a view of us was watching and I was desperate not to make a fool of myself.

The tall man seemed to sense exactly what was happening and with a little chuckle, reached his hand down to grab mine, pulling me to my feet before I fell. I smiled gratefully at him, my face again burning, and thanked him. Lennon introduced him to me, then the two of them turned and walked towards his house, leaving me to follow. I quickly tugged up my jeans, smoothed my loose t-shirt, and caught up with them.

I looked around into some of the homes scattered randomly by the roadside as we walked. They all had hard-packed dirt floors and there were animals everywhere, including inside the houses. There were more children than I could count, none who had sufficient clothing or shoes, and many who had interminable sniffles. The homes themselves were really falling down "houses", many more equivalent to "lean-tos" or shacks.

After about an hour of conversation and a tour of the stranger's land, Lennon headed back towards the bike. I had been able to follow only a few words here and there of the conversation – much less than when I was talking with people in the NECOG office. My head was hot and spinning. I was ready to head back. I didn't feel like I was ever going to be able to communicate with the people in the colonies.

Soon we were on the bike headed back to Santo Domingo. Lennon tried to talk to me, shouting over his shoulder to be heard above the noise of the bike and road. I tried to respond a few times, but it seemed clear from his chuckles and shaking head that I hadn't understood correctly what he was saying. I was very conscious of the fact that I was still using his waist to hold on to; I wondered if he minded.

The NECOG office was in front of us again much more quickly than I remembered. I got off more easily this time. As Lennon parked the motorcycle, he turned and smiled at me.

"You're a nice passenger", he said in Spanish that I was amazed to understand. "I look forward to going with you again."

"Thanks – me, too", I responded, also in Spanish, trying not to blush too deeply. I suddenly wanted to say more in a rush of emotion – to tell him how excited I was to be working with him, and to thank him for his kindness that day. But I couldn't find the words. I hoped the dazzling smile I gave him conveyed my thoughts. Then my smile froze as I noticed faint handprints on Lennon's white shirt, where I'd been holding on. He didn't seem to notice.

Lennon smiled back and I walked back towards my office, stepping lightly, stifling an embarrassed and giddy laugh.

Chapter 10

It was very dark all around me as I stumbled over to the stairs. There were no streetlights outside – only the light from the moon to see by. I didn't want to turn on the lights and wake up Mark – I just had to pee. I was dreading going to the outhouse in the middle of the night like this, but really saw no other option. I'd already been awake for 20 minutes trying to talk myself out of having to go. It was no use – if I waited, I was sure I'd wet the bed.

I grabbed a small flashlight and headed very carefully down the stairs. As I got to the bottom and turned towards the back of the house, I figured it was safe to turn on the kitchen light without disturbing anyone. I shined the flashlight to where the switch was to make sure there weren't any waiting surprises – like cockroaches or the huge poisonous spiders the natives called tarantulas. The light flicked on after a moment, and I screamed.

Large rats scattered in three directions off of our small eating table, carrying pieces of the bread with them that I had carefully wrapped in plastic only hours before. I took three or four stumbling steps backwards, trying not to fall down, gasping and forcing myself to stop screaming in disgust and horror.

I heard Mark upstairs cursing at the mosquito netting over the bed as he struggled to free himself from it, yelling to me to find out what had happened. Next door the lights came on and I heard our landlord fumbling with his door. Both appeared quickly.

"Rats!" I yelled, a little meeker now. My skin still felt like it was crawling but I was beginning to feel embarrassed for my outburst that had so obviously scared the two men as much as the rats had startled me.

"Oh, for God's sake!" muttered Mark, coming the rest of the way down the stairs. He turned and told the landlord that everything was under control. The older man eyed me warily before turning back to his house. "You're such a city girl!"

"You're just mad because it is now crystal clear who has won the argument for getting a cat!" I said triumphantly. "Those suckers were huge! And they ate my breakfast for tomorrow!" I moved gingerly towards the table to examine the remains.

"What are you doing down here anyway?" yawned Mark. "It's like two-thirty in the morning."

"I have to pee!" I exclaimed. "And you have just won the honor of escorting me to our outhouse! Ain't no way I'm going out there alone – that's where the rats went!" I started towards the back door, hoping he would just follow me. To my surprise, he did without comment.

Once I had finished and we were back upstairs in the bed again, I couldn't resist cementing the deal. "Come on, Mark; let's get a cat. Just think – less nights like this for you", I said in a singsong voice I knew irritated him. Mark grunted and rolled away from me.

I smiled into the darkness, knowing I had won.

Mark borrowed our neighbor's motorcycle to go the few kilometers out to the farm where we'd heard there was a good, young mouser cat available. I had been getting lessons from Lennon and Eduardo on how to ride, so I drove it out with Mark on the back. I was trying to explain to him how to do it as we went. He had refused to carry the cat back – he hated cats and was allergic to them – so he was going to drive the bike back while I carried the cat.

Mark had learned as a kid how to ride a dirt bike and was sulking as I tried to show him what I knew. He still didn't like the idea of having a cat in the house. He thought they were dirty and flea-ridden. I had assured him that if his allergies turned out to be too bad, we would get rid of it. He expressed his skepticism on all points.

It took us a little while to catch the cat once we arrived. The family told us he was a good mouser, about seven months old, and to just feed him enough table scraps to keep him hunting. When the kids finally caught the lean feline, they shoved him into a burlap sack and handed the squirming, screeching bundle to me. I was not accustomed to barn life and was horrified at carrying the cat in the sack, but saw no alternative.

"You better know how to ride this bike as well as you say you can, mister", I said to Mark between clenched teeth as we walked back to the motorcycle. "I'm not sure how long I can hold him in here. He's pretty pissed."

During the ride, the cat began to howl loudly and I had some difficulty holding onto the sack. We were going slowly both because of Mark's comfort level on the motorcycle and so as not to jar the cat more than necessary. Dark clouds were gathering ahead of us.

We were still three kilometers away from town when the drops began to fall. By the time we reached our house, we were both drenched and the sack had fallen silent. I was afraid the little cat had gone into shock or suffocated.

When we got inside, I gently set the sack down on the floor and we closed all of the doors so the cat couldn't escape. I wanted him to learn that this was his home for a couple of days before he went out so that he wouldn't just head straight back to the farm.

I opened up the sack carefully and looked inside. I saw two huge, terrified eyes staring back at me set in wet orange fur. "Oh, come on out, you poor little guy", I cooed at him. "I'm so sorry we put you in there. Come see your new home!"

Slowly, a small orange head peeked out of the bag and looked around. Little by little, paws, a lanky and lean body, and a long tail followed. His fur was light orange and striped – definitely a little tiger tomcat. The pupils of his eyes were so dilated from fear and the darkness of the sack that I couldn't tell what color they were. He was wet, unsure of where he was, and a little unsteady on his feet, but I was very relieved to see that he was basically fine. I continued making encouraging noises to coax him out.

He began sniffing around the room as we watched him and he us. He didn't go too close to Mark, seeming to sense his hostility. Instead, he circled behind furniture and walked around me, looking for potential hiding places.

"He looks like Flea from the Red Hot Chili Peppers with that blond orange spiky fur!" I said, smiling. "He's going to be a real cutie once he gets cleaned up."

"He probably *has* fleas", muttered Mark. "He better keep his mangy butt off our bed if he knows what's good for him."

"Well, then there's something we can agree on", I said lightly. "His name will be Flea. You have your reasons in mind when you think about him, and I have mine. Come on, Flea", I continued, standing up. "Let's see what we can find for you to nibble on."

Mark stood watching us go into the kitchen, looking like he had just lost some turf – to a cat.

It took Flea a few nights to find his way onto our bed. When he did, he wisely chose my side to nestle into. As long as he was outside of the mosquito netting, I thought I could get away with it. I was pretty sure he didn't have fleas. And even if he did, I missed having a cat curl up against me so much that I didn't care about fleas or Mark. Somehow his warm little body comforted me more than Mark's turned back. I drifted off into a content sleep.

Sometime in the middle of the night, I awoke to something jarring the bed and Mark cursing. I opened my eyes and squinted down to the foot of the bed in time to see him kick Flea into the footboard of the bed hard enough to break his back.

"Stop it, you lunatic!" I hissed at him as I backhanded him across his chest. "You're going to kill the poor cat!"

"I told you he can't sleep on this bed!" Mark growled back at me, giving the poor animal a final push off the bed. "And don't hit me again or I'll hit you back!"

I was already getting up out of bed to see if Flea was hurt. He was moving towards the stairs and, startled by my movement, he went down them quickly before I could catch him. I went back to the bed and stood facing Mark with my hands on my hips.

"First of all, don't be so mean!" I said. "The poor cat's just looking for a little warmth. He was outside of the netting at the end of the bed. What was he hurting? And second of all, I'll hit you anytime I see you hit that cat! You want to hit someone – you go find someone your own size." He was glaring at me and clearly not going to respond, so I went back around to my side of the bed and climbed back in.

It was a long time before either of us slept again.

Chapter 11

3/9/97

Dear Mom & Dad,

Work this week was fairly interesting, if not a bit stressful and frustrating for me.

On Monday, Mark observed classes at the Institute for most of the day. I was at NECOG observing the Social Promoters - Lennon and Eduardo - writing an *informé* (a monthly report) with Juan Carlos. I made my first mistake (well, major one, anyway). Juan Carlos had a headache and had been ordering the secretary, Alejandra, and other people (except me) around all morning. Finally, for about the fifth time that morning, he picked up his intercom and barked, "Bring me a coffee!" I said, "You can't say please, Juan Carlos?" He just smiled, then went over to the intercom and very mockingly said, *"Por favor, Alejandra"*.

She came running into his office wanting to know what that was for. He told her that I had suggested he use "please" with people. She informed me that he was the boss and therefore didn't have to say please to anyone because he is superior because of his position!! **AARGGHH!!!** (Stop laughing, Dad!) So seeing as I was already nibbling at my toenails, I decided to go for the knee. I told them, since they're religious folk, that we are all equal before God, to which Juan Carlos responded that yes, but not before men. I was furious! Luckily it was lunchtime, so I was able to escape.

Juan Carlos had to go my way in the truck, so he gave me a ride home. In the truck (after mocking me some more in front of the other male employees), he quietly told me we all have things to learn from each other. Feeling pessimistic, I said nothing, but took it as a reprimand. Mark, feeling optimistic as usual, took it as a concession, when I told him of the incident later.

Time will tell. The issue has not surfaced again. However, that could be because Juan Carlos was in Managua for the rest of the week.

Which brings me to the rest of the week! Tuesday and

Wednesday, and actually Thursday, we did very little! We had to submit plans for the month of March (on the 4th day of March). Mark's was easy; he's being flooded with requests for English classes from the regular teachers (turns out there are about 10-11 schools in town, but only one that teaches English).

If our public school working friends in Detroit think it's bad there, check this out. Teachers must decide in about 7th grade that they want to be teachers. The course of classes then changes to exclude English. Since this class is required for a diploma, they never receive one; only a teaching certificate, basically binding them to that career forever. It is possible to go back to school, but the Institute's rules right now say that they must enroll as full students in order to take English, which means five years of repeated courses just for a crummy English class! Not to mention that they are taking the same classes that many of them teach!

The union is negotiating with the director, but for now, they've approached Mark to teach them anyway, because they want to actually learn English, which doesn't happen in the crummy classes. So he'll have 50-60 teachers on Saturday mornings, plus the English teachers twice a week, and more classes to come!

Anyway, for the rest of his schedule he just copied what days the Social Promoters go out to the two banks he's supposed to work with, and when the Peace Commission meets (so he can "advise" them), and ya! (as people here are fond of saying).

Since my Spanish sucks wooky, at least in my opinion, I'm relegated to following around folks on the Women's Pastoral Committee (WPC) for the month. This is an area of my job anyway, so I guess its okay. They are a busy bunch, so I won't be bored, and two of them, Juanita (Juan Carlos's wife) and Jamileth (Ya-mi-let), have professed once again a promise of teaching me Spanish. However, I think they think I'll learn by osmosis, so I've started studying a little with Mark.

I will get to observe a seminar with the Ecological Brigade leaders for two days on the 13-14th. At least I'll learn some terminology, meet them, and maybe set up some meetings for next month. The rest of the week I basically observed meetings, classes with the street kids who are illiterate, and helped artistically with the planning of the next week of classes (I was the official illustrator). It was an okay week, just linguistically frustrating!

Juan Carlos has agreed to let us drive to Managua to pick up the in-laws! He also said we will have to take another trip there beforehand so he can make sure we know the way. We will be going to Juigalpa (H-we-gall-pa) on the 19th for a meeting with the Regional Director, so I think that's the trip. After Juigalpa, the roads are mostly paved and more or less clearly marked, so we'll be okay from there. However, this is not certain; we may make another trip. I'll keep you informed .

Well, if nothing else, life here is never dull or quiet! There's a Fair in town, and it's about 1 1/2 blocks away. Between it, the discoteca next door to it, and the weeklong festival of the 32nd anniversary of Santo Domingo, it's NEVER quiet! If there's one thing Nicas do well, it's throw a party. There is music at ALL HOURS (even at 4 a.m.) and fireworks, too, with the festival. Luckily, the festival ends tonight.

In addition, as I sit at our kitchen table with the back door open (no screen doors, folks), the kids are playing in the yard, roosters are chasing chickens, mothers are calling their kids, birds sing, the breeze blows, and cooking fires crackle. Whenever I feel down, I just stop and look around. It's <u>so</u> beautiful and enchanting, you have to love it! Well, all except the latrines, I guess. But in spite of all of the crawling, flying, biting and whining animals, the sun always shines, the people are always ready to smile and chat for a while (even if you are Spanish-challenged) and, except for the big trucks that go rumbling by, the air is always sweet.

On that happy, contented note, I'll sign off. As always, missing you lots, love you all lots, and keep in touch.

Love,

Ellen

Chapter 12

I woke up feeling like I would rather roll back over and stay in bed – preferably for the remainder of the day, if not the rest of the week. I had no energy, and no desire to face another day in Santo Domingo.

I lay in bed listening to the sounds of the street outside – women yelling at their children, pots and pans clattering, motorcycles carrying men going to work at the various organizations around town. The sun was streaming brightly through the front window and the sky was already a blinding bright blue so unmarred by clouds that it didn't look real.

Mark was already up and gone. He had a meeting with some of the English teachers. I rolled over and stared at his side of the bed. I felt sad. He seemed to be having such a great time, getting more enthusiastic about his work there each day. Well, as enthusiastic as Mark got.

It was Friday. The weekend would be coming next, thank God. I wasn't really expected in the office. I wondered if that was contributing to my feeling so down. No one seemed to really have much in the way of expectations of me, other than that I kept showing up. I was suffocating under the constant façade of zealous Evangelical posturing that went on everyday, by some who came to the office, and by many of the pastors and lay leaders we worked with around the area.

I sighed and rolled over again, reaching for my pack of cigarettes. I never smoked in bed, but thought, what the hell? Mark wasn't there to disapprove, and neither were any of the judgmental folks in town who thought smoking was a sin, and totally improper for a "lady". I had to chuckle at that thought, even in my subdued state.

There didn't seem to be any middle-ground choices for church. As Sunday approached, we faced yet another round of invitations from the pastors and lay people at NECOG to visit their congregations. I found the services depressing, exhausting, and completely lacking in spiritual presence. I wasn't exactly a person of well-formed faith, but I knew what made me feel inspired, and I hadn't found it yet in any of these church services. They were stereotypical classic hard-core Evangelical churches – they were so over-the-top that they were like caricatures of themselves. The screaming, hollering, Bible-thumping (literally) and writhing around that went on at the front of the church was scary and very uncomfortable. I shuddered at the thought of facing another Sunday.

The Catholic Church was located just half a block from our house. In fact, in lieu of an address like those we had in the States, ours was "half-block east of the Catholic Church, the two-story house". It cracked me up every time. Sorry be the person who didn't know where the Catholic Church in town was!

I had heard music coming from the immense church at various times. It was like other buildings in town – it had walls, but there were large "windows" all along the sides. The windows were really made up of dozens of cinderblocks that had patterned and decorative openings in them. It still seemed strange to me that it never got cold enough to need to have a way to seal up the building. Even with all of the rain, it would have seemed to me that there was a need to keep out the elements. That just wasn't the way of thinking. The buildings seemed to be built more to accommodate nature rather than try and defy it. It was an attractive and intriguing philosophy.

A thought struck me suddenly, and I sat up. *That's it! We can go visit the Catholic Church! Then we won't be lying when we tell the other pastors that we already are visiting another church on Sunday!*

Suddenly, the blinding blue sky and noises of the street outside were appealing again, calling me out, inviting me back into daily living. I smiled and put out my cigarette. Maybe this wouldn't be such a bad day after all.

I was relieved when Mark told me that visiting the Catholic Church was just fine with him. He, too, was irritated by the displays in the other churches we visited. As the son of a mainline Protestant pastor, he struggled with it in different ways than I did, but it was no more inspiring for him.

We managed to find other ways to spend our time in the first part of the day on Sunday, probably more out of relief at not being forced to attend another service than anything else. We were leisurely around the house and I made a big breakfast. It was nice to relax.

We knew there was an afternoon service, so we planned to attend that one. I put on a long tan dress that had fit me well when we arrived, but that I noticed was starting to hang a little more loosely.

We walked to the church and could hear the choir warming up. Some of the music sounded similar to what we'd heard in other churches, and I began to worry a little bit that maybe this wouldn't be so different after all. But my dad had been Catholic his whole life and I had enough experience in the Catholic Church to know that if anything, it was in danger of going to the opposite extreme.

We found seats near the back. The space was cavernous – much bigger on the inside than it appeared from the outside. There was a group of young people, many teenagers, up at the front in what appeared to be a choir "loft" kind of area to the left of a simple stone altar. There were only a handful of people gathering for the service – maybe 30 or 40 in a space that I guessed could easily hold 1,000.

The priest was fairly young – he appeared to be in his 30's – and was very soft-spoken. I had a very hard time understanding him at all. Mark chuckled softly as he began to speak. I looked at him quizzically, and he leaned over to tell me that the priest had a Castilian accent. That was where Mark had learned his Spanish, so he actually understood the priest better than he understood people in town. As I focused my attention back to the front of the church, I smiled at the irony.

I was able to follow the main parts of the Mass, and for once was grateful for my dad having taken me along with him occasionally. It was low-key and calming. The music was very much in the style of other music I'd heard in churches, but I began to realize that this was probably more due to being in Nicaragua than any sort of religious distinction.

During a moment of silent meditation, I bowed my head and closed my eyes. In that quiet moment of absolute stillness in the church, I was overwhelmed by the sense of spiritual peace that I felt. It moved me quite suddenly and unexpectedly to tears. The moment passed and the Mass moved on, but I remained emotional and moved. Mark didn't seem to notice, and I quickly wiped my eyes.

The Mass ended. We filed out quietly and walked towards home as dusk fell. I had a small smile on my face, and Mark asked me what I was thinking about.

"I'll be going back there again," I said, my smile broadening. "I think I just found my new church home."

Chapter 13

3/17/97

Dear folks at home -

Well, here we are writing to you on the e-mail! Right now I am in the office at NECOG typing this in advance. We will be going to Juigalpa on Wednesday until Friday, and we will be using the e-mail there. Mark is teaching a class right now, and I don't really have much work to do right now, so I thought this would be a good time to write.

Last week went by very quickly. Most of the week, I worked on a workshop presentation that I will be giving in April (3rd and 4th) with the Social Promoters, Lennon and Eduardo. My part is on the negative effects of fire (controlled or otherwise) on plants, animals, soil, water and all living things. Eduardo will present on prevention of forest fires, and Lennon will present on creating tree nurseries. The seminar will be for 30-50 (we're never sure how many will show up until they arrive) ecological brigade workers from the colonies. I'm very nervous about doing an entire 2-3 hour lecture in Spanish, but it's all scripted out - I basically just have to read it.

I also attended a few meetings around town, and one that both of us attended in a colony about 45 minutes away by motorcycle! We went with Lennon and Eduardo to a meeting of the Peace Commissions from this region. It was very interesting. The people in attendance were the "real" *campesinos* (country folk). Most were illiterate, all were mud-coated. They were there to talk about the work that they've done in the past year, and what they'd like to do in the coming year. They truly spoke from the heart. Several said there could be no peace in their communities because there are no schools, no medicine, and now practically no food because the freaky weather we've been having has destroyed most of the bean crop.

If that isn't bad enough, they are also vulnerable because of their extreme isolation to attacks by roving groups of bandits that rape, kill and rob the people of the villages. Most expressed a feeling of being at their wits end, but somehow they manage to keep going. It was an extremely interesting and moving meeting. I came away feeling like we lead a life of luxury and ease here in town. Those people are at the base of economic status.

Without moving off the subject too lightly, we are going to be gone a week and a half total. We will go to Managua from Saturday a.m. till Monday morning, staying with Dan and Vicky Johnson, another NPCA couple working for NECOG, Managua. Monday a.m. we are going to the Pacific Ocean for a much-needed vacation! That week (Holy Week) means a week off from work here in Nicaragua. We will stay at the ocean probably until Friday, and then come back here by bus. It only costs $5 each to take the bus, and it's supposed to be a fairly comfortable ride. Better than the truck or that horrible plane again!

Lots of love,

Ellen

Total immersion into a foreign language and culture was a full-time job unto itself for me. In the first few weeks, I came home with a headache almost every day from the sheer concentration and mental exertion it took for me to be in conversation with people around me in Spanish. Mine was broken and often incorrect, but most people seemed thrilled that I was even making the effort and encouraged me to keep going. I contemplated leaving for an immersion class offered in another part of the country, but quickly realized that six weeks away from Santo Domingo would disrupt our lives more than I wanted. The few people I told about the idea of going emphatically announced that they could do a better job of teaching me the language if I just stayed.

Mark was having struggles of his own with the language, which was embarrassing and frustrating for him. He had a degree in Spanish, and had studied abroad in Spain for a semester in college. He was certified to teach it. But the dialect, accent and style of speaking out in what he called the "Nicaraguan Outback" was so different that he was having a tough time relearning the language he thought he'd been able to speak for years. The priest at the Catholic Church seemed to be the only person in town he understood easily.

I had been studying French in Paris while Mark was in Spain during college; I had studied Spanish formally for only two semesters in college, and yet here I was, picking it up very quickly. He never said anything to me, but other people frequently commented that my Spanish was surpassing his. There was still plenty that I didn't understand, but it seemed I was catching up. I could tell it was hard on his ego.

Before either of us realized it, two and a half months had passed, and Mark's parents were on their way down for a visit. I communicated through letters and faxes with my parents on a weekly basis. As the visit approached, my letters contained a running wish list of things that I wanted them to send along. I didn't care much for the food we had on a daily basis – I had never really learned how to cook, and yet there was an unspoken expectation I could feel from Mark that I continue to do the cooking, just as I had in our small apartment in Detroit. And not only cook but cook from scratch! We did not have a refrigerator – just a small three burner camping stove to cook on. I didn't have a clue what tricks other people used to save food day to day, so I ended up trying to just cook small amounts each day all from scratch – boiling hard, dried beans for over an hour; cooking rice for half an hour; sometimes buying a little piece of meat or a couple of eggs and frying them up as well. It took five times longer to prepare the meal than it did to eat it and, by the time I was done cooking, I often had no appetite.

So in addition to asking for some favorite non-microwave-required foods, I noticed that my pants were much looser than before. I had no way of knowing my new size, but the baggier my clothes were, the hotter I was, so I asked them to send a few clothing items I had packed away from when I was a slightly smaller size. It would be nice to have a few "new" things.

Juan Carlos had made sure we both paid close attention to the route on the last trip the NECOG staff had made to Managua. He had decided to let us borrow his pick up truck to go and get Mark's parents from the airport in Managua. I was sure this was intended to impress them since Mark's parents not only lived in the area of the Partnership Office sponsoring us, but his father was a retired pastor as well. With the roads the way they were across the country, the 350-kilometer trip that would have taken roughly three and a half or four hours on highways in the States took over eight hours by truck here. And it took 16 hours on the bus.

The roads were not marked and maps were difficult to come by, so people generally navigated their way across the country by knowing which towns they would pass through on their way from one place to another, and then follow the sporadic signs pointing towards that town.

Just to keep things interesting, most splits in the road were not marked with where they led or the direction in which they went. Usually the next sign for an approaching town would come eight to ten kilometers after the split. And in case that didn't make it complicated enough, when giving directions, Nicaraguans were famous for telling each other to "just go straight" at the split. The only problem was that the splits always went either right or left!

It was, therefore, with a little trepidation and a lot of naïve optimism that Mark and I set off driving on our own to Managua to pick up Mark's parents. Miraculously, we managed to get all the way into Managua without getting turned around. Once in Managua, however, the National Police, who were notorious for stopping foreigners in particular to harass them, stopped us. As we stood helplessly by, the two police officers tore apart Juan Carlos's truck allegedly looking for drugs. When they were satisfied that the truck contained nothing, they left us to reassemble the inside of the truck – the seats, steering wheel, gear shift box, and all luggage had been removed and thrown to the side of the road.

Mark's face was flushed dark red with anger as we tried to put things back together. Luckily, we had made good time and were a couple of hours early arriving in town so we would not be late in getting his parents; a fact of which I cheerfully kept trying to remind him. It did not ease his rage. He finally snapped at me and kept struggling. I walked away and lit a cigarette.

Once we were back in the car and on the road, he realized it was only another 500 meters to the airport. While this did not help ease Mark's frustration with the police, it did mean that we would be able to get his parents on time.

I watched the anger boil in Mark's blood by stealing glances at his neck where it gathered in an angry brick colored patch. I had stopped talking when he snapped at me at the side of the road but I could sense his tension and knew not to say anything else. I was feeling tense myself – my in-laws were not my favorite people. My mother-in-law seemed to always be measuring me against some imaginary stick that I wasn't allowed to see. She was known to make comments about my weight, which I just thought was rude. Not everyone was meant to be short and petite. My father-in-law was amiable enough but had a way of asking me questions that made me feel like I was being interrogated.

I was looking forward to seeing familiar faces and to the things I hoped they would bring from my family, but I was not looking forward to the tension I knew would plague the house over the next week. I tried to tell myself that I didn't care what they thought, but knew that their arrival was the reason I'd dressed so carefully, selecting clothes that complimented my shrinking figure. I hoped the knee-length denim skirt and top I had put on would give me confidence as we waited for them to come out of the airport terminal. I desperately wanted another cigarette before they got there but knew there wasn't time. Like my own parents, they didn't know I smoked.

They arrived without ceremony, smiles and hugs all around. I suppressed a smug laugh at how they were dressed – they looked like I had when we had arrived a few months before – dressed for mountain climbing when all they would be doing that day was riding in a hot truck and hanging out in a hot city.

After all of the luggage was piled in, I volunteered to sit in the back of the truck with Mark's father. I hoped the amount of wind and noise from the road would kill any chance for questioning. As he climbed back there with me, I realized that little would stop him after not seeing us for over two months.

"So! How's life treating you guys? Tell me everything!" he said jovially, while struggling to find a comfortable spot among the suitcases.

We stayed in Managua for a couple of days before heading back to Santo Domingo. My mother-in-law was having some stomach troubles, so we were delayed in heading out by an hour or so, which annoyed me. Night had fallen by the time we made it back, and we all just collapsed into bed after a quick dinner. Mark's parents took the only bed in the house while Mark and I each got a hammock. That was fine with me – I found the cocoon of the lightweight cloth both comforting in its hugging snugness and breathable enough that I never felt claustrophobic.
Plus Flea liked the hammock, too and would come and nestle into the crook of my legs whenever I got into it. He provided extra warmth and a feeling of being loved that was free from the complications of the relationship with my husband. As I climbed with cramped legs into the soft hammock, Flea came bounding in the open window and looked at me with expectant eyes. I smiled and kissed the air, calling him to come and curl up. I was still smiling as I drifted off to sleep, the soft rumble of his purr on my foot.

Chapter 14

I awoke to the usual sounds of our neighbors preparing breakfast and the household rising for a new day. The roosters were crowing as usual while a child next door was being scolded for some mischievous deed. I stretched in the hammock and peeked out into the early morning light. Down by my feet, Flea stretched and yawned, too, before curling back up into a ball at my feet, willing me to do likewise.

I sat up and scratched him behind the ears before swinging my legs over the side of the hammock, forcing the cat to also disembark. As I watched, he walked over to Mark's sleeping form in the other hammock, sniffed, and turned to look back at me as if to see what I thought of his curling up with Mark instead. I raised an eyebrow at the small cat and whispered, "Yeah, right" under my breath. Flea seemed to agree with my assessment, so he jumped into the window and walked out onto the closest tree limb, off to find breakfast.

I felt rested. I had come to love this time of day in Nicaragua – the sounds and smells of early morning household activities around us, yet the solitude of an otherwise still sleeping house of my own. I quickly dressed and went downstairs to make some coffee and steal a quick smoke before anyone else got up.

The first few days of the visit had gone smoothly so far. I was proud of myself for having maintained a cool head and avoided making sharp retorts to my mother-in-law's subtle insults. On a visit to the NECOG office, they had both gotten the chance to hear me speak Spanish for the first time. Their surprise was evident on their faces, but only my father-in-law could manage a compliment. His wife simply looked away and started another conversation with her son.

As I gathered up the clothes from the past few days to do the washing by hand in the giant concrete sink, I heaved a deep sigh. Normally, doing laundry only every couple of days was fine – Mark and I didn't go through that many clothes. But now I would be washing for four. I didn't understand why the in-laws couldn't just take their own damn laundry back home to wash it, but Mark seemed eager to show off in some weird way how we did our laundry.

I had finished washing the shirts, had the underwear all soaking in Clorox and was starting to work on the shorts and pants when my mother-in-law came into the kitchen.

"Well, good morning! You're up early," said the older woman, an amused smile on her lips as she watched me sweat in the early morning heat. She herself was dressed in a cool cotton jumper, quite comfortable and refreshed. She looked like she was wondering for the thousandth time why her son had chosen this unladylike woman for his mate.

"I've been up for an hour," I replied lightly. "There's coffee on the stove if you would like some." I glanced over my shoulder as my mother-in-law tried to casually sniff the pot where I had brewed coffee. "It's fresh," I added sourly.

"Oh, I'm sure it is," came the reply with a little embarrassed laugh. "I was just enjoying the aroma." She helped herself to a cup. To me, it seemed she did so with trepidation. "So what's on our agenda today?"

"Well, I'm just about done washing the clothes, which means I'll be going to wake Mark up so he can come wring them out for me," I began.

"Oh, no, don't do that!" interrupted his mother. "Why would you do that? The poor boy works hard enough! He needs his sleep. You know he's never really been much of a morning person. I'm sure you can handle this yourself, can't you?"

As I struggled to compose myself, scenes from my own 12-14 hour long days of hiking through farms and working in the blazing sun in jeans and work boots flashing through my mind. Mark had apparently not been very honest with his parents when sharing with them how each of us spent our days – he spent his in offices and classrooms, many of which were air-conditioned.

"Actually, it's one of the small ways in which we share responsibility for keeping our house up," I said instead of screaming at the woman, as I desired to do. "After he wrings out the heavy clothes, he mops the floors while I hang the clothes. And you see, since I've already been up for over an hour working and he's gotten to sleep an extra hour, it all kind of balances out."

"Well, I just think it's unnecessary," said the older woman with apparent disapproval in her voice. "I'm sure there are plenty of other things that Mark does around the house to, quote unquote, share the responsibility with you. He went to bed after you did, so he hasn't gotten as much sleep as you have." She acted as if I was really being too demanding of her poor Mark and did not try to hide the annoyance in her voice.

I was ready to attack the woman. *What business of yours is this anyway?!*, I wanted to scream at her. Instead, I took a deep breath and trying to sound innocent said, "Okay, then, how about if you give me a hand with this since you're already up?"

"Sure, no problem," came the cocky reply. I mopped the floors while my mother-in-law struggled mightily to get enough water out of the heavy garments that they weren't still streaming. She was still wrestling them as I went upstairs with a triumphant smile on my face to get dressed.

As I passed Mark's sleeping form, I couldn't help but kick him gently and say, "Hey, how about getting your lazy ass up and going to help your mother. The poor woman's been fighting with your jeans for half an hour to get enough water out of them that they'll dry."

"What?" a sleepy head popped up out of the hammock. "Did you put my mom to work? Why didn't you come wake me up?"

"That's a question you should ask your mommy," I sneered. "I'm done arguing with her about how my own god damn marriage works!"

Mark blinked a couple of times, trying to clear his eyes and mind of the sleep still in them. "Oh, boy," he sighed. "This doesn't sound good. What happened?"

"I'm not going to discuss it right now," I hissed. "I'm going to Santa Estelita today with Lennon. I'm going to be late if I don't leave now." I finished yanking on my boots and walked out the door.

Mark heaved another sigh and dropped back into the hammock.

It was going to be a long visit.

Chapter 15

4/15/97

Dear Mom and Dad -

This is not a letter to share with everyone. This is a letter in which I get to express myself, and you as parents get to console me and keep my despair to yourself. (In other words, this is a bitch session!)

Mark's parents arrived just fine on Saturday. We made it to Managua all right, as I wrote in the e-mail message. Unfortunately, they so monopolized our time after their arrival that, due to our deadlines, I was prevented from checking the e-mail again on Sunday, so I missed any message that you may have sent back .

Monday they started telling Mark all the things that we should do around the house to improve it. They want us to paint inside, and not only that, but they want us to hurry up and do it while they are there so that they can take pictures. Of course, they've offered to do it for us. The problem is that we can't adjust the house without consulting our landlord, and with something like painting, we have to talk about adjusting the rent because it's an improvement. That's a much bigger deal here than in the States, and it takes time. They also want us to rebuild the back steps, which we've done several times. They are about as good as they are going to get! This is Nicaragua!!! And rural Nicaragua at that!!

Then, of course, there is a lot of small stuff, like the fact that I'm up at 6 a.m. everyday washing clothes. I am married to their son. He chose me to be married to. Therefore, it is not their station to tell him that I shouldn't ask him to get up and help me every morning. When they say this, he doesn't stand up to them and say, "Well, WE have discussed this and decided that she washes clothes and I clean the floors every day. It's our routine." Or better yet, "BUTT THE HELL OUT! THIS IS NOT YOUR HOUSE NOR YOUR MARRIAGE!" **ARGGHHHH!!!!** Instead, he just says, "Hmm." What a wuss I married!

Speaking of which, yesterday, after our morning bible study and other events I'll talk about in a minute, we went in the truck to Santa Estelita. Since Mark needs practice driving the truck, he drove. Juan Carlos didn't come. It was the four of us, plus Lennon and Eduardo. We went to talk to someone who is a local Social Promoter and see what he's doing on this piece of land. (It was actually a very interesting experience, but since this is a bitching letter, I'll talk about interesting stuff later.)

Anyway, Mark was driving pretty badly. He was crawling over places that were flat and fairly smooth, and speeding over bumps. He was also running the engine hot by constantly driving in second gear. When I said something to him about it, he proceeded to drive faster over all kinds of road, and his mother blamed me when she didn't feel well later on because I had told Mark to "drive faster". Once again, **ARGGHHHH!!!!**

Today I get a break in the morning (right now) and this afternoon I think they'll be here. However, I am going tree planting with Lennon Wednesday and Thursday, and with Eduardo on Friday. I'll have plenty of time with them in the mornings and evenings, though, I'm sure.

All that, PLUS we have not received hardly ANY mail, and as of tomorrow, we will have been here for **nine weeks**!!!

That's all. I promise to have a "good" letter for you to share before they leave.

Love,

Ellen

I was walking off my anger at my mother-in-law when I reached the NECOG office. Even my excitement about going out to the colonies with Lennon wasn't enough to completely vanquish the demons she always managed to awaken in me.

He stepped out from the shadows of the building from where it seemed he had been watching me and smiled at me as I approached, catching me off guard. I was startled to see him emerge from nowhere.

"Oh, good morning. I didn't see you there," I stammered in Spanish. I felt my face instantly flush under his penetrating stare.

"Good morning," he said softly. "Ready to go?"

I climbed onto the back of his motorcycle, more gracefully now that I'd had some practice. We were out of the town before he spoke.

"So what are you so mad about this morning?" he said with amusement in his voice.

"Oh, Mark's stupid mother is such a bitch," I spat, all of my anger from that morning flooding back at the chance to talk about it with a sympathetic ear. "She keeps trying to get into the middle of things that have nothing to do with her. And her momma's boy son doesn't seem to have enough of a spine to stand up to her and put her in her place."

Lennon laughed loudly with genuine enjoyment of the image. He had already observed that Mark was not the type to stand up to anyone on anyone's behalf, not even his own. He listened to me search for the words to describe to him what had happened. He waited for me to get it all out of my system before laughing again and speaking.

"I can't believe how fast you have learned Spanish, *gringita fea!*" he exclaimed over the noise of the motorcycle and road. "I don't think I've ever met anyone who learned it so quickly! Surely they must be impressed by that!"

"Gringita fea?" I shot back. "Why are you calling me a 'little ugly American girl'? That's not nice!" I laughed and play-punched his shoulder, but I was hurt.

Lennon laughed again. "Its meant in irony," he explained, pausing for a moment. I was reviewing his comment in my head, trying to see if I was understanding him correctly. I was just about to ask when he continued, "You are very beautiful. To call you 'ugly' is an obvious contradiction to the truth."

I blushed. I had never been comfortable with anyone complimenting my looks. It hadn't happened that much in my life, frankly, and I surely didn't believe that I was anything special in that department. But I had gotten compliments often since arriving in Nicaragua. I chalked it up to being foreign, something "exotic". I wasn't sure if Lennon meant it in that way. I decided to push any thoughts about it out of my head.

We bantered back and forth during the hour-long ride to Santa Estelita, Lennon, I think, intentionally pushing my buttons occasionally just to hear the spark come back into my voice. I started to realize that he was flirting with me.

I was increasingly attracted to him and had no idea what to do with the emotions he stirred up in me. I felt like I was going to burst if I didn't tell him about it, even though I had no idea what I wanted to have happen as a result.

We arrived early for our meeting with a local group of farmers to talk about the upcoming tree nursery program we'd be launching. I kept thinking about Lennon and being attracted to him. It was hard to sit still in the meeting. I felt like I needed to unload how I felt. I had never been one to harbor feelings from afar.

I got through the rest of the day in Santa Estelita, my head filled with romantic images of holding hands, flattering compliments, chaste kisses and warm hugging embraces. I was glad that Lennon was in charge of the meeting – it gave me more opportunity to watch him lead the farmers through the steps for preparing their tree nurseries. Not only did I find him physically appealing, but also he shared my values about reforesting the stripped land. It made him attractive on an entirely different level.

During the ride home, we chatted about the meeting and our plans for that colony. He told me about the classes he was taking at the University in Juigalpa, the nearest large city, to get his degree. I told him about my own college studies and my desire to impact real change in the world through my experiences in Nicaragua.

As we approached Santo Domingo again, I began to feel a little depressed. While Lennon was really flirtatious out in the *colonias*, he tended to be much more reserved in the office. We passed the hospital where his wife Patricia was standing in the doorway of her small office. We both waved, my depression settling even more heavily over me.

Chapter 16

I shook my head as if I could shake away the thoughts crowded inside. I was coming to our house where Mark and his parents were sure to be waiting. I had to pull myself together. But the front door was closed and when I opened it with my key, there was no one inside. Instead, I found a note that they were off looking at one of the schools where Mark was working with some teachers. The note also suggested that we could meet up to go to dinner someplace together. I smiled wryly at that part – Mark had volunteered to cook that night.

At first I was relieved to find the house empty, but as I looked around, my relief turned to anger. The house I had left so tidy and clean that morning was now strewn with clothes, papers and magazines, and the sink was full of dirty dishes. There was mud tracked throughout the rooms. This was not the first time I had come home and found the house in this condition after leaving it clean in the morning. Something had to change.

With every item I picked up, my blood boiled a degree higher. All of the previous offenses Mark had committed flashed in my mind – the unspoken expectations that I do all the shopping, cooking and most of the cleaning; the closed look in his eyes whenever I tried to talk to him about doing things differently; the silence with which he met my desperate arguing, trying whatever I could just to get him to engage with me as some shred of proof that our relationship was still alive.

He doesn't care, I thought bitterly. *I'm working my butt off out in the stifling hot colonies for long hours while he's holed up in some air conditioned office with those fucking computers! Do I want to do housework when I come home? No! Do I want to cook and clean up for his stupid ass? No! So why do I keep doing it anyway?!?*

Suddenly I stopped, rocked by my own thought. Why *did* I keep doing it? I thought about every single other woman I knew in Nicaragua, both working full-time outside of their homes and a few that stayed at home, like Juanita. They all had *empleadas* – young women or older girls who came to their homes to cook and clean for them on a daily basis. I had been encouraged on other occasions by a couple of them to get an *empleada* for myself, but I hadn't quite been able to bring myself to do it. The concept of being humble and not building a fiefdom around ourselves had been so thoroughly drilled into our heads at the orientation training we'd received before coming that I just hadn't ever considered it an option. But it was becoming clear that this was too much. I couldn't do it all. I suddenly realized I was going to have to ask for help. It was a very sobering thought and one that made me uncomfortable.

When Mark returned with his parents, the house was clean again. I waited for one of them to say something about my efforts, but no one seemed to even notice. I managed to get through dinner at one of the local eateries with a fake smile and pleasantries, my anger still boiling below the surface. Once we returned home and settled in for the evening, I could wait no longer.

"What exactly do I have to do or say to get you to quit living like a pig?" I exploded. "I'm really tired of leaving the house cleaned and picked up only to come home after a usually very long day to find it once again looking like an ape lives here! What is your problem?!" I was trying not to scream at him, knowing that his mother would be straining to hear every word from the other room.

Mark stared at me with a dumbfounded look on his face. He had not seen this coming and was embarrassed that his parents might overhear me scolding him like a child.

"Keep your voice down," he replied. "What is your problem now?"

"*You* are my problem!" I screamed at him, unable to control my anger anymore. I no longer cared who was listening. "You are the most inconsiderate asshole I've ever voluntarily spent time around! When I left this morning, the house was clean – the floors had been mopped, the laundry done, and there were no dishes in the sink. I come home a few hours later to find that a tornado has been through here! I can't live like this any more!" I knew my temper was getting to the point of no return where I would say and/or do something I regretted, but I didn't care. My patience with Mark and nerves felt stretched like a rubber band about to snap.

Mark just stared at me. His brows were furrowed and the corners of his mouth turned down slightly. I could see him clenching and unclenching his jaw.

"You aren't even going to say anything??" His silence only fueled my rage.

"What can I say?" he hissed back at me. "Anything I say you're going to twist around and use against me, so why the hell should I even bother?"

The two of us just stood glaring at each other, hands balled into fists and planted on hips, each of us trying to get a grip on our anger while I wondered how we had ended up in this marriage. He was probably wondering the same thing. I was the first one to break the silence.

"I'm working extremely long hours at an extremely physical job," I said, gritting my teeth to try and calm myself, my fists clenching at my sides. "You essentially sit on your ass every day. And yet, I'm the one that's expected to magically get everything done around here. I can't do it anymore."

Mark regarded me in silence for a moment, his light brown eyes cold with anger. "Well, why don't you just hire an *empleada* then?" he asked. "Everyone else has one. I don't understand why you insist on trying to be superwoman."

I would not have been more shocked if he had thrown cold water on my face. Suddenly all the wind was gone from my sails. I was expecting to have to fight him for this, expecting it to be a decision that we came to together, reasoned through, justified to ourselves. Suggesting that I simply take the action myself and solve "my" problem both deflated and further angered me. Deflation and the exhaustion of the day won out.

"Fine," I said disgusted. "I'm gonna do that tomorrow. Thanks for your help." I picked up my bag and headed for the stairs. "I'm going for a walk."

4/18/97

Dear Mom, Dad and other people reading this -

This has been a busy last couple of weeks. Mark's parents are preparing to leave today for Managua. They will leave for the States in the morning on Saturday. We had a very nice visit with them. They painted our living room for us, and left us enough paint to do the kitchen ourselves. They got to visit a lot of places in and around town, and I think they enjoyed themselves.

I started my regular visits to the campo yesterday. Lennon is in charge of the North Zone, in which there are nine colonies, and Eduardo has the South Zone, which only has six. Yesterday Lennon and I went to Santa Estelita to start giving out the materials for tree nurseries. Part of my job will be going back several times over the next year to each colony to see how they are progressing. I have to keep a detailed list of who grows what and how it does, and also if they are keeping up on the project. If they don't, it's my duty to report that to Juan Carlos who will then not allow them to receive nursery materials the following season. These are important resources for them as they help protect their crops when the trees are big enough to transplant.

This afternoon after Mark's parents leave I'm going to two more colonies (Lennon again) to do the same thing. I'm learning a lot; I'm constantly impressed how technically informed these peasant farmers are about the environment and different ways to preserve it. Granted, some still don't take very good care of it, but there are a few I've met that really have it together, and I have a lot to learn from them. I've already received several invitations to come back.

Mark's been mostly playing tour guide this week, but he continues to teach English classes. We are supposed to be getting a computer for the office any day now, and then he will work on teaching everyone how to use it. I've been teaching Alejandra, the secretary, how to use ours a little, as she prefers to learn with a woman! She's embarrassed to ask questions of Mark; too much *machismo* exposure has made her somewhat afraid to not understand things in front of men. So she smiles and nods when Mark teaches her, then comes to me to ask her questions. Juan Carlos finally saw what was going on and took me aside to tell me that, if I would be so kind, it was fine with him if I just taught Alejandra instead of Mark. At times, he can be a master of diplomacy.

Speaking of, I want to tell you about this strike we're experiencing. It started Monday morning, so it's a good thing we came back Sunday night or we would have gotten trapped in Managua. The strike is being staged by, ironically enough, the *Contras* and the *Sandinistas* together. It is a protest against the current president who is allowing ex-patriots of Nicaragua to come back and force poor people out of their homes or off their land to reclaim what the previous government (well, two governments ago) confiscated when they left the country. Some fear there will be violence in Managua where a higher homeless population cannot be tolerated; the poor will revolt.

However, we seem to have landed ourselves one of the more secure spots in NECOG here in Santo Domingo. Not only do we have a more isolated and calmer spot, but also we have Juan Carlos to protect us, and the best and the most well-known Peace Commissioners in the country.

We visited the strike, which is in every city of any size, on Monday with Juan Carlos. He was allowed to pass without a problem, after greeting all his old *Sandinista* buddies that he worked with in Peace and Reconciliation during the Civil War. (He worked as a disarmer.)

On the way back from the colony we went to visit, I was driving. As I approached the blockade into town, the men would not let me pass. Then Juan Carlos poked his head around from where he was more or less hiding, and suddenly the club-toting serious faces broke into smiles and jokes, and the tree branches blocking the road were pulled aside! If it had been the *Contras* (or ex-*Contras*), everyone says that there wouldn't have been a problem to pass either. Juan Carlos, NECOG and the Peace Commissions have such good relations with everyone on all sides that we would have been safe with him wherever we were. I am constantly amazed at how people respond to him with complete respect and trust. And now that he's begun to say please and thank you around the office a little bit, he's becoming downright lovable!

We're becoming better friends with many people here. Mark had his motorcycle lessons two weeks ago, and my turn is coming soon. Juan Carlos is anxious for me to learn, although I'm not sure why since I have to borrow one of the SP's *"motos"* to go, and they need them almost every day. Oh, well; it will be good to know how anyway. I can now ride with either of them without fear. Especially Lennon, with whom I tend to go more right now; I have total confidence in him.

Anyway, these friendships, and the beginnings of mail arrival (we finally got your letter, Mom, a whole month after you sent it!) make life more and more enjoyable here. We both feel well adjusted. I had a day of homesickness shortly after the arrival of Mark's parents, but was comforted by everyone in the office and I feel much better. Mark continues to do fine, but I suspect he may feel a little "down" after his parents leave. Anyway, we know now that we can count on our new friends to take care of us when we're in need .

Love you all lots...

Love,

Ellen

Chapter 17

Though our neighbors did not speak any English, they had caught the word "*empleada*" during the loud argument. I was home early from work the next afternoon, writing a letter home. Mark and his parents were off at one of the schools where he taught, and then he'd be taking them to the local "airport" to fly back to Managua. What mattered was they weren't there to bother me. Neither of the out-laws had said anything about the previous night's argument, acting as if nothing was unusual about me and Mark screaming at each other. Unfortunately, they were right.

There was a soft knock on the open front door. I leaned over from my spot at the kitchen table to look into the front room and see who was there. Our landlord and next-door neighbor stood awkwardly next to a woman who looked to be well into her thirties. She stood about 5'2", an average height for Nicaraguan women, and of average build. Her arms and legs were muscular from hard labor, and her dark eyes watched me from a solemn face.

I got up and went to the door, smiling at the landlord. "Good afternoon. How can I help you?", I asked in my best Spanish.

The man was clearly uncomfortable. He shifted from one foot to another and cleared his throat a couple of times before managing, "Well, um, I was wondering if you might want a hand with, ah, things around the house. I know you, uh, work long hours, and, um, well, there's a lot to do." His face was flushed and he was having a hard time meeting my eye. I was concentrating on understanding the small man and my brow was furrowed. It was not helping him feel better. He rushed on, "So this is Mireya. She is a long time acquaintance of my family and a hard worker. She's here to offer her, ah, services to you as an empleada. I, uh, would, um, highly recommend her. She is a good, Christian woman." He quickly stepped aside, and it was visually apparent that he was relieved to have my focus be shifted to someone else.

"Hello, *Señora*," Mireya said softly, looking up at me. Her gaze was steady and framed by a brown face and very black hair. "I am a good *empleada*," she said simply.

I recovered from my surprise at the situation quickly and smiled. "That's great," I said, "but I'm not even sure what an *empleada* does, or how much you charge. I'm very new to this." I laughed nervously and wished Mark was there to at least make sure I understood this woman correctly.

Mireya smiled back. Her two front teeth were edged in silver and they peeked out from a dimpled and suddenly beautiful face. She laughed lightly – the sound had a musical quality. "I can do as much or as little as you like. I can cook, clean and do the laundry. I can shop for the food if you leave me money, or you can buy what you want me to cook. I can iron your clothes for you or just wash and hang them. I can sweep, mop and scrub your floors and shower every day, or I can just do it once a week. Whatever you like, really." As she spoke, her hands animated what she described. She was clearly in her element explaining her skills, and I liked her immediately.

"What will you charge me?" I asked hesitantly, not sure how to phrase the crude question with more grace.

Mireya laughed softly again. "Well, it depends on which of my services you use. We can start at C$250 per month and adjust as needed if you like. I can start today, too." I had to ask her to repeat the figure – numbers were a challenge for me to grasp the first time I heard them. I did a rough mental calculation – Nicaraguan Córdoba were exchanging between 10 and 11 per US dollar, so Mireya was going to charge about U$25 per month to liberate me from the shackles I felt attached me to my household duties.

"Yes!" I exclaimed. We spent a few minutes outlining her starting duties – mop the floors daily to keep the unending dust and mud under control; wash clothes daily; prepare lunch and dinner daily. I thought it would be easier on Mireya if I just bought the food myself and left it for Mireya to prepare. Besides, I wasn't sure if I trusted her enough right away to give her weekly grocery money – that would take a little time.

We agreed that Mireya would start the following day and bid each other good day. I returned to my letter writing, my mood completely lifted. I reread the last paragraph I'd written to try and regain my place, but found I no longer felt like ranting about Mark. I crumpled up the piece of paper and threw it on the floor, pulled out a fresh one and started over.

Chapter 18

The first few days that Mireya came to the house, I was careful to follow Juanita's advice. Since she normally arrived after we had already left for the NECOG office, I left detailed notes of instruction for her on the kitchen table each day. Juanita had convinced me that empleadas in general were not to be trusted with anything – with money, to follow direction, to work independently, not to steal your stuff. I was careful to put away my more private possessions in my trunk. I even locked it every day.

The notes I left were basic.

"Good morning, Mireya – I hope you are well today. Please buy rice and beans, plantains, cream and cuajada today. Here is enough money to cover the costs. Mark and I will both be home for lunch today. Thank you. –Elena"

Mireya made no comment; she just did exactly as I asked in the notes each day, and said very little when she served us lunch. We insisted that she sit and eat with us, which made her visibly uncomfortable. I took her silence for a lack of education and years of service that had trained her to be that way.

Near the end of the first week, I was not home for lunch due to a trip out to a *colonia*. Along with my usual daily instructions on what to buy and how much, I had told Mireya in my note that morning that I wouldn't be there, and that I would see her the following day.

When I came home that evening, there was a note from Mireya waiting for me. Mark pointed to it on the table.

"I can't really make out what she's saying. Her handwriting is even worse than mine."

I guffawed. "Wow, that's pretty bad. But your Spanish is better. I may need your help in deciphering it." I picked it up and squinted at it.

Her writing was like that of a young child – fat looping letters that were a visible struggle to write. The letters all sort of ran together and I had a hard time making out individual words. I asked Mark to help me, and between us we pieced together –

"Doña Elena – Thank you for your note. I hope your trip out to Calero today was a success. I bought what you requested and made enough food to leave you for dinner. I did not have enough to buy detergent, so I got it on credit. Until tomorrow, Mireya."

It took me several readings to figure out and absorb what she had written. I found myself wondering what level of education she had completed, and thinking that I shouldn't judge her by her ability (or lack thereof) to write. Then I was embarrassed to even have to mentally tell myself not to judge her.

The following day I left her enough money to cover the food and the detergent, and neither of us mentioned it again.

At the end of the second week, we were having lunch as we usually did. Mireya was her usual quiet self. Mark and I were politely chatting in Spanish so as not to be rude. She made no effort to be part of the conversation, and we didn't really do much to encourage her.

As I finished telling Mark about an upcoming trip out to one of my colonies in the coming week, Mireya suddenly looked up at me, directly in the eye, and said softly, "Doña Elena, when I worked for the family from the Netherlands, they found it to be more convenient for them to not have to worry about planning their menu each day. They enjoyed giving that boring task over to me so that they could focus on their more important jobs and taking care of the children."

She stopped speaking, her steady gaze never leaving my face. I was still processing what she had said. I wasn't sure that I had understood her completely, so I glanced over at Mark to see what he thought. He was openly staring at her as well. She took our silence for anger at her boldness.

"Excuse me, I did not mean to overstep," she said quickly, looking down at her plate. "I only thought –"

"No, Mireya, not at all," I interrupted. I laughed nervously. "I just wanted to make sure I understood what you suggested. Can you tell me again?"

She looked up, visibly relieved. "I have noticed that you both work long hours, and that you, Doña Elena, travel out to those *colonias* frequently. I was thinking of ways that I could make your life easier, and one suggestion I had was that you allow me to plan the meals for you. It would be one less thing for you to worry about." She paused for a moment. "We could try it for a week or so, and if you are not happy with my choices, we can go back to the way we're doing it now."

I thought about all of Juanita's warnings about *empleadas* as I looked at Mireya. I was a little stunned by how eloquently she spoke, and more than a little embarrassed for being stunned. My face flushed. Juanita had told me firmly not to tell any *empleada* that we were new at this kind of arrangement, but as I looked at Mireya's gentle face, I trusted my own instincts.

"I think that sounds like a great idea, Mireya," I said, smiling. "Thank you for suggesting it! This is the first time we've ever had someone work for us in our home, and we are not sure of how to handle things. Any other suggestions that you have for making this work better for all of us would be great."

Mireya's face immediately relaxed and lit up in a beautiful smile. Her soft laugh was musical, and I found myself wanting to trust her completely. She looked down again, a little coyly, and then glanced up again, something else clearly on her mind.

"Did you have another suggestion, Mireya?" I asked, my own smile expanding.

"Well, just that another thing my family from the Netherlands used to find made their lives a lot easier was to not worry themselves with the details of how much of various household supplies we had on-hand." She hesitated, and I nodded that I understood. She continued in a rush, her face more serious now, "I know that you have probably been warned by people who want to protect you from dishonest *empleadas* that you should never trust any of us with much of anything. While I would never insult you or your friends by suggesting that they were wrong, I hope that so far I have done nothing to suggest that I am dishonest."

I laughed again, a little more nervously this time at how close she was coming to the mark with what Juanita had said. "No, of course not. What did you have in mind?" While I tried to keep my tone light, I felt a little bit like I was being set up for something.

"There are some days when you have left sufficient money for the food you've requested, but I've also needed to buy detergent to wash the clothes or floor cleaner. I've either had to go without those supplies, or have taken them on my own credit with vendors that know me personally and gotten the money from you after the fact." She paused and searched my face to make sure I was understanding her. I nodded.

"It might be easier for all of us if we talked about what supplies I need each week, and you could just leave me enough money for the week." She rushed on, looking both uncomfortable and determined at the same time. "I am an honest woman, Doña Elena, and I will continue to bring you whatever change there might be at the end of the week. I will not steal from you." She made this last comment with a fierce edge to her voice, looking me directly in the eye.

I watched her for a moment, and she held my gaze. I believed her, and told her so.

We listed off the items that she would need in the course of the coming week, and I was again taken aback by how sharp her mind was. My embarrassment deepened at mistakenly assuming her silence meant she was not very bright. She was intimately familiar with how much every item cost from the various vendors, and deftly calculated and recalculated how much she would need based on where she would have time to shop each day. Her confidence came through very clearly, and I quickly found myself believing that maybe Juanita wasn't right about all *empleadas* after all.

Chapter 19

The house was quiet. The sun was shining brightly, coming in through Ellen's bedroom windows, making her feel carefree and happy. She was playing with Mandy, dressing her in a new tennis outfit she'd just gotten for her tenth birthday. She was talking quietly to the doll about how nice she looked.

"Ellen, can you come here for a minute please?" came the very distant voice, straining to be heard up through the clothes chute all the way from the basement to the top floor. A quiet cough followed. "Ellen?"

Ellen froze for a moment; her reverie interrupted, then went bounding lightly over to the clothes chute, and opened the little door. She poked her head carefully into the small space, and looked down at the elderly man looking up at her with a smile.

"Hi," he said, his smile widening. "I was wondering if you could come down here and give me a hand with something for a moment."

Ellen felt a little finger of fear snake through her belly. Swallowing it back, she called down, "Sure, Uncle Gerald, I'll be right there."

She descended to the main floor cautiously, looking around. She felt uneasy. The house was empty except for the two of them. Her mother and Aunt Jenny were out grocery shopping together and wouldn't be back for an hour or so. Her brother was playing at a friend's house, and her father was at work. She swallowed hard again and turned to go down the stairs to the basement.

Her heart was thudding in her chest. He was standing at the bottom of the stairs with that smile still on his wrinkled, whiskered long face. She looked at his watery light eyes and wobbly chin. He reached one shaky hand forward towards her.

"I just need a hand lifting something in your dad's workshop. I can't quite manage it myself. Can you give me a hand, like a good girl?" His tone was syrupy sweet.

She hesitated, but then went forward to meet him. Her hand instinctively went up to take his.

"Thank you, sweetheart," he said softly. "You're such a good girl. Come here and let me give you a little hug."

He was folding her into his huge frame with those shaky

hands. He leaned down as if to kiss her cheek, aiming for her mouth instead. Her mind was screaming at her to run as she felt his slimy tongue pass over her lips. His hand groped the front of her shirt. She broke away and ran quickly up the stairs.

"Ellen, honey, wait! Where are you going? I thought you were a good girl! I thought you were going to help me?" This last sentence he said in a singsong voice. She felt as if she were going to vomit. She was terrified, not knowing where to run. He started up the stairs, still calling her in a singsong voice, "El-len..."

Her eyes darted around the dining room where she was rooted, desperately trying to think of what to do, of where she could go to get away. He now stood between her and the back door, and the front door was locked with a key. She'd never get it open in time.

Instinct took over and she ran around into the hallway, sprinting up the stairs as fast as her little legs would take her. As she passed the opening at the top of the basement stairs, he grabbed at her arm, but she yanked it away before he could take hold.

"Ellen, why on earth are you running from me? I just wanted you to help me! I was just trying to show my appreciation!" He was panting slightly from coming up the stairs. He was not in good shape from years of smoking and being overweight, and was over 70 years old.

"Don't touch me!" she screamed at him, running into the bathroom upstairs next to her bedroom. It was the only door she could think of that locked, and she was struggling to make the lock turn. The house was old and door locks inside of the house were not something her family ever used. She fumbled with it now, worrying that either she wouldn't be able to turn it in time, or that she would get trapped inside. Either way, she was desperate to get away.

"El-len..." that singsong voice again, getting closer. He was actually coming up the stairs! He never came up to the second floor! Boy, wait until she told her mother!

She got the door lock engaged, and backed away from it slowly, her heart in her throat, wringing her hands. She was shaking from head to toe.

"What do you want? Leave me alone!" she yelled, hearing

uncertainty in her own voice.

"Ellen, what are you getting so upset about?" He was just outside of the door now. He was trying to turn the door handle. She clamped her hand over her mouth to keep from throwing up. "Huh? Tell me what's wrong?"

Ellen was momentarily shocked into silence. "What's wrong? You tried to kiss me and touch me, that's what's wrong!" She was incredulous.

A soft laugh. "No, I didn't, honey." More laughing. "I was merely trying to say thank you for helping me, and if my hand accidentally slipped and touched you in a place that made you uncomfortable, I'm sorry." Pause. "Ellen, honey, it was just an accident. I didn't mean to scare you. Why don't you come on out here so we can talk about this, huh?" His tone was amused and soft, like he felt sorry for her confusion.

Immediately uncertainty crept in. Did she mistake his intentions? Was it all an innocent accident? He was her "Uncle" Gerald, after all – long-time neighbor and family friend! He wouldn't hurt her, right? She took a hesitant step towards the door. He heard her.

"That's right, sweetheart, come on out so Uncle Gerald can make it up to you. There's nothing to be scared of, I promise."

"I won't come out unless you go back downstairs," she said, trying to make her voice sound strong.

His soft laugh again, amused. "Okay, Ellen, you win. I'll wait in the living room for you so we can talk about this, alright?" His tone was disarming.

She waited to hear him start descending the stairs before she crossed back to the door and tried to quietly undo the lock. His footsteps hesitated, and she immediately flipped it back into place. He chuckled and resumed his descent.

This time she waited until he had reached the bottom of the stairs before turning the lock open. She paused, listening, straining her ears to hear him. She heard silence.

She quietly crept down the stairs and when she peeked around the corner into the kitchen, he was standing right there, leaning up against the counter, watching her with a concerned look on his face. She froze.

"Ellen, come here. Now, I'm not going to hurt you." He held

his arms open, using his principal voice, though he had long been retired. He watched her. She took a tentative step towards him.

"That's right, there's nothing to be afraid of." She kept moving towards him slowly until he could reach her. He put his hands on her small shoulders and looked down at her with his watery gaze, straight in the eye.

"Ellen, I'm not sure what you think happened down there, but I assure you it was nothing. If you think something else happened, why, it's because you have a very active little imagination!" He paused, smiling a little. "Now," he squeezed her shoulder, "give me a big hug and I'll forget all about this little misunderstanding of yours."

She nodded dumbly, thoroughly confused. She allowed him to pull her into his arms again, and this time, really wasn't sure if he was trying to touch her budding breasts, or if his shaky hands were slipping.

Chapter 20

I was sitting home alone one evening, reading and listening to music. Mark was off teaching an English class. I heard the sound of a motorcycle like Lennon's approach and went towards the door, my heart rate instantly elevated. It was him – he was slowly dismounting from his bike in front of our neighbor's house across the street, but he was looking directly at me. I ducked back into the doorway again, suddenly feeling foolish and giddy. I walked back towards the kitchen and grabbed a cigarette from the pack on the kitchen table. The light was off in the front room but on in the kitchen, casting sort of a twilight glow in the living room. I heard his footsteps on the grass leading to my front door and heard him clear his throat. I tried to appear as casual as possible, suddenly busying myself at the sink.

"Hey, *gringa fea*, what are you doing?" came the voice from the shadowy figure at my door.

I turned around, faking a surprised look on my face. "Hey, Lennon, what's up?"

"I just came to see Julio across the street and saw you so I thought I'd say hello."

I hesitated, looking at him carefully. "Actually, I'm glad you came by. I've been wanting to talk to you about something."

"Well, let me look in on Julio and I'll stop back by before I leave."

"Well, I would prefer to have some privacy for this conversation and Mark may be back by the time you're done over there. Can you come in for just a minute?" I couldn't believe what was coming out of my mouth, which was suddenly extremely dry.

Lennon looked over his shoulder towards Julio's house, then opened my front door and stepped inside. He looked a little nervous.

"Lennon, I don't know how to tell you this, but I need to talk to you," I began softly, letting the words flow as they came to me. I walked towards him as I spoke, motioning him to take a seat in one of the rocking chairs in our living room. "I know that we are both married and I don't expect that to change, but I find myself very attracted to you and I don't know what to do about it." I spoke the words in a rush, as quickly as they would come to me in the still-foreign language. I couldn't look directly at him, but stole glances to try and gauge his reaction. I just knew he would either let me down easy or share my feelings, but either way, I was pretty sure that I could trust him.

Lennon hesitated before he spoke, waiting for me to look at him. "I'm so glad you said something, Elena," he said softly, looking at me through semi-lowered lashes. "I've been feeling the same way and have not wanted to make you uncomfortable by saying anything. I find myself watching you all the time and have started to wonder what your name would sound like with mine at the end – Elena de Calderon."

Suddenly I realized that I'd been holding my breath, and at his corny, Fabio-like line I almost guffawed out loud. I was flooded with relief that he appeared to share my feelings, but somewhere deep in my heart a small voice spoke a warning. I quickly told it to shut up.

I smiled at him, savoring the giddy feelings of knowing someone else finds you attractive. I felt confident that I could handle a little romance with Lennon – nothing physical had to happen, right?

He gently took my face in his hands, closed his eyes, and brought his lips to my forehead. I flushed with a mixture of embarrassment and giddiness. As he pulled back, he wrapped his arms around me and hugged me firmly but gently. I closed my eyes and breathed in his scent.

He pulled away quicker than I would have liked, standing to go. "I have to get over to Julio's house before someone suspects something. I'll see you tomorrow," he whispered. He reached out and gently touched my face again. It seemed so weird! I felt both wildly alive and like I was in a movie. Before I could dwell on it too long, Lennon suddenly strode towards the door and said in a loud voice, "Okay, Elena, well, I'll see you in the office tomorrow then, and we'll discuss this issue further then. Good night!" And with that, he banged loudly out my front door, calling to Julio who had emerged across the street.

Emotions were warring inside of me as I sat watching him go. Part of me felt guilty as sin, as badly as if I had slept with him; part of me was still racing from the sheer recklessness of the encounter. Somewhere down deep, I felt ashamed and immediately regretted having said anything to him.

But I was whistling as I turned up the music and began dancing in my living room.

I found that I was obsessing about Lennon. There was no other way to put it. Every time I heard the sound of a motorcycle pass by wherever I happened to be, I turned to look with hope rising in my chest that it would be him. There were a lot of people in town with the same model of bike. I was learning the subtle distinctions in the sounds of their motors, but that didn't make him appear any more often.

And when it was him passing by or arriving somewhere near to where I was at the moment, I tried very hard to act casual, both to keep him from knowing how deeply he was penetrating my mind as well as to keep up appearances that nothing was happening between us to anyone who might be paying attention. I didn't always do a very good job.

I noticed as the days passed that he seemed to find a lot of reasons to visit my neighbors diagonally across the street. He was friends with Julio, the man of the house, but I had never noticed him spending any time there before that day in my living room when I told him how I felt. I fantasized that it was because of me that those visits started. Suddenly the woman of the house, Felicia, became friendlier where before she had never really spoken to me. Her children often began to appear at my door, just to say hello or to return Flea who they claimed often wandered into their yard.

One day as I was heating up the food that Mireya had made earlier in the day for our dinner on the stove, I heard Lennon's motorcycle arrive across the street. I rushed to the concrete cutout blocks in the front wall of the house to peer unseen outside. My heart was racing as I watched him slowly dismount from the bike in his usual fashion. He glanced over at my house with a blank expression and kept moving towards Julio's house.

Since Mark wasn't yet home, I decided dinner could wait. I put a CD into the combination radio/disc player we had on the bookcase and began tidying the living room. I wasn't really expecting him to come over but wanted to be able to keep an eye on what was going on. I felt like a silly schoolgirl with a crush that was turning into an obsession but couldn't help myself. I had to know what he was doing.

After a few minutes, one of the kids came over. "My mom says if you aren't too busy maybe you could come over and visit for a while", said the little girl. She was a very beautiful child dressed in dirty and ill-fitting hand-me-downs, her clothes for doing housework. She was 10 years old but looked to be only about seven due to malnutrition.

"Sure," I said, trying to keep my tone light. "Just let me get myself ready then I'll come over." The girl smiled and nodded, then turned back towards her house and skipped away. I flew up the stairs to the bedroom to check myself in the mirror. I ran a brush through my hair and put on a clean shirt before heading back down. Being terrified of the steps to our second floor seemed like a distant memory from another time as I jumped confidently down them two at a time.

I walked slowly over to the house, not wanting to appear eager, relieved to see Lennon's bike still parked out front. I wasn't sure what I was going to say when I got there. I wiped the sweat off the palms of my hands onto my jeans.

They were all sitting around in the semi-open air kitchen at the back of the house. The roof of it was made mostly of palm trees and it had two walls and a hard-packed dirt floor, something more common in the *campo* than here in the "big city". Lennon was sitting, legs spread casually, and watching me from a chair leaned up against a wall. Julio was sitting nearby and Felicia was cooking something over their wood fire stove. It was really more of a campfire with a tripod set up over it and a flat grill that balanced from chains just over the flames. The three kids ran around in the adjacent yard, playing some version of tag.

They all greeted me warmly, the woman especially with a big grin. She seemed to have a conspiratorial look and I wondered what the conversation had been like before I arrived. I glanced at Lennon but his face betrayed nothing, as usual.

We chatted for a while about this and that, and then Lennon mentioned that they were all going out dancing the next night, which was Friday. His wife Patricia would be coming, too. He invited Mark and me to come along. Julio added that they would be walking over to Lennon's house first for a few drinks, since it was more or less on the way to the club, and that we should walk over with them. I tried to imagine what Mark would say. He didn't really like the music that was played in clubs here (you could hear it all over town as it blared from the discos into the wee hours), and I knew he wasn't much for dancing, especially not to Latin music. I didn't know how either, but I loved to dance and was willing to try. Besides, I really missed just going out with people.

I accepted on our behalf and told Julio just to come knock on our door when they were ready to head over. We chatted for a few more minutes, and then Lennon stood up to leave. I wanted to leave, too, but I didn't want to leave his presence. I jumped up and made an excuse about needing to get dinner started before Mark got back. I followed Lennon out to his bike. So did Julio.

"Well, so okay, I guess I'll see you guys tomorrow then," I said, not wanting to leave but afraid to be any more obvious. I started to turn to walk back towards my house when Lennon reached out and touched my arm. He held out his hand to shake mine. I couldn't suppress a little laugh.

"Until tomorrow, *gringita fea*," he said seriously. He shook my hand with a very somber look on his face that I couldn't read. I thought with regret about the fact that I would be going to one of Eduardo's *colonias* the next day and wouldn't get the chance to even ask Lennon what that was about. I shook his hand tightly and tried to make my expression as somber as his. I half succeeded. Julio extended his hand next, so I shook that, too. Then I turned to go. Julio looked amused; Lennon was hard to read. I broke out in a light sweat.

When Mark came home a little later, I had dinner ready. After some light chat about how our respective days had been, I mentioned the visit across the street and our invitation to the following evening's festivities.

"I don't want to go to the stupid club," he said flatly. "They play bad, bad music." He had a little half-smile on his face and I hoped he didn't really mean he didn't want to go.

"I know, I know," I replied. "But don't you miss just going out with people?" I was trying not to whine.

"I miss going out with our friends back home, but I don't really consider any of them our friends", he said with a frown. "I've never really had a conversation with the people across the street, and Lennon just seems shallow. They aren't exactly the type of people I would gravitate towards as friends."

I sat looking at him feeling a mixture of genuine surprise to hear him speaking in such an openly elitist way, and mild embarrassment that I had somehow failed to detect these same character flaws he seemed to see so clearly. "Are you serious?" was all I managed to get out.

He looked at me, alarmed surprise on his face. "Well, yeah! I mean, I guess I was just hoping we'd become friends with deeper people." He returned to his plate.

"I can't believe how elitist you are being!" I exclaimed, finding my voice and indignation at last. "You just said yourself that you've never even had real conversations with any of them. How dare you judge them without even talking to them? What are we supposed to do – just sit home all the time until the so-called 'deeper' people reveal themselves? Well, you can do that without me! I'm going out dancing!" I pushed my chair back from the table and threw my plate into the sink with a clatter.

"I didn't say I wouldn't go!" he said with kind of a pathetic whine in his voice. "I just... I thought you would understand." With that, his head was back down, hung over his plate. I left the room.

Chapter 21

When I came home from work the following day, I raced upstairs to find something to wear. *I must be losing weight*, I thought to myself, as I tried on several dresses only to have them hanging off me. I finally settled on a pair of black pants that still fit me decently and a denim top that showed off my mid-riff when I moved. I knew the other women would be dressed in tight-fitting clothes of various styles and this was the closest I could come with my current wardrobe. I planned to get some new clothes when I went home for my friend Toni's wedding, but that was a few weeks away yet.

Mark made no comment on my outfit. We had dinner to warm up left from Mireya, as usual, but I was too nervous to eat much. I ended up giving Flea most of my plate of food.

Julio and Felicia came over around 7 p.m. and we all headed out together on foot towards Lennon's house. I didn't actually know where he lived yet. I could hear Julio trying to talk to Mark behind me as we walked. Mark seemed to be struggling to understand him. I wasn't exactly in a position to criticize anyone's Spanish, but I had noticed that occasionally I seemed to have an easier time understanding someone who spoke in a more dialectic way than Mark did. It was an interesting switch for us.

Before too long we reached Lennon's house. It was a little nicer than ours – it had a front porch with a tiled floor that was swept clean, and curtains hanging from the windows. We didn't really have any windows on the main floor of our house; something that had made me feel claustrophobic from the beginning. I just kept the front and back doors open all the time to combat it.

As we approached, we could see Lennon sitting inside the front room watching TV. Patricia, another woman, and two small children were inside as well. As introductions were made around the room, I watched Patricia carefully. It was the first time we'd seen each other up close. She was quite short and very pretty. The two girls were eight years old and 11 months old. Both were very striking, a beautiful combination of their parents.

We settled in for drinks and chatted. Patricia had a lot of questions for us, especially me, about the work I was doing. She seemed particularly interested in the details of what I did out in the *colonias* where I traveled with her husband. Although she smiled and seemed friendly enough through the inquiry, I detected a note of urgency to her questioning. I wondered if she was suspicious of all women with whom her husband had professional contact. I wouldn't admit, even to myself, that she had anything more to worry about with me. I felt like I was having an out-of-body experience sitting in this woman's living room, almost as if I was posing as someone else. In this state, I was strangely amused at the situation.

After everyone had consumed a few drinks, Lennon and his wife gave the other woman, their live-in nanny and housekeeper, instructions for the evening, and we all walked towards the disco. The music was blaring loudly even from several blocks away. The night air was quite warm and with the alcohol we'd consumed, conversation was coming much more easily to everyone. I noticed Mark having an intense conversation with Julio about something in politics. As we walked, Patricia linked arms with me and quizzed me about my opinions on Santo Domingo and Nicaragua. I tried to keep tabs on where Lennon was.

The volume of music at the disco quickly swallowed the evening's conversation. We found a table together and proceeded to consume several more drinks through the course of the evening. It took a few songs to get going, but eventually I dragged Mark out onto the dance floor with me. I would have rather taken Lennon, but it just wasn't a good idea. Mark tried to move with the music but was hopelessly clumsy compared to the Latin men around us. I laughed hysterically and didn't feel able to stop.

Julio asked me to dance next and showed me how to follow his lead to learn a little salsa. Before long, I was completely absorbed in the steps, oblivious to everything around us. I got to dance with Lennon as well, but was concentrating so hard on doing the steps correctly that I didn't have time to flirt. Out of the corner of my eye, I noticed Mark dancing with Patricia, who was watching us very closely. A slow dance came on next, and Lennon just took hold of my waist and pulled me into it before I could pause. I noticed Patricia grab Mark and force him into it as well. I snorted a short laugh. When Lennon looked at me quizzically, I nodded in their direction. Patricia looked determined and Mark looked defeated.

Dancing with Lennon that first time was magical. I felt giddy and my heart was pounding in my chest. It was like being in high school all over again with a boy that I had a huge crush on.

We didn't talk much – partly because the music was so incredibly loud, and partly because I don't think either of us really knew what to say. Instead, I just relished the moment; the newness, the exhilarating feel of Lennon's touch. I was afraid to hold on too tightly or too loosely – I didn't want to do anything to break the spell of the moment.

When the song finally ended, I reluctantly let go. Alcohol was making me bold enough to try to hang on longer, but Lennon was firm in breaking away. I was crestfallen, and then immediately startled by how emotional I was getting. Julio was coming towards me to dance again as we were heading off the floor, and I gratefully took him up on his offer.

We closed the club down around 3 a.m. and headed back, stumbling along the rocky road. At the main road, we parted company with Lennon and Patricia. They wrapped their arms around each other and headed off home. I felt a twinge of jealousy that I was helpless to combat. Mark didn't even try to hold my hand. There was a lot of stumbling and laughing as the four of us made our way back. We parted after loud *"¡Buenas Noches!"* in the street.

The music was still ringing in my ears and I was partially deaf as I headed up the stairs to bed. I felt quite drunk as I peeled off my sweaty clothes and dropped them to the floor, simply seeking the bed.

"So, did you manage to survive the evening?" I murmured to Mark as he came up the stairs. I was already face down on the bed.

"Yeah, it was better than I thought," he replied. He didn't sound half as drunk as I felt. "Julio and I talked a lot about politics. He's more interesting than I gave him credit for." There was a note of surprise in his voice.

"Imagine that," I slurred, already falling half asleep. "A poor, rural Nicaraguan who can match your political debating."

Mark barked a short laugh. "Point taken."

Chapter 22

The first trip I took with Lennon after that night of dancing was to Carabas. We set out together on his motorcycle, chatting all the way. The conversation was full of so much overt flirtation that I was blushing for most of the ride. It had a surreal quality to it – I was having a hard time believing that he was so into me. Some part of it seemed like a dramatic act.

We got to the Campesino Bank, our usual first stop, and went in to say hello to Albert, the older man who worked there every day. He and Lennon had known each other for a long time. They joked around for a while as I looked on, a smile plastered on my face as I tried to keep up with their banter. I was also still giddy from the ride. Which probably explains why I didn't catch what Lennon said next.

Before I knew it, he was jerking his head towards the back of the bank, motioning for me to follow him. Albert busied himself with some paperwork, deliberately not looking at us. I looked at Lennon. There was an intense look on his face but not one that I found threatening. I followed him.

"I thought the meeting with the Brigade was supposed to start in a few minutes," I said softly.

"No," he whispered. "It won't start for another hour."

Suddenly I felt as if I had walked into a trap. We were standing in front of a cot that was hidden from view of the rest of the bank by a partition. The bed looked freshly made. Lennon sat down on the edge of it, taking my hands and gently drawing me to him.

"What is this?" I asked, trying to keep my tone light and my nervousness hidden.

Lennon smiled. "Nothing," he said. "Come sit with me." He patted the bed next to him.

As I sat down, he slipped an arm around my waist and put his other hand on my cheek. His kiss was sweet and warm. There were alarm bells going off in my head – what if we got caught? What if Mark found out? What if Patricia found out? What were we doing?? But they were soon silenced or at least forgotten in the heat of the moment. My nervousness melted under Lennon's gentle but firmly guiding hands, and I gave into the heat.

After it was over, I was flushed with shame. He got up quickly, cleaning himself with a small dry washcloth he found nearby, then handing it to me without a word. He was talking to me, telling me we had to get up and go get something to eat before the meeting started. I somehow got the gist of what he was saying, but I don't remember hearing him talk. I just remember a loud pounding of guilt ringing in my head.

We put ourselves back together and he sauntered casually back up to the front of the empty bank as if nothing had happened. I followed him, my head hung and my cheeks burning. He turned around and glanced at me and quickly spoke.

"No, Elena, not like that," he said quietly. "You must walk with your head up, smiling and meeting people in the eye as you always do. It is when you depart from your normal behavior that people begin to suspect something. Keep your head high and no one will know."

Gee, I thought, *for someone who just told me back there that this was his first time being unfaithful, too, you seem to know an awful lot about how not to get caught*. Regardless, his advice made sense, so I tried to quickly compose my face and body language as a member of our Brigade walked through the door. He smiled at us both and turned to conduct business with Albert. I followed Lennon outside.

I don't remember what happened during the meeting that day. I was concentrating very hard on pretending nothing had just happened – I hadn't broken my wedding vows, I wasn't a marked woman, and I wouldn't do it again. These were the lies pounding in my head as I listened to the meeting and kept a bland smile plastered on my face.

On the ride home, I was quiet. Part of me was completely absorbed by my overwhelming feelings of guilt. The other part of me was wondering if our encounter had meant anything to Lennon. I found that my feelings for him were desperately stronger than ever and I was dying to know how he was feeling. I finally asked him. He was silent for a moment, appearing to choose his words carefully. I braced myself for his answer.

"I'm falling in love with you, Elena," he said over his shoulder.

I was stunned into silence. "Pull this bike over," I shouted over the wind. "We need to talk!"

As the bike came rolling to a stop beside endless fields, I asked him to repeat himself. He just turned and looked at me. "You heard me," he said.

"Lennon, I don't know how to do this," I babbled. "I'm consumed with guilt right now and yet I'm more drawn to you than ever before. I don't know what to do!" I felt like I was getting hysterical.

"*Amor*, you need to calm down," he urged, putting his hand on my face. "I've never done this before either, but I've had a lot of practice watching other people do it. While I've always been disgusted by their bold behavior and the way they seem to act like they have no regrets about what they're doing, I have picked up a few tips along the way that I think can help us now. You just need to trust me."

As I looked into his eyes, I found the comfort that I so desperately wanted to find there, and let myself be comforted. He kissed me, told me we needed to get back, and off we went again. My heart was still pounding and I was still feeling ashamed of myself for giving in to a passionate moment, but I tried to be soothed by his words and think about holding my head up high. By the time we reached Santo Domingo and rode past the hospital where Patricia worked, I had a smirk on my face, having convinced myself we would pull it off. She was standing outside of her clinic, watching the road as she talked with other people, and I raised my hand in a wave as we went by.

Chapter 23

I decided to stay home one morning before heading out to one of the *colonias* right before lunch. I didn't really have anything to do in the office, and I wanted to just take a break and be at home.

Mireya had been with us for almost a month, and everything had been going really well. I had no reason to distrust her, but found myself watching the clock as I cleaned up my breakfast dishes to see what time she would come by. She did not know I was at home that morning.

As ten o'clock came, her eldest daughter, Estelita, came to the door. She was a little breathless and looked nervous. I wiped my hands on a towel as I walked into the front room, beginning to feel a little alarmed.

"Good morning, Doña Elena," she said, catching her breath. "I looked for you in your office but they told me you were at home this morning, so I ran over here."

I reached the front gate and unlocked it as I said, "That's okay, honey, come on in. Where is your mom? Is everything okay?"

Estelita stepped into the house, her glance darting around at everything, including up at my face. "My mother is not able to come today, so she sent me in her place to do her job for her. She is hoping to be able to return tomorrow. What would you like me to do first?"

"Wait, wait, hold on," I said, holding my hand up. "Is your mom okay? Is she sick?" I was feeling less alarmed and a little more irritated now. I wasn't sure I wanted to leave this barely-12-year old girl in my house alone to do the cooking and cleaning. I know I wouldn't have been mature enough to do that safely alone at age 12.

Estelita would not look me in the eye. "She's just not able to come today," she repeated. She sounded like she was carefully reciting only what she had been instructed to say – no more.

I decided not to push her. "Well," I said, "I actually am on my way out to the *colonias* in a little while, and Don Marco is not going to be here for lunch today either, so go ahead and go back home. Let your mother know that she should come back as soon as she's able, and that if there is anything I can do, she should let me know."

Estelita was reluctant to go. "But my mother sent me here to do her work! She will not be happy with me if I go home without doing it."

"Okay," I said, turning and walking back into the kitchen. "I'll write her a note that you can take to her, explaining everything." I took a piece of paper from my small notebook and carefully began writing a note. I chose my words carefully so as not to get Estelita in trouble or offend Mireya.

The girl was still reluctant to go, but she finally took the note and let herself out of the front gate. Once she had carefully closed it behind her, she trotted off down the street, note in hand.

I watched her go, wondering if this was the beginning of trouble.

Later that evening when I came back from the colonia, I found Mireya waiting at my kitchen table. Mark still wasn't home – he was off working with Alejandra in the office on her new computer.

As soon as I saw Mireya, the same feeling of alarm from that morning came back. She was sitting, watching the door, her hands clasped tightly on the table in front of her. Her face was drawn, her jaw set tightly. The knot in my stomach got bigger as I reached the gate and began fumbling with the lock.

She got up and quickly came over to help me with it. "Doña Elena, I'm sorry if I startled you. When you sent Estelita home with your little note, I felt that I needed to come by and give you an explanation."

I ushered her back into the kitchen so we could sit at the table together. I shook out a cigarette and lit it, saying, "No, Mireya, I was just worried about you. It didn't seem that you were simply not feeling well; it seemed as though something might be wrong and I was worried about you, that's all."

Mireya wrung her hands together, her dark eyes darting around as if not sure where to focus. She was visibly nervous and looked as if she were trying to decide how much to trust me.

"Mireya, if you're in some kind of trouble, please tell me so that I can help you." I reached across the table and gently touched her hands. She jumped a little. I quickly withdrew my hand and said, "I'm sorry."

"No, no, Doña Elena, it is me that is sorry. I did not mean to make you worry, and I am sorry that I am so nervous right now." She craned her neck to look out into the front room. "Did you lock the gate? It's after dark now."

I was starting to feel scared as I got up to check the gate. It was locked. I came back to the kitchen table saying, "Okay, Mireya, now you're starting to scare me. What's going on? Please tell me!"

After a pause, and a deep breath, she said, "Doña Elena, I was with the father of Julio and Roberta for 10 years. Estelita is not his child; she was born before I knew him.

"My ex is not a nice man. After a lot of abuse, we separated. Every now and then, he comes back. He is not welcome in our home, so he gets very angry and sometimes violent when I tell him to go away.

"A couple of days after I started working for you, he came to my house late at night. We were all in bed sleeping and the house was locked up tight. He started pounding and yelling – he was drunk – and when we wouldn't open the door, he broke it down." She paused, her breathing a little heavier, her fear palpable. Cold fear was gripping me, too.

"Oh, my God, Mireya," I breathed out. "What happened? Are you and the kids okay?"

She nodded, "My neighbors heard what was happening and came to tell him to leave. He was so drunk that after using his energy to break down my door, he didn't have any left to harm us, so he left."

"The reason I couldn't come to work today is because I filed for a restraining order against him, and today was the court date. I had to go to court to explain why I need this restraining order. I had to wait there most of the day. I just got done a couple of hours ago and then I came here." She paused, clearly struggling to go on.

"I had to wait most of the day," she repeated. She looked up at me finally, her shame and pain written all over her features. "And he was right there, on the next bench, waiting, too." She was whispering now, trying to hold her chin up and her tears back at the same time. I was having trouble holding back my own.

I gripped her hands – "Why didn't you tell me when this happened? You can come to us with anything – we will help you, Mireya! I don't want you or your kids to be in danger."

She shook her head. "I know, Doña Elena. At the time, we were so new together and I wasn't sure if you would believe me." Her head hung down again.

My fear had turned to hot rage against this unknown man. I had had too many experiences and heard too many stories of women not being believed for one reason or another when they were victims of some type of violence or abuse. I clenched my jaw and lit another cigarette, trying not to make Mireya think I was upset with her.

"Mireya, I respect your decision at the time to do what you felt was going to keep you safe. I hope that you know now that I trust you and I do believe you. Thank you for trusting me enough to share the truth about today and that night with me." I ducked my head to try and catch her eyes, which were focused down on her hands as if she were waiting for a verdict. When she finally looked up at me, I said again, "Thank you for trusting me. Is there anything you need?"

She smiled and finally relaxed a little bit. "No, thank you. I should probably get home to my kids now. They are at my sister's house. I was afraid to leave them home alone."

"Mireya, is the door fixed? Do you need a new door?"

She smiled again, a little sadly, and rose from the table. "No, thank you, Doña Elena. We are just fine. Enjoy your evening now. I'll see you tomorrow. Good night."

I walked her to the front gate and unlocked it to let her out into the twilight. She closed it behind her with the same gentle care that I had seen in Estelita earlier in the day. She gave me a quick smile, and started to walk away.

Suddenly she turned and said quietly, "Doña Elena, be sure you lock that gate until Don Marco comes home." I nodded and then quickly turned the key as she stood watching to make sure I would.

Satisfied, she nodded, and then walked off towards her home.

Chapter 24

I walked from our house to work the same way every day. Down to the corner by the Catholic Church, down the street next to the Catholic Church, then down the street that ran in front of the church. There was only one house on that last block that ever had any signs of life to it where I could often see a woman in her mid-30's on her porch, usually in a hammock or a chair, with some combination of children nearby. As I passed, she always wished me good day and smiled.

One day, I decided to stop and speak to her. She seemed flattered and a little flustered, but invited me onto her porch, which was enclosed with bars. She said her name was Auxiliadora, which I had a hard time pronouncing. She laughed in a way that made it obvious that she laughed a lot, and said that most of her friends just called her Dora. She had four children, which she proudly introduced. I knew from experience that it was inappropriate to ask a woman about the father of the children, so I simply smiled at them and didn't ask questions. I told her a little about myself and why I was in Santo Domingo, to which she listened politely. I told them all I had enjoyed meeting them and made my way back to the street.

Dora called after me that I was welcome to stop by any time to chat or have a drink. I thanked her and waved as I headed to the office. I was excited to meet a new friend – someone who seemed normal and real and nice.

Our friendship grew over a few weeks time. I stopped to chat with her either coming or going from work most days. She had a boyfriend named Oscar that I knew because he worked for one of the other organizations in town that sometimes overlapped with NECOG. I had seen him in the *colonias* as well as around town on his motorcycle. He seemed like a nice fellow but I really didn't know anything about him. He was always very polite and seemed to treat Dora well when I saw them together.

One day she disclosed that Oscar had a wife and children of his own.

"Do you think less of me now that I told you that?" she asked, cringing a little bit but still smiling.

At this point, I had been with Lennon a few more times and felt in no position to judge anyone else's decisions either to myself or to their faces. In fact, I saw it as an opportunity to have a confidant at long last that I could talk with about Lennon.

"No," I said, returning her smile. "I don't think less of you at all. In fact, maybe I have a secret of my own to share with you." I hesitated, waiting to see how she would react.

Her eyes narrowed and I could tell that she already suspected something. "Do tell," she said with interest and a little cattiness.

"Well," I hesitated, still unsure if I should break the secrecy to which Lennon had sworn me. "Maybe you're not the only one seeing a married man." I looked away down at my lap.

She smacked my arm. "Are you kidding me?!" she screeched. "Who is it?" she hissed. "It's Lennon isn't it?!"

My mouth dropped open. "How did you know that?" I stammered. I was suddenly wondering how many other people had figured it out, including my own husband.

Dora laughed. "Don't worry, *gringita fea*, you're not as obvious as you think you are. I'm just, shall we say, experienced in this area and have a good eye." I was still wondering who else had figured it out. I must have looked really mortified and worried because Dora laughed again and said, "Really, Elenita, don't worry! No one else has guessed."

We chatted a while longer. I was still sweating thinking about who else might have figured out my secret. The familiar guilt and shame were creeping back with the knowledge that someone else now knew our secret. Somehow it made it more real.

As I stood to leave, Dora touched my arm and said, "Really, Elenita, your secret is safe with me. I would never do anything that would bring you harm." She had a serious and sincere look on her face. Then it changed to a sly smile as she added, "And if you two ever need a place to, you know... well, my house is your house, little one..."

5/10/97

Dear Mom and Dad,

This is a letter not to be shared. Mark is in Managua for the weekend, and hopefully you "spoke" with him on e-mail. I just couldn't bring myself to go. First and foremost, I need a break from him. Second, the 48-hour trip was an idea that overwhelmed me, especially since I had a migraine yesterday. Third, I wanted some time to write letters, relax, and receive any phone calls that might come from a man named Lennon Calderon.

There are so many things to explain that I'm not sure where to start. I guess I'll just jump right in and hopefully it will all come out eventually.

Lennon is the Social Promoter for the South Zone. Eduardo is the SP for the North Zone. I need to visit all of their colonies and do projects in them. Eduardo didn't go to his colonies hardly at all in April, so I went with Lennon most of the month.

We hit it off as friends immediately, starting back in February when we arrived. Our personalities are discomfortingly similar; we are both outgoing, dominant types and we have a good relationship. He is almost as stubborn as I am, and equally a sucker for romance and details. How we found this attraction to each other, I'm not sure. He is very handsome (at least, I think so), and just about an inch taller than me. He got married at 18 when his girlfriend got pregnant, and they have been unhappily married (as of late) for the past almost eight years. They both talk of separating/ divorce, but it has yet to happen. He tells me the only things keeping him there are his two daughters - ages 8 years and 11 months. Patricia, his wife, is one of the most unhappily married women I have ever seen. They have no friendship. She openly admits to having no faith or trust in him at all. All they do is fight. These are all observations, not lines I'm being fed.

So we went out to the campo six times in April. Most places take at least 45 minutes to get to on the motorcycle (an added attraction; it's so sexy!), and we talk non-stop on these trips - about ecology, the fires, projects we're doing or want to do. He is in school in Juigalpa on the weekends studying agricultural development and when he finishes in a year, he'll have the equivalent of an intense bachelors degree. Not quite a masters, but more advanced than us. He's studying genetics right now, so we talk about that, too. We have yet to run out of things to say! He's one of my two best friends here, Dora being the other.

People started talking about us, saying we were having an affair because we went around together so much. They have since stopped talking as I am now going with Eduardo. Small towns are the same here as in the States; if people are bored, they'll find someone to talk about. Also, the four of us, Mark, me, Lennon and Patricia, hang out a lot together, so that helps. It's not Lennon that they see with me.

I don't know how to explain my feelings for him. Strong is a good word. There is a spark between us that is different than anything I have ever felt, probably because we are both so strong in terms of personality. He's very special. He drives his motorcycle like a maniac when he's alone, and probably slower than necessary when I'm with him. He says he's afraid of me getting hurt. He also thought you'd be pleased to know he takes very good care of me when we're on it, knowing you don't like them.

Mark remains Mark. Not one romantic cell in his body nor thought of it in his head. He's still shy about making friends, so my Spanish is now equal to his, and I often understand more. This has him down. Our relationship problems are ever-present and ongoing, as you know, but I won't try and tell you that my interest in Lennon is not at all connected. I'll just ask that you remember back to all the things I complained about in the States. Living together, working together and knowing all the same people, along with many people seeing us as one person, especially in the office, is too much. Consequently, I spend a lot of time here at Dora's house to have a break. Now that Mark will be teaching computer and English classes four nights a week, I hope the situation will improve. We remain mostly on good terms, but I must confess to you that the spark, if there ever was one, is practically non-existent. I don't know what this means for the future. If I want to be content with security for the rest of my life, which is the primary thing Mark provides, I have it.

Enter my frustration. I feel like I really missed out by dating only one person in college. I realize no one could have told me different at the time, and as I grit my teeth, I say, "You were right, Mom." But moving beyond, what do I do? For one, we had started talking about a child seriously, but you can bet that's absolutely out of the question now. I pop those pills religiously. But what can I really do? The logical answer is nothing. Of course, there are other options. Lennon talks about running away to Costa Rica together, or the States, except he speaks about four words of English. If I separate from Mark, will I regret it for the rest of my life? Is that a chance I'm willing to take? If we separate, the church will instantly bring us home. Do I stay? Do I leave Lennon behind and try to just believe it's my lot in life to stay married and be unsatisfied or/and unhappy?

Mom, you said to remove myself from his presence. Well, what happens when I do that, as I will be away from him for the next week and a half, and have been for the past week, and I'm sitting here thinking about him practically non-stop? When it's him who's calling me just to see how I'm doing and saying sweet things and not Mark?

He is not without faults (I would say it again, but I'm running out of room). But who is? I can see already what some of our problems would be, but what if it doesn't matter? Have you ever felt like this? If you have, I hope it was for each other and that's what's made it work for 30 years. But the question that haunts my dreams at night and my thoughts in the day is: What if I married the wrong person?

Okay, I'm done. The advice hotlines are open and waiting for your "call" (in a letter addressed only to me, please, and actually please send it to Dora's house because I really wouldn't want Mark to read it). The question of "what to do" is the topic. A speedy reply is requested.

All my love to you both,

Ellen

Chapter 25

About a week later, Juan Carlos announced that we would all be traveling to a place called La Cruz outside of Managua, the capitol, for a three-day planning session with all NECOG staff from around the country. There was a lot of excitement and buzz around the office as everyone rushed to get things ready to go. I was excited to go, too. It made me feel like Mark and me were really a part of the NECOG staff and not just some outsiders. Mark wasn't as excited; he felt like he was working on projects that didn't have anything to do with NECOG's overall work plan. He was grumbling about all the classes he would have to miss with his students instead.

I found myself more annoyed and less patient with Mark than ever before as the trip approached. We hadn't been intimate since my trip out to Carabas with Lennon, but that wasn't unusual for us. The absence of physical closeness was seeping into the rest of our relationship. I still felt guilty every time I looked at him, but lately the guilt had begun to feel more like pity than shame.

The trip itself was hard. There were eight of us piled into the back of Juan Carlos's pick-up truck, riding hard over the rocky roads. We traveled three hours to Juigalpa the first day, arriving at the NECOG office there in time to have dinner with the staff and bed down for the night on the floors of the office. I was sure there would be cockroaches crawling all over us, and that we would be eaten alive by mosquitoes. We were not prepared and carried no sleeping bags or mosquito netting or anything. It was a long and uncomfortable night. The women were bedded down in one room, the men in another.

When 4 a.m. came and someone shook me awake, I was so stiff that I could barely get up off the hard, cold floor. I couldn't stomach any breakfast at that hour, so I passed on it and headed for the truck, hoping to find a comfortable spot. I didn't see Mark anywhere. I wanted a cigarette but was afraid to smoke in front of all these Evangelical pastors and members. There was a conversation about the Rapture going on in the back of the truck already. It seemed I did not fall into the category of those who would be saved from hellfire and suffering. Oddly, the realization made me want to laugh instead of cry.

Mark finally came stumbling out, looking even worse than I felt. He was scratching several mosquito bites on his arms and looking very grumpy. He sort of grunted a greeting at me and continued to scowl. I just looked at him thinking how incredibly different our relationship was than what I had imagined or hoped my married life would be like. I had noticed several other couples where the man had shown great concern for how his wife had slept. A couple men had even asked me. But not Mark. I just shook my head and climbed up into the truck.

A long, hard and bumpy eight hours later, we arrived in La Cruz with NECOG staff from around the country. Members of our own delegation had come and gone during the trip, and our numbers had swollen to 18. I was afraid the small pick-up truck would give up under the weight of us all, but it held out. As we dismounted, people greeted each other warmly as long-lost friends and colleagues out there in the world fighting the good fight seem to do. I felt like an outsider again until we caught sight of Ana and some other members of the Managua staff that we had met when we had first arrived in Nicaragua. It seemed like years ago but really only four months had passed. Hugs, kisses and smiles were exchanged all around as they asked how Mark and I were surviving our post out in "no-man's land". They were impressed by and very complimentary of my progress with Spanish. As I basked in pride, I noticed Mark's mildly jealous look. My pride swelled even more and I felt cruel.

The conference finally got underway with a worship service. It was far more toned down than what we were used to seeing out in Santo Domingo, and I found myself moved instead of removed. The conference itself was a little over my head linguistically. I just tried to follow along and keep up. There didn't seem to be any other representatives of partnerships like Mark and me present. I wondered if they were more removed from NECOG's actual activities like Mark.

On the second day, Mark woke up feeling very hot. He was flushed a deep red and when I touched his head, he was burning up with fever. He didn't seem to want to stay awake. I went looking for Ana.

"I'm not sure what to do," I told her. "He seems really sick but says he just needs to sleep."

"Has he been bitten by any mosquitoes lately?" she asked, her expression one of genuine concern.

"Actually, yeah, he had a bunch of bites on his arm after we spent the night in Juigalpa," I was now getting concerned, too.

"I think we should get him seen by a doctor," she said briskly. "Let's get him up and dressed. I'm taking him to Managua." She headed back to our room and I followed.

"What do you think is wrong with him?" I was concerned but also disappointed at the thought of missing the conference. *And time with Lennon*, I admitted guiltily to myself.

"I'm not sure," she said, "But we need to get him seen and find out."

When we reached the room, Mark was back asleep again. His head was still very hot and flushed, and he was buried under all the blankets in the room. I shook him gently and told him he needed to get up and go with Ana to the doctor. His eyes stayed closed but he frowned and slurred that he didn't need to go anywhere. He just wanted to sleep.

Ana stepped over to him and shook him more forcefully. "You need to get up and come with me, Marco, now." She spoke emphatically and firmly. She grabbed one of his arms and tried to pull him into a sitting position. I took his other arm and helped her. His eyes were open now.

"Where are we going?" he asked in English. His speech was slurred as if he were drunk.

"Ana is going to take you to see a doctor," I answered. "Do you want me to go with you?" I was hoping he would say no.

"You can stay here, Elena," Ana replied. "One of you should be part of the planning process for your region. I'll have Marco back by lunch time."

I felt jubilation and shame come rushing in at the same time. I looked back at Mark. He was just trying to keep his eyes open as we pulled his shoes on. I helped Ana get him off the bed and out the door. Her truck was parked far away so she told me to stay with him while she went to get it.

As she went jogging off, Mark looked at me, his eyes dark. "Why aren't you coming with me?" his speech still slurring. "You don't need to be at this stupid conference."

I felt indignant. "And why does it not surprise me that you would think that?" I said angrily. "You, who doesn't work with any programs integral to NECOG's mission while I'm busting my butt to get a sustainable reforestation project off the ground! I'm staying because Ana said I should and because I want to find out how to do my job better. If you weren't so arrogant, maybe – " My words got cut off in my throat as Ana pulled up. My face was burning with anger combined with this terrible shame I couldn't shake. A part of me knew I should have gone with him – period.

Back at the conference everyone wanted to know where he was. As I told people, I watched surprise spread over most faces that I had not accompanied my husband. I quickly told people that Ana had said I should stay and that she expected they would be back by lunchtime. But my face burned each time.

When lunch came and went without their return, I began to get worried. Finally one of the other regional directors that had a text pager came over to me and said that I had a message from Ana. I took the pager and read the message. It said, "Marco – possible malaria – staying in hospital overnight – more later – Ana". Malaria! I couldn't believe it. I was suddenly sick with guilt and panic. How could I have stayed behind! Everything I thought I knew about malaria came rushing into my head and I became convinced Mark was going to die. I desperately pulled on the regional director's arm.

"What does this mean?" I shouted. "Is he going to die? I have to get to Managua!"

She looked at me strangely while slowly shaking her head. "No, he won't die. He'll probably have horrible headaches and a high fever for a while, but most people don't die from malaria unless it goes untreated. And none of us can leave to take you to Managua. If you wanted to go, you should have gone with them at the beginning. It's too late now. But I'm sure he'll be fine. Just try to relax."

I realized there was a small crowd of people watching us and I tried to get a grip on myself. I nodded my head, overcome with guilt and unable to speak, and blindly walked away. I walked right into Lennon.

"Hey, what's wrong?" he asked, concern written all over his face. "You look terrible."

I choked back a sob and managed to tell him what had happened, including how I was feeling. "I'm a terrible wife and a terrible person," I blubbered.

"No, you're not, *gringita fea*," he chuckled. "If you were, you wouldn't be feeling so badly right now. I'm sure he'll be fine. Ana will make sure he's attended to, and then she'll probably come back and get you. Until then, let's get you something to drink. You need to calm down. Remember - act normal. This isn't worry that's consuming you – its guilt."

He had steered me over to the table where there was coffee. I stood and watched as he whipped up the grains with just the right amount of water to make a poor man's equivalent of espresso, which he knew I loved. As I sipped the hot drink, I began to relax a little bit.

The rest of the day went quickly. At one point Lennon and I were in a small group session together with other people that neither of us really knew. I was surprised at his gentle flirting. When he went up to the front of the room to make the presentation for our group, he winked at me from the front. Realizing how obvious he had just been, he tried to play it off as if he had something in his eye. I guffawed before I could stop myself and the whole room was looking at us. The burning came rushing back but not as badly this time.

After the day's activities had ended, I got a message to call Ana at her home. When I did, she told me that Mark had been treated and released, and was resting at the home of Jane and John, an older couple who also worked for the National Protestant Church of America (NPCA) that had been in Nicaragua for a long time. They lived in Managua. I asked if I should come and Ana told me no. She pointed out that the conference would end in another day and that I should just come to Managua then. She told me who to talk to for a ride and said that she'd be staying in Managua as well to catch up on work and to look in on Mark for me. I thanked her and hung up feeling a mixture of relief and freedom.

As the evening wore on, I had just about given up on finding Lennon in my casual search when he walked past me and slipped a note into my hand. "Meet me at the edge of the road in 15 minutes" it said. I was suddenly giddy.

I tried to be as nonchalant as possible in making this little rendezvous by the road. I was smiling broadly by the time I got there. He was already waiting in the darkness.

"Hi," I said, suddenly feeling shy. "Where are we going?"

"Oh, I just thought we could take a little walk in the moonlight," he said, wrapping his arms around me and kissing me lightly.

He took my hand and we started walking. I told him about Mark and what Ana had said, and confessed my feelings of freedom upon hearing that I would not have to go to Managua until the following day.

"That's not good, Elena," Lennon said with a frown, surprising me. "You should be there with your husband. People will think you stayed behind to be with me."

"Well, Ana was the one who told me to stay behind in the first place," I countered, beginning to feel a little bit stupid.

"That doesn't matter because most people don't know that. They would assume a wife would go with her husband. You should have gone."

"Why are you saying this to me now? Earlier you seemed fine that I hadn't gone. What changed?" I was feeling wounded. I let go of his hand.

"Don't move away," he said in a softer tone as he grabbed my hand again. "I'm just saying that maybe you should have thought more clearly about this earlier." We walked in silence. A moment later he said, "Oh, here we are."

We had arrived at the ruins of some old building. It wasn't very big and there were really just half walls still standing. Lennon said it was probably part of an abandoned farm. The moon had come through the clouds and was shining very brightly. Stars were everywhere. It was easy to forget that he had just offended me as he lowered me to sit on the floor with him and began to kiss me. This time, it wasn't giddy passion that allowed me to move from one thing to the next – it was pure need; need to feel loved, to feel comforted.

My back was rubbing up against the concrete floor as we moved. It was rough and I could feel the skin being scraped. I told Lennon, and he put his hands under my spine, fanning out to buffer my back from the ground. When it was over and we got up, I touched my finger to my spine at one particularly sore spot and could feel moisture. I hoped it wasn't coming through my shirt. More importantly, I would have to remember not to show my back to Mark until I came up with a good explanation. I pointed it out to Lennon and he suggested I tell Mark that I slipped and fell while he was in Managua.

As we walked back to the conference center, all was dark inside of the buildings. I found that I was not as consumed by guilt and shame as I had been the first time. There was no chastising in my head, scolding me for being weak or unfaithful. I wondered absently where that little voice had gone.

5/28/97

Dear Mom and Dad,

It's now Wednesday, and I talked to you last night to tell you about Mark. We talked more with the French couple who are doctors. They said that there is no way to tell if it is malaria for sure. They said that because of the anti-malaria medication we take, a test wouldn't show up positively. They also said that anti-malaria meds do not prevent run-of-the-mill malaria, which is probably what Mark has. It only prevents cerebral malaria, which can kill you. It could also be Denghi Fever, which is common here, too, and not treatable outside of liquids, rest and avoidance of aspirin.

Bottom line: he's going to be fine. He felt a little better today when I left for this meeting in Juigalpa. I wasn't going to go, but he told me to go since there is nothing I can do for him. Between our friends, our empleada and the Frenchies, he'll probably get plenty of taking care of today.

And now for the less rosy side of life here...

Often in the evenings, Mark feels like resting or doing something different (and usually solitary), and so I often walk over a block to Dora's house by myself after dinner. Apparently, our landlord, "the spy", saw me leaving alone and returning "late", which means like 9 p.m., accompanied by a man other than Mark. If he had looked closely, he would have seen that it is the 15-year old son of Dora who walks me home to see that I get there safely.

Anyway, instead of speaking to one of us about it, he chose to come to Juan Carlos and tell him an elaborated version of what he saw. As rumors fly about what I must have going with Lennon, Juan Carlos took me aside to tell me to be "more careful". He basically told me that I shouldn't leave the house alone unless I'm going to the store. I don't know what he expects me to do when I'm home alone in the evenings while Mark teaches class. The whole situation makes me angry. As you all know, I am not accustomed to being told what to do in my personal life. We'll see what happens. Mark was annoyed as well, but being the calmer of the two, he calmed me down and suggested we just play it by their rules for a while. After a prolonged struggle, I conceded.

We begin to see the uglier side of NECOG with time. Being an evangelical institution, they consider themselves above gossip and being judgmental. However, we are finding, as in every organization, religion, etc., there are some who take these ideals more seriously than others. Unfortunately, our boss seems to be one who is above it at times, and not at others. I'm still trying to decide if he has our best interests at heart always.

More later. Lots of love to you both,

Ellen

Chapter 26

They tumbled clumsily onto the narrow, twin bed in her college dorm room, groping each other awkwardly. She was trying to pull his pants off; he was working on her bra. With nervous giggles, they each struggle with the other's clothing.

"Here, why don't you –"

"No, wait, I'll just –"

More nervous giggles. They finally reach for their own clothing. He pulls off his jeans, bending at an odd angle to reach his feet. She shrugs out of her blouse, cheeks flushing a little, and unclasps her bra, unsure of whether or not to remove it completely. Though not their first time together, they are still new at this.

She hopes that her roommate won't suddenly decide to come back to the room. But as things progress, she begins to relax a little. He's very gentle. As he works his way down her body, she inhales deeply, willing herself to let go of the nerves and enjoy the moment.

She closes her eyes, concentrating on enjoying his touch. She sighs softly, turning her head to one side and closing her fingers around the sheets. Her breath quickens.

He seems to be encouraging her to relax further and enjoy his touch. She does, her face openly displaying her pleasure. She moans softly, biting her lip, approaching bliss.

"Oh, my God, what is that look on your face about?" He shatters her reverie, like he just poured a glass of cold water over her body. "What is wrong with you?"

She freezes, eyes snapping wide open, face flushed a deep shade of red, no longer from ecstasy but rather now from shame and embarrassment.

"I.. I don't know," she stammers, reaching for the sheet to cover her body. "I guess I was just enjoying… the moment." She finishes lamely, not sure what to say or where to look. What happened? She wonders.

"You just had this look on your face," he mutters, not sounding so shocked or startled anymore. He lies down next to her, not touching her, face up to the ceiling. "I don't know, it looked like something was wrong with you."

She feels utterly humiliated. "No," she says softly, a tear slipping down her burning cheek. "Nothing was wrong. I'm sorry I scared you." She rolls over to face the wall. She feels like something must be wrong with her. She is confused, ashamed and deeply embarrassed.

After a few minutes, he gets up and begins to dress, saying nothing. She turns on her side, watching his strong, muscular back as he works on his clothing.

"Why are you leaving?" she asks softly, reaching out to touch him, but hesitating.

"I don't know," he mumbles, and pauses. "I have to get up early tomorrow. I think it would be better if I go back to my own room." He still does not turn to face her. She fights to keep from breaking into tears, her feelings of shame and confusion deepening. She knows that he does not have an early class the next day and would normally not hesitate to point out the contradiction, but the moment has robbed her of the will to argue. She does not speak, not trusting her own voice.

"I'll see you tomorrow," he says more gently, turning now towards her, leaning over to kiss her tenderly. He brushes hair off of her forehead, looking into her eyes. She is thankful for the darkness that hides her burning face.

"Don't be sad," he says, a little more business-like now, standing up, gathering his keys and backpack. "I'll see you tomorrow," he says again.

She watches as he makes his way to the door. Her face crumples as he leaves, no longer able to hold back the tidal wave of desolation that she feels. For once, she's grateful that he's just not the type to look back.

She is crushed under the mixture of emotion, and she lets it wash over her. Her mind races – maybe there really IS something wrong with her. Maybe she doesn't know how to be intimate. Maybe her face and body are really so unattractive in their natural state that she shouldn't be having sex! Even as the absurdity of each thought tries to enter her mind to give her some relief from her anguish, his words come back to her, taunting her.

"What is that look on your face about? What is the matter with you?.... it looked like something was wrong."

Chapter 27

My clandestine meetings with Lennon became more frequent and had an increased sense of urgency, at least for me. I found that I was feeling almost desperate to be not just in his company, but also in his arms, and felt that I couldn't get enough. I felt like a woman obsessed but powerless to do anything about it.

It didn't take long for me to try and find a casual way to mention to him that I had confided in Dora, who he seemed to like, so that I could tell him about her offer. He was angry that I had told her at first, yelling at me as we rode to a colony one day. My punishment was to be denied that afternoon. He left me sitting at the bank in Carabas with Albert while he went off to meet with someone. I obeyed like a chastised child, and sat listening to Albert's vague lecture on adultery. I was mildly amused that he couldn't bring himself to just scold me outright for what he knew was going on with me and Lennon, but didn't dare say it out loud. I didn't give him any help. Instead, I just patiently listened and tried not to smile my amusement as he told me about his own broken marriage and relationships, ruptured from his adultery. I found it curious that I didn't feel more guilt than I did.

When Lennon returned from his meeting, he continued to give me the silent treatment. We got back on the bike and rode home in silence. I tried poking and cajoling him into talking to me, but he wasn't giving in. I finally just talked to his rigid silent back about Dora's offer. He made no response. I gave up.

I was lounging on Dora's porch a few days later, chatting idly with her, when Lennon rode slowly by on his bike. He glanced in our direction, then kept going. I started to jump up, but Dora grabbed my arm.

"Make him come to you," she said softly, watching his progress down the road. "Don't let him know how eager you are to kiss and make up. Make him pursue a little."

I settled back into the hammock, knowing she was right but unable to slow my heart rate that had just sped up a little. As we watched, Lennon doubled back and came to a rolling stop in front of the house.

"Doña Dora," he called from his motorcycle. "Good afternoon. How are you today?" It was like he couldn't see me there, which made me want to jump out of my skin.

"I'm fine, Don Lennon," she returned easily. "And you?" There was a hint of a smile on her lips; she knew how to play his game. She casually stretched her arm over to where I was settled into the hammock and took my hand. It was a gesture of protectiveness and friendship, and clearly conveyed the message to him that he shouldn't ignore her other guest.

"May I come in for a moment?" he asked, not acknowledging her gesture. He waited for her to nod her agreement before swinging off his bike. He left it parked in front of her house as he approached. I never took my eyes off him, trying to burn my gaze into his face and force him to look at me.

"Perhaps I could get a drink of water from your kitchen, Doña Dora?" he asked as he entered the gate onto the porch.

"Of course you may," she replied, keeping up whatever maddening façade they were trying to maintain. I was becoming more outraged every moment, but I held my tongue and my position by sheer will. He went through to the house and we heard him in the kitchen getting some water. I wanted to go back there, but Dora held my arm. *Wait for him*, she mouthed to me. I looked away angrily.

"Perhaps I could come by tomorrow and visit, say around 10 a.m.?" Lennon asked Dora as he came back to the porch. This time he was looking directly at me and I understood that he wanted me to meet him there. I wasn't ready to give in to him that quickly but didn't want to say no either. I just glared at him. Not for the first time, I felt totally manipulated by this man.

"As you like," murmured Dora with amusement, watching the exchange of wills take place. With that, Lennon turned and left quickly, not looking back as he started his bike and turned the corner.

"What the fuck was that all about?!" I exploded as soon as he was out of earshot, heaving myself out of the hammock.

"Hey, calm down, *gringita fea*," Dora replied evenly. "There are people listening around us. Lennon knew that, so he played it cool and tried to tell you to meet him here tomorrow." She paused, then smiled. "I think he plans to take advantage of my offer to you."

"Well, who says he's going to get anything but a swift kick?" I shot back. I realized that I was very angry yet oddly thrilled by the situation. I knew I would be there the next day, and that I wouldn't give him a swift kick. Dora let me pace for a while, watching my anger turn and my face flush. She just smiled.

I was there the following day at 9 a.m. Instead of going to the office, I simply stopped at Dora's house on my way. Mark was off teaching a class. All but the youngest of Dora's kids went to school in the morning. The youngest wasn't yet old enough to go, so she was watching cartoons on the small television in the living room as she scooped up *gayo pinto* with her tortilla.

Dora was making her bed with fresh sheets as I entered. She smiled at me as I reached to help her. I felt embarrassed at the situation. I had never had someone else aware that I was about to have sex. I wasn't sure what to say, so I remained quiet.

"I have to run to the market for a few things," Dora said lightly, seemingly sensing my discomfort. "I'm going to take my daughter with me. If you could just wait here for me to get back..." she trailed off.

"Of course," I answered quickly. I breathed a small sigh of relief. At least we would be alone in the house. "Will you stay until he gets here?" I asked. I had grown so accustomed to having other people around virtually all the time that being alone, especially in someone else's home, left me with a slightly panicked feeling.

Dora smiled. "Yes, Elenita, I will stay until he arrives," she said. "Have you eaten breakfast?"

"No," I confessed with a weak smile.

"Well, there's *gayo pinto* on the stove and I'll get some eggs in the market. You'll probably have an appetite when I get back!"

We were still chuckling when the motorcycle pulled up, its motor purring softly. Dora motioned me to stay put in the bedroom as she went out to the front door. I heard them talking softly as she helped Lennon maneuver the bike into her living room. She closed the front door behind them. It was the first time I had ever seen her front door closed. The house was much darker. I was a nervous wreck for some reason. This was by far the most planned encounter Lennon and I had ever had. I was terrified that someone was going to come to the door and discover us.

My fears melted away a little bit as he came into the room. He had a lusty look in his eye, and he came right to me. His first embrace left me breathless and my fear forgotten. He had me half undressed and onto the bed before Dora and her daughter were out the door.

When we were both sated and sweaty, he spoke to me for the first time but I wasn't ready for him to break the spell of what had just happened. I put my hand gently over his lips and closed my eyes. The stinging slap to my wrist nearly made me jump out of my skin. My eyes flew open and I turned to him angry and stunned.

"Don't you ever hush me," he growled. He got up and began dressing himself. Words escaped me for only a moment.

"Who the fuck do you think you are?" I hissed at him. "You don't hit me! I was enjoying the afterglow and I just wanted another moment of quiet! What the hell is the big deal?" I began reaching for my own clothes.

He didn't respond. He just finished dressing and left the room. My head was reeling as I tried to understand what had just happened. He came back a moment later and grabbed me by the shoulders a little roughly. "Hey!" I protested.

"I was going to tell you that I love you and you ruined it."

That stopped me cold. While we had both talked about falling in love, we had never said those words to each other. Somehow that made it the worst kind of adultery. My face flushed with a strong mix of emotions – I felt like I loved him too, yet I was ashamed and embarrassed and confused about how we had gotten so far into this. He released my shoulders and walked out again. I was too stunned to follow.

I stayed in the bedroom as he pulled his bike back out into the street, slammed Dora's front door behind him and sped away. I curled up on the bed and cried. I'm not sure how long I was like that before Dora was suddenly at my side, cooing to me and wiping my face as she pulled me into her ample bosom. I told her what had happened through choked sobs and broken sentences. I didn't know what conclusion to reach so I simply stopped talking when I told her that he had left. She pulled me off the bed, handing me a handkerchief to wipe my face, and pulled me by the hand into the kitchen. She made me a hearty breakfast of *gayo pinto*, eggs, warm tortilla and a hunk of *cuajada*. It was heavenly. I realized how ravenous I was and finished every bite. I felt much better.

I looked up to find her studying me with her head slightly cocked to the side. I knew that meant she had an idea but I was unprepared for what she suggested.

"You know, you are now regretting how the situation unfolded because you wanted to tell him that you love him, too. At the same time, you are now unsure of the status of your relationship and terrified that you have lost him. Also at the same time, you are feeling confused and conflicted because of the gringo." The gringo was what she called Mark, never by name. I nodded mutely, tears welling up in my eyes again when she continued. "What we need is a social gathering – a fiesta – where you can be in the same room with Lennon. You need to be dolled up for this party and have a good time so that he can see you aren't suffering. You need to show him that you are more in control than he thinks. It will drive him crazy and he'll be crawling back to you! Trust me!" She wore a big smile on her face, pleased with her own plan. I wasn't as convinced.

We talked about the details of this hypothetical party. Mother's Day in Nicaragua is celebrated on the same date each year, unlike in the States. It is a time to have parties, often large ones, and invite lots of friends. It is not necessarily a day spent with one's own mother, but rather celebrating the mothers in your midst. Certainly people recognize their own mothers on that day, but the whole day isn't necessarily dedicated to spending it with mom unless you are a young child.

So Dora's big plan was to have a party and invite several couples, including our neighbors Julio and Felicia from across the street. Her Oscar was also included as were a few other friends, along with Lennon and Patricia and Mark and me. We planned the menu, divided up the tasks involved in preparing for the event, and set off our separate ways.

I wasn't convinced that Mark would like the idea of attending this party. He had only met Dora very briefly and had not really talked with her. With his general wariness of everyday regular Nicas continuing to permeate his view of our small world, I didn't feel optimistic.

I arrived home for lunch to find Mireya cooking over our three-burner stove. I loved having her there. It was wonderful to come home to a clean house and clothes hanging out to dry, but more than that, I liked having someone in the house when I came in. Mireya seemed shy and didn't really say very much, but I could tell from watching her that she missed very little. That day she was preparing one of my favorite dishes – *pescasón*. It was made with slices of a local squash called *chayote* with slabs of *cuajada* cheese in the middle, dipped in batter and fried. Not the healthiest dish, to be certain, but there was little I enjoyed more than this delicacy. Mireya was the first one to make it for us and she knew how much I enjoyed it.

Mireya handed me a note from Mark when I walked into the kitchen. It said that he wouldn't be coming home for lunch – he was going to be meeting with some of the morning teachers over lunch. School is taught on a schedule that allow kids to help out at home, on the farm or with small side jobs in Nicaragua, so half the kids go in the morning (roughly 7:00 a.m. – 12:00 p.m.) and the others go in the afternoon (roughly 1:00 – 6:00 p.m.). Many teachers teach both shifts.

I was relieved that Mark wasn't coming home. I wasn't sure how I was going to pull myself together from the events of the morning to face him with something resembling normal composure. Mireya watched me out of the corner of her eye reading the note, and she saw my relief. She gave me a curious glance and asked if everything was all right.

"It's fine. Marco is working over lunch with some teachers, so it will just be you and me today." I insisted that Mireya eat with us each day, though many people did not allow their domestic help to eat until after the family had been served and cleaned up after. She had been uncomfortable with this idea at the beginning, but clearly pleased that I had insisted.

"How are you doing today, Señora?" she asked, clearly not wanting to pry, as we sat down together at the small kitchen table.

"Oh, I'm okay," I sighed. "I had an interesting morning." I was dying to confide in her but conflicted. I sensed that she would be an excellent confidante; one about whom I would never question loyalty, not worry that she would gossip about me, and certain that the wisdom I saw in her eyes could benefit me. At the same time, I knew it would be changing the nature of our relationship fundamentally to do so and I was afraid she'd be too uncomfortable. She was watching me without watching me, trying to appear nonchalant, but her curiosity was nearly palpable. I decided to take the risk.

"Mireya, I need to confide in you because I think you would have really good advice for me. But I'm afraid to put you in an awkward position and I don't want you to leave. What do you think?" I turned to face her, my desperation I'm sure was evident on my face.

"I think you need to decide for yourself whether or not you think me trustworthy," she answered softly, looking me in the eye. "*I* know that I would never betray you or Marco, but you need to feel that yourself. Until you do, you should not confide in me." She continued to watch me, her gaze steady.

"The problem is that I need to confide in you about my relationship with Marco and I don't want to put you in the position of picking sides between us."

Her steady gaze continued as she thought for a moment. "We are women," she said simply. "We take care of each other."

I realized I had been holding my breath. I smiled at her and took another bite. I felt an inexplicable wave of relief wash over me suddenly and I was afraid I was going to cry. I concentrated on chewing.

"I'm not as.... Pure as you might think I am," I said finally, still not looking at her.

"None of us are."

"I've been having an affair with Lennon." I looked up at her to see her reaction. She never missed a beat.

"I suspected that you were interested in him. Be careful of how much you show it. It will be obvious to some." She paused and took a bite. I could tell she wanted to say something more but was hesitating. I urged her to go on. "It makes me a little sad," she said finally. "Marco seems like such a nice man and the two of you are such a handsome couple."

"Marco is not a bad man. He just doesn't give me what I need."

We went on to have quite a long conversation about Mark, love and relationships. I learned more about what she had been willing to endure at the hands of her ex-husband in order to keep their marriage together. She had suffered a lot of physical and emotional abuse from him. I asked her what finally made her decide to leave. I was not prepared for the story she told me.

Mireya walked home from the hospital in the dark. She carried a sheet over her arm, having been prepared to spend the night there watching over her father-in-law. He was recovering from surgery. With no real caregivers in hospitals to take care of patients outside of the necessary medical care, families usually took turns. Tonight Mireya had volunteered. She liked her father-in-law – he was kind to her. Which was more than she could say about his son.

The beatings had been getting more frequent and more violent, and she gently reached up to touch the freshest bruises under her jaw as she walked. She wasn't sure how much longer she could endure this. At the same time, she didn't know where to go or how to get away. Her eyes welled up with tears as she thought of her three young children. He never came after them, even Estelita, her oldest. Estelita wasn't his; she was the product of the kidnapping that Mireya had endured 12 years before.

Mireya walked a little more quickly, wringing the sheet in her hands. She felt uneasy, walking alone in the dark. She could see the small house and turned in to climb the steep dirt path.

She could hear her husband's low voice talking in a soothing manner as she approached. It was so out of character for him that her heart immediately dropped into her stomach. She wanted to run the rest of the way up the path and burst through the door, but her legs suddenly felt heavier than lead. Her breathing quickened as she made herself keep going towards the closed door.

It was when she heard her 11-year old daughter's voice, soft but a little scared, that she managed to lunge the last few steps and get to the door.

It was locked, which was unheard of unless they were all sleeping or not home. She didn't have her key, so she knocked urgently.

"Who is it?" came the sharp response from her husband, all gentleness gone from his voice immediately.

"Mireya," she responded softly. "Mireya," again more strongly this time.

"What are you doing back here? You're supposed to be at the hospital taking care of my father!" She could hear him coming out of one of the bedrooms, striding towards the front door. She tried to compose her face.

"I was, but he told me to go home," she answered, willing her voice not to shake. "He said that he didn't need me to watch over him tonight, that he was feeling much better." She paused as he unlocked the door. "He thought you would like to have me here at home instead." She looked into his stormy face, searching for some clue as to what had happened.

She walked into the house, brushing past him, looking for the children. "Estelita?" she called.

The three children were in the room they shared. The two little ones, Julio and Roberta, were each curled up asleep in Julio's bed. Estelita was sitting up, perched on the edge of the small twin bed that she shared with Roberta. Her dark eyes were huge as she looked at her mother.

"What happened?" Mireya breathed, afraid to speak too loudly, and afraid to hear what her daughter would say. Memories of being raped by the son of a woman that she had been sent to work for by her parents came flooding back as she watched her daughter wring the cloth of her thin nightgown in her hands. Mireya had only been 13 when that had happened.

Estelita stared up at her with large eyes, afraid to speak.

Mireya went to her, gripped the girl's shoulders firmly, and said, "It's okay, my child. Tell me. What happened?" Mireya was barely able to keep her panic in check.

"He offered me money if I would let him touch me," the girl whispered, her head hung low.

Mireya's mouth went dry and her anger threatened to boil over. "Did you let him?" she asked through clenched teeth.

Estelita's head snapped up, hurt written across her young face. "No, mama!" She shrugged her shoulders, trying to break her mother's grip. "Ow, you're hurting me!"

Mireya relaxed her hands as relief flooded through her. She stood again and turned towards the bedroom doorway where her husband was leaning. Her anger was no longer in check.

"Get out of my house, you son-of-a-bitch!" she growled at him. She was waving her arms at him as she came towards him, pushing against his small frame. "Get out and don't ever come back here again!" She was starting to yell now, beating into his chest, adrenaline and rage fueling her strength.

"GET OOOUUUUUUT!" she howled in fury.

He looked at her with contempt, turned on his heel, and left.

Mireya slammed the door shut, bolted it, shoved a chair under the handle, and collapsed on the ground, her fear and sadness and pain consuming her. Estelita came to her mother, and together they cried and clung to each other until both were spent.

I could hardly breathe as I listened to Mireya's story. I felt like I was in a nightmare; the one where my legs wouldn't move and I was powerless to get away from an unseen monster. Only when Mireya reached over and gently touched my hands did I realize that I was wringing them together, twisting my shirttail in my lap. My own experience of being molested at the same age as Estelita came rushing to the forefront of my mind, and it was like I was in the room again, trying to get away from my attacker.

I jumped as she touched me, startling both of us. I gave a short, nervous laugh as I shot to my feet, knocking my chair over and fumbling for my pack of cigarettes.

Mireya looked alarmed. "Doña Elena, are you alright?" She stood up, reaching her hand towards my arm without touching me, then drawing back again.

I had found a cigarette and was pacing back and forth, trying to catch my breath and calm down. I hadn't really been suppressing the memories; the man had continued to harass me verbally all the way through my adolescence, teenaged years and into adulthood – all the way up until I went to Nicaragua. I didn't know why I was so suddenly upset; I just felt very agitated. For Mireya's sake, I shrugged it off.

"Oh, nothing, Mireya, really," I said, flashing her a quick smile. She did not look convinced. I said the first thing that came to my mind. "It's just that I'm so outraged by people who do things like that to young children!" I puffed on my cigarette, continuing to pace. I was starting to calm down a little bit.

Mireya was watching me warily. "Well, I guess what I was trying to tell you, Doña, is that we all do what we feel is best for ourselves in the moment. No one else will do that for us." She paused, still watching me pace. "I don't judge you for your choices with Lennon."

I stopped pacing and stared at the wall, fixated. Something was trying to click in my brain, but it was just beyond reach. The harder I concentrated on making some connection that seemed very important, the foggier it became in my mind. Finally, I shook my head and gave up.

I still felt very guilty about my own seemingly lame reasons for carrying on with Lennon, but I was oddly comforted by her words. I was beginning to see that Mireya was an incredibly wise woman; one whose opinions I valued, and whose respect I wanted to feel I deserved. I walked over to where she was still standing, watching me. I leaned over and gently hugged her. She hugged me back, and tears came unexpectedly to my eyes.

"Thank you for telling me your story," I whispered, closing my eyes. "It means so much to me that we can speak openly with each other. You have no idea."

She patted my back as she held the embrace. "Oh, Elena, I understand loneliness." She paused. "Yes, my child, I do."

Chapter 28

They lounged together on the couch in his rented studio apartment, a bright shaft of moonlight coming in through the window and flooding the room.

"I don't know, I'm pretty excited about this opportunity," said Ellen, running her finger down Mark's arm lightly. "You heard them in Santo Domingo. Juan Carlos made it pretty clear that they were offering us the jobs – both of us! I think we should do it!"

Mark was thinking about it, turning over the possibilities slowly in his mind. The idea was actually growing on him, but Ellen watched him warily. He knew that she was interpreting his silence as an inclination towards a negative response. "Well," Mark started to say, but Ellen cut him off.

"Look, I think it would be really great! They clearly want you to come and teach English, and you won't be taking anyone's job that is a native because they specifically said they want a native English speaker for the job! And as for me and the reforestation project, well, I'd love that and frankly, without very many college-educated people who could do the job, I wouldn't –"

"Stop, stop!" Mark said, laughing softly at her enthusiasm. It was one of the things that he really loved about her, but sometimes it got to be a bit much. "I'm just thinking about it – I'm not saying no."

"Oh," said Ellen, instantly looking embarrassed. "I was just trying to tell you why I think it's such a great idea, that's all." She looked wounded, almost like a small child that had been rebuked.

"I know, and I'm glad to know that you're excited," he said, in a softer tone, patting her arm. He paused to gather his thoughts. "I think we should talk more with Esther about it. I want to understand a little more what the expectation from the Partnership would be. Remember, we'd be going there primarily to represent them. Our day jobs would be secondary, I imagine."

"Well, let's call her then!" answered Ellen quickly, brightening immediately. She sat up. "It's not too late – I think we should call her now! We'd be able to catch her at home!" She got off the bed and started heading towards the phone.

"Well, hold on a second," said Mark, a little annoyed now at how spontaneously she jumped into things sometimes.

Ellen hesitated, turning back to him, waiting for his reason to delay the call, impatience written on her face. "What now?" she said, her annoyance coming through clearly in her voice.

Mark looked at her, torn as he always was between loving her willingness to act decisively, and thinking of her as childish and impetuous. As he watched, a flirtatious, pouty look came across her face, and love won out – this time.

"All right, what the heck – go ahead and call her," he said, smiling slowly at her excitement. As she turned back to the phone, he shook his head, wondering to himself for the millionth time how they managed to stay together.

"Hi, Esther? It's Ellen. How are you?" Ellen paused, listening.

"I hope I'm not calling too late, but Mark and I," she turned back to look at him and flash him a big grin while she continued talking, "were just talking about Santo Domingo and the trip, and how exciting it all was!" She had a big smile on her face. She paused, listening again, her smile freezing, and slowly starting to fade a little.

"Uh, huh, well, we thought it was a pretty clear invitation from the local Partners," she said, her brow starting to furrow, a hand going up to rest on her hip in a defiant way. Uh, oh, thought Mark. Here we go. He sighed softly.

Ellen continued on, not noticing his expression or body language. She was looking at the wall now, and looked intent on making her point. Mark had seen the same look directed at him a thousand times.

"Well, what I heard them say was that they'd love to have both of us. It was clearly an invitation being extended to both Mark and me." There was a slight tremor creeping into her voice now that usually indicated she was about to start yelling. Mark braced himself. This was also familiar to him.

A moment later, Ellen's head snapped up and she turned to look at Mark, eyes wide open, and a stunned expression on her face.

"I see," Ellen said softly, still starting at Mark. "Really. Hmm." She paused, eyes glued to Mark. "Well, that definitely is something to consider." Another pause. "Uh, huh, okay, Esther. Well, I'm sorry for interrupting your evening. I'll let you get back to your family now. We'll be in touch."

She turned to hang the phone up and slowly turned back to Mark. Her expression of surprise was more one of worry now. Mark waited, watching her. He wasn't sure he wanted to know what she was about to say.

"Well, that was interesting," she said. She looked a little nervous, like she didn't want to tell him what Esther had said. She wouldn't really meet his eye; she just kept glancing his way. Mark was finding it difficult to catch her eye, but didn't say anything. She looked like she was waiting for him to encourage her to tell him. He was just watching her warily.

After a few seconds, her impatience won over. "Okay, well, first she argued with me about whether or not the invitation was even issued by the Partners in Santo Domingo for both of us to come. She thinks that only you were invited." She rolled her eyes, her irritation at a different interpretation of the exchange clear. She paused briefly before plowing ahead. "And then she went into something about how we would have to be married to even go! Isn't that ridiculous?"

She was trying to look incredulous, but it wasn't going so well. Instead she looked once again like a small child, her face openly vulnerable.

Mark was stunned. He wasn't sure what to say. Any response immediately felt like a trap. He suddenly felt very tired.

"You know what, it's been a really long day for both of us," he said, looking away and settling back into the bed. "Let's figure this out another day." With that, he turned over and closed his eyes.

Ellen just watched him for a moment. Tears began to well in her eyes as she slowly made her way back to the bed. She climbed in and spooned up behind him. He shifted slightly. She pulled away a little.

Both of their minds were racing.

The clock read 1:24 a.m. before she fell asleep.

It read 3:56 a.m. before he did.

TOP: the back of Ellen's house in Santo Domingo

MIDDLE: the backyard of the house, shared by several houses in the row

BOTTOM: the air strip used by the little commuter plane that ran between Managua and Santo Domingo

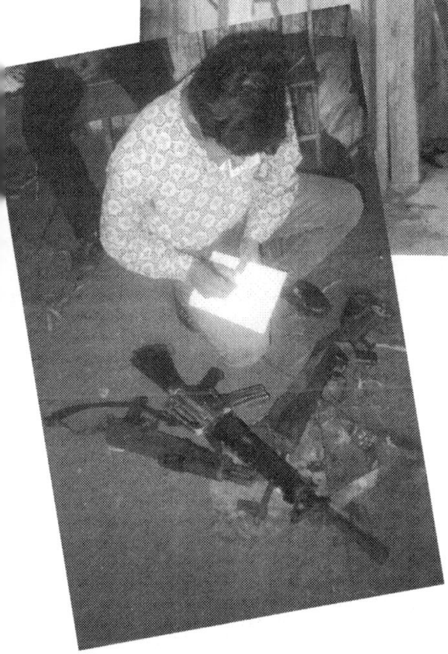

TOP: a typical house out in the rural communities outside of Santo Domingo

MIDDLE: child doing homework in his living room in Santo Domingo

BOTTOM: one of NECOG's Peace Commissioners signing papers to collect weapons from former soldiers out in the rural areas outside of Santo Domingo

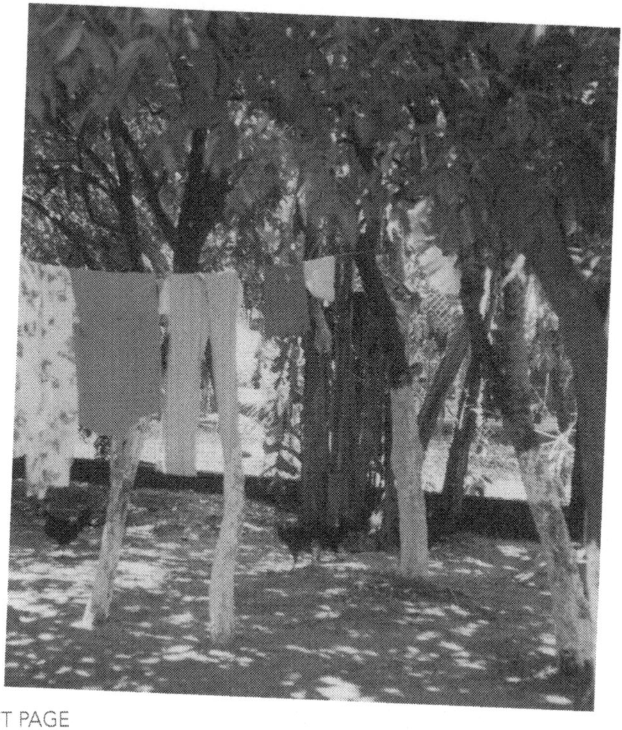

LEFT PAGE
TOP: the main "city" street in Santo Domingo

MIDDLE: the NECOG office in Santo Domingo where Alejandra, Lennon and Eduardo worked. Ellen's office was to the left.

BOTTOM: the open road outside of Santo Domingo

RIGHT PAGE
TOP: laundry drying on barbed wire in Ellen's backyard

BOTTOM: an abandoned home in a colony outside of Santo Domingo

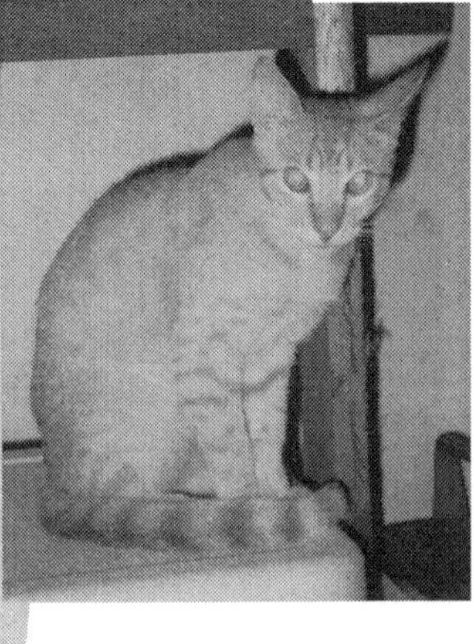

TOP: Ellen, on the camping trip with Mark, Pedro and Joaquin (October 1997)

MIDDLE: Flea, Ellen's cat

BOTTOM: Ellen in her Santo Domingo living room (March 1997)

TOP: Mireya and Ellen (April 1997)
BOTTOM: Ellen and Mireya's children (December 1997)

Chapter 29

Mark's reaction to the idea of Dora's party was mild in comparison to what I had imagined. I had convinced myself that we would not be going together because he would be so against the idea. Instead, he surprised me by simply shrugging his shoulders and saying that it was fine with him. He was mildly curious about who else would be in attendance, and as I listed off the other guests, careful to place Lennon and Patricia in the middle of it, he showed no reaction.

Lennon and I did not have the occasion to go out into the colonias together during the 10 days' time that passed between our meeting at Dora's and her party. It seemed as though the more I sought out chances to be alone for a few minutes with him in the office, the more steadily he avoided me. I wasn't sure where we stood or what was going on. He had left so angry from Dora's house, yet angry because he hadn't gotten the chance to tell me that he loved me in the way he wanted to do it. I felt very confused and depressed, and with each day he avoided talking to me, I felt worse.

By the time the party arrived, I didn't want to go. It took strong convincing from Dora that I should pull myself together, put on a nice dress and get my butt over to her house to help her get things ready. After seeing that my depressed state was causing Mark to look at me with suspicion, I tried to follow her advice. I put on a long, tan dress that fit much more loosely than it had when we had arrived but that I still thought was my best dress at that point. I left my hair down. It had grown out past my shoulders and lightened from dark brown to a reddish blondish brown from the sun. When I washed it and let it dry naturally, some of the curl from my last perm still made it wavy.

I walked over to Dora's house about an hour before the party was to start to give her a hand setting up. Mark was going to walk over with Julio and Felicia. When I got there, she looked me over with a critical eye and pronounced me fit to be seen, then turned quickly and beckoned me to follow her into the kitchen.

"Drink this," she commanded, pushing a glass of what appeared to be cola towards me. "You need to relax and get out of the dumps! You're never going to make Lennon come crawling back to you looking so down at the mouth! You are in danger of truly being *la gringa fea!*"

I sniffed the contents and almost coughed. The smell of rum was very strong. I wondered if the cola had been added only for color. Dora was frowning at me, so I dutifully took a small sip. It was too strong. I almost gagged. "Do you have any lime?" I choked.

"Yes, my child," Dora laughed, getting me two small slices from the counter.

I managed to continue taking small sips, larger ones when I stopped to think about how depressed I felt over the Lennon situation. It began to go down much more easily and soon Dora was refilling my glass.

Before I knew it, guests started arriving. Lennon and Patricia were among the last. Their kids and nanny were with them. Patricia looked flustered but was all smiles. I wondered if they had had sex before they came over. Lennon's face betrayed nothing as usual.

Everyone began eating and drinking, and soon the volume of the party was considerably higher than it had been at the beginning. Someone had turned Dora's stereo up and loud, wailing Ranchero music was blaring out at us. The mournful tunes were fitting of my mood, which I still couldn't shake. If anything, I felt like the alcohol was pushing me further down instead of buoying me up as Dora had planned. I mostly stayed towards the kitchen and didn't talk to many people.

Finally Dora found me and grabbed my arm hard, pulling me outside behind the house.

"What is the matter with you, Elenita?" she hissed at me. "You are sulking in the kitchen and everyone knows something is wrong. You better get out there and start mixing. Slap a smile on your face and hold it there, and hold that chin up high. You are going to make your husband suspicious and your lover glad that he walked out on you. Now pull it together!"

I just glared at her. I felt like I was in a drunken haze and in danger of falling down. Suddenly this struck me as terribly funny and I started to guffaw.

"That's better!" she proclaimed. "Now march in there and mingle!" She slapped my butt as I turned to stumble towards the house.

When I got to the front of the house, I could see that Mark had been pretty steadily hitting the bottle as well. He was talking loudly in slurred Spanish with Julio and Oscar. They were listening intently, more to understand him than from being riveted, I suspected. This thought made me once again burst out with a loud guffaw. Julio and Oscar smiled up at me with affection. Oscar winked.

I went to the food table, determined to eat something to slow down the alcohol coursing through my blood. I hadn't eaten anything for several hours and was starving, but nothing on the table really appealed to me. I was too nervous. I was painfully aware that Lennon was watching me, and working hard at acting like I didn't care. So I tossed back my hair, something I knew he thought was sexy, and proceeded to take a few things from the table.

As I turned to take a seat nearby with Dora, I cast a cold stare in his direction. He looked startled. Dora smiled coyly at me as I sat down and murmured, "Good girl, good girl."

Soon he caught my eye again and looked pointedly at the kitchen, then got up and started walking back there. Dora noticed and made a loud production of asking me to help her fill some trays back there as well. I got up and followed, my stomach churning.

When he saw Dora appear, he quickly walked back to the front of the house without looking at me. I was dumbstruck! With the alcohol in me, I decided to be bold. I turned on my heel and followed him back out to the front of the house. I walked up to where he had quickly taken a seat next to Patricia again, who was deep in conversation with their nanny.

"So how have you guys been?" I asked too loudly, interrupting Patricia mid-sentence. I perched on the arm of her chair. She looked up at me a little startled.

"Fine, and you, Elena?"

"Haven't seen much of you guys since our big trip to the disco a few weeks ago! You been avoiding us?" I was aware that I was slurring my words and talking too loud but was unable to stop.

"No-o-o," she said slowly, glancing over at Lennon with a questioning look on her face.

"Well, I just wondered. It seems like every time I've seen Lennon lately, he's turned and walked the other way rather quickly. I was just wondering if maybe we'd done something wrong." Now other people were beginning to pay attention. This was not the kind of direct conversation people had in this culture unless they were picking a fight. I noticed Dora heading towards me. I didn't give her the chance to get there – I simply got up without waiting for Patricia to answer and walked away.

A few minutes later, I had tossed back yet another drink. They were going down much too smoothly now. I went back over to Lennon and Patricia. I was like a moth drawn to flame – I couldn't stay away from them. I knew somewhere in the back of my mind that I was behaving in a way I would later regret but was unable to stop myself. I felt numb and desperate to know where things stood with Lennon. Since he wouldn't leave her side, I felt compelled to talk to him wherever I could reach him.

"So! Are you guys having a good time?"

Two pairs of dark eyes stared at me – one was filled with confusion; the other with warning. I heeded neither.

"You know, Patty, - I can call you that, right? Patty, I just think you and your husband there are the greatest. I really enjoyed myself when we all went out together. When are we going to do that again? You're such a great couple together. So devoted. So faithful..." I was staring directly at Lennon now. Patricia's eyes were going back and forth between us.

"I just love you guys!" With that proclamation, I leaned over and kissed each of them on the cheek, practically falling into Patricia's lap as I went towards Lennon. He did not move a muscle.

"Elena, are you okay?" she asked, her voice concerned and suspicious at the same time. "Maybe you should slow down a little on the drinks."

"Oh, Patty, alcohol numbs the pain of life. Don't you know that by now? It numbs the pain. I have pain and I want it numbed, so I'm drinking it away. Isn't that right, Lennon?"

"Elena, I think Patricia is right – you should slow down. You're going to get yourself in trouble."

"Oh, and wouldn't I love to find trouble with you!" I teased, smiling coyly at him. Alarm flashed across his face and made it look comical to my distorted vision. I guffawed loudly, spitting accidentally on Patricia. I found this even more hilarious and laughed so hard I fell off of the edge of her chair where I'd been perched. Dora was immediately there picking me up, trying to drag me into the kitchen. I pushed her hands away and headed over to Mark, landing right in his lap. He had been watching the whole exchange and looked at me darkly.

"What's your problem?" he growled at me in slurred English. "You've had too much to drink."

"Look who's talking! You can barely put a sentence together in Spanish! Why do you think Oscar and Julio have been hanging on your every word? Tell me it wasn't because you thought you were that interesting!" I got up and started to walk away. His hand shot out and grabbed my arm and pulled me back. I landed hard on the chair next to him.

"You don't talk to me like that!" he snarled. "And I'm sick of your flirting with Lennon! Talk about people thinking you're interesting – hah! You think you're that good-looking? Funny? Well, take it from the one you've been with the longest – you're not!" With that, he threw my arm back across my body. He tossed back the rest of his glass.

A part of me instantly felt small and ashamed, while the rest of me was filled with rage. My face burned. I was thankful that he had been speaking in English; while everyone in the room knew we'd just had an unpleasant exchange, at least they didn't know the details. I leaned over to Mark, determined to make him feel as small as he'd made me feel.

"At least Lennon is interested in talking to me and thinks I'm pretty. You better watch out – he just might steal me away from you," I breathed into his ear. I turned away and started to get up when his hand came down and smacked me hard on the thigh.

"Where the fuck do you think you're going? Sit your ass down. You're done flirting for tonight."

Oscar and Julio were instantly on their feet and grabbed Mark by the shirt. They had him up against a wall before the look of surprise had time to spread across his face.

"No one hits women here, and especially not Elena," said Oscar softly. Only his eyes and his fists in Mark's face betrayed his anger. Julio was right with him.

I stood back and watched, feeling triumphant but rattled as they talked to Mark and he held up his hands in defeat. We had been dancing a little too close to the truth for my comfort. I wondered how much Mark knew or at least suspected.

They finally all sat back down and Mark got another drink. I walked back into the kitchen with Dora on my heels. I was shaking and badly wanted another drink but was scared of what else Mark might do. I decided it was time to sober up. I got a glass of water.

I avoided Mark for the remainder of the evening. I watched him carefully out of the corner of my eye as I tried to sober up. He continued to drink at a steady pace. Julio and Oscar were keeping a close eye on him. At one point Oscar asked me if I wanted to sleep at Dora's house that night, or if I wanted him to walk us home. I tried to laugh it off and say that in all the years I'd known Mark, I'd seen him pick fights with other guys but he'd never laid a hand on me. While I tried to convey confidence to Oscar, I realized that I was sobering up for a reason. I wasn't quite sure *what* Mark would do when we got home. I hoped it would be nothing more than pass out. I couldn't imagine that he would hurt me, drunk or sober. It just wasn't Mark – he was a pacifist.

When just about everyone else had gone, it was time for us to leave as well. I had noticed Felicia wanting to leave a couple of times. Julio had glanced over at me each time and brushed her off. When I finally walked over to Mark to ask if he was ready to leave, Julio motioned to Felicia that it was time for them to go, too. She shot me a look of disgust that caught me off guard. She had been so friendly up to that point. I wondered if Julio's defense of me had made her jealous.

The events of the evening had left me drained. As the four of us walked the few short blocks home, the mild worries of feeling threatened by Mark evaporated in the cool night air. It was after 3 a.m. and we all just wanted to get to bed. Mark could hardly walk from intoxication. One arm hung over Julio's shoulders and the other hung heavily over mine like a yoke.

I was thinking about Lennon, and how he would go home with Patricia and not give me another thought; thinking that agreeing to this party was a foolish mistake on my part; thinking that Lennon wouldn't want me any more. I had sobered up, but was close to tears and feeling very emotional.

We bid Julio and Felicia goodnight at our front door, Julio asking me once more if I would be okay. I assured him we would be just fine and we walked inside. I was locking the door behind us and had just turned around to head for the stairs when Mark's hand slapped me heavily in the face. I stumbled back, catching myself on the door.

"Tha's for bein' a fuckin' slut, hangin' all over Lennon like that and makin' me look like a goddamn fool," he slurred, his eyes smoldering but barely open.

I touched my lip, which was split and bleeding a little, as I got back on my feet. Something in me snapped in that moment. I growled at Mark, "You stupid son-of-a-bitch!"

Mark was trying to focus on me, his body swaying slightly. He looked less certain of himself. "Hey, I'm sorry, I din't mean to hurt you, baby." He was speaking more softly, and took a step towards me.

"You stay the fuck away from me!" I yelled, hot rage consuming me. "What's the matter with you?! You don't hit me!" I was shrieking, unable to control myself.

Mark stepped back again, some of his anger returning. "Well, you shoun't have been hangin' all over that asshole Lennon all nigh', and none o' this woulda happen'!" He was pointing a finger in my direction, but not able to control himself enough to make it go straight at me.

I slapped his hand away, swinging as hard as I could. I only caught his finger, so the effect was enormously unsatisfying. I swung again, but missed completely as he took a step back. "Hey!" he protested.

"Maybe if you actually paid me any attention, or acted like you cared about me, or ever noticed me in any way, I wouldn't resort to flirting with anyone else!" I was still screaming at him. I felt sick. Mark just looked at me, trying to focus, saying nothing.

"Ah, riveting silence, as usual!" I yelled.

I stepped back, breathing hard and having a hard time catching my breath. I turned blindly to the door and fumbled with the lock until I got it open. I was so consumed with rage I was afraid I would kill him if I stayed any longer.

When I opened the door, our landlord neighbors and Julio were heading our way. I stepped out and quickly shut the door behind me.

"Everything's fine," I stammered. "We just had a little misunderstanding. Marco's had too much to drink. He just needs to sleep it off and he'll be fine. I just need some air."

Our landlord looked at Julio, genuine concern and alarm on his face. He slowly turned and walked back to his house. Julio looked at me. I could tell he was thinking the worst about what had happened. I was suddenly thankful for the lack of streetlights and porch lights on our block.

"Are you sure you're okay?" he asked.

"I'm fine. It's him you should be worried about!" I managed a small laugh that sounded harsh and forced to my own ears. "No, really. I'm fine. And he'll be fine, too, once he gets some sleep. I left my purse over at Dora's house. I'm going to go get it."

"Do you want me to walk with you?"

"No, I'm fine, Julio, really. It's only a couple of blocks away. I'll be fine. Go to bed with that beautiful woman of yours. I'll see you tomorrow." With that, I walked away, not waiting to see if he'd do the same.

The further I got from the house, the more the reality of what had just happened both descended on me and seemed to blur. Had I just imagined this whole thing? I choked back sobs, more from self-pity and the realization of what my life had become than sorrow. How could it have come to this? I had witnessed plenty of very physical fights between Mark and his fraternity brothers in college. But never had I imagined that his physical rage would be turned onto me. I suddenly felt overwhelmed, vulnerable and very naïve.

When I got to Dora's house, it was completely dark. I paused outside her gate and could hear she and Oscar inside giggling softly. My lack of faith in the reality of my memory of what had just happened at my house won over, and I kept on walking. I was probably just being stupid.

I wanted very badly to talk to Mireya. I was sure that she would understand and be able to comfort me and reassure me that everything would go back to the way it had been in the morning. But I only knew the general area of where she lived and Santo Domingo didn't have telephone booths with phone books and addresses listed. There weren't even any house numbers, let alone street names. I wandered around for a while until I was sure that Mark had either passed out or gotten himself up to bed. Fatigue finally won over and I headed home. There was no light on in the front room of our house. I tried to peer in through the open cinder blocks but couldn't see that high. I took a deep breath and opened the door as quietly as I could.

My eyes adjusted to the dark and I could see that Mark was not around. I crept up the stairs as quietly as possible. I could make out the form of Mark sleeping on the bed. I slipped out of my dress, put on a t-shirt and shorts, and crept back down the stairs. There was no way in hell I was getting into bed with him.

We had two hammock chairs in the living room, hung from the strong beams above. I curled up in one of them and was soon joined by Flea who came slinking down the stairs. I tried to cover up as best as I could with a sheet and prayed that the mosquitoes would leave me alone for one night without netting. As exhausted as I was, sleep eluded me for a long time. It wasn't until the early morning light had begun to creep into the sky that I finally fell into a dreamless sleep.

Chapter 30

The next morning, I was up and moving long before Mark came down the stairs. When he finally came stumbling down the stairs, I was on my way out the door. I turned as I heard him coming down, and he stared at me. I could almost see the wheels in his head trying to turn.

"I'm going out," I said flatly, clipping my words. "There's coffee in the kitchen." I turned to go.

"What happened last night?" he asked, his voice still full of sleep. I turned back towards him in time to see him rubbing his eyes and yawning. I resisted the strong urge to punch him in his exposed gut.

"What happened? What are you, some kind of moron?" I was incredulous. "Which part? The part where you hit me, or the part where we argued so loudly that the neighbors came over?" I was staring at him, my rage from the night before coming flooding back. My hands were braced on my hips.

At the words "hit me", his hands flew down from his face and he stared at me, mouth slightly open. "What? I didn't hit you!" It was his turn to sound incredulous.

"Didn't hit me?" I was back to yelling, and took a step towards him. "What's this, you fucking asshole?" pointing to my lip, sticking my chin out so he could see the split. It was barely visible by that point, but that was not helping me feel any less furious.

His face fell and he immediately looked wary. "I don't remember hitting you," he said very slowly. "I'm sure that if I did, it was a complete accident."

I barked out a harsh laugh. "Oh, I'm pretty sure there was nothing accidental about it, sweetie pie," I said, a mean smile on my face. "How convenient that you don't remember. I supposed you don't remember our argument either?" I was spitting my words at him.

He continued to watch me warily, "No-o-o," he said slowly. He thought for a second. "I barely remember getting home, and I have no idea how I got upstairs." He watched me, pausing again. "I'm going to assume you didn't help me."

I bared another laugh out. "No, I did not. I went for a walk to cool off, and now I'm leaving again. I don't want to be in the same space as you right now." With that, I turned on my heel and walked out the door.

On Monday, Lennon came to me while I was alone in our little office trying to put together my monthly summary of what I'd been doing and a plan for the upcoming month. I had been scheduling a lot of days in the colonias assigned to him, determined to get our relationship back on track.

I told him what had happened, sticking my lip out so he could see the barely-visible split. I embellished that I had exacted a revenge of my own and that he needn't feel too macho and go after Mark himself. Once he realized that I was not seriously hurt, he turned tender, kissing my bruised lip gently and murmuring sweetness into my neck.

We spent a lot of time together over that next month, going to the *colonias* frequently. I learned who was in his network of friends out in the various *colonias*, and with whom his relationship was more formal. From his friends we often got meals in exchange for cigarettes, which he smoked, too, and usually buying soda pop for the children. There were always children around; there didn't seem to be a single household without them.

In June, it was time for me to take a trip back to the states. A college friend of mine was getting married and had asked me before we went to Nicaragua to stand up for her in the wedding. She had been in my wedding and I was thrilled to oblige. It was the first wedding I'd ever been in. I was also eager to step on a scale, which we didn't have – I knew I had to be losing weight but I was afraid to guess how much. My clothes all fit much more loosely than before, and I even fit into Mark's jeans – a first.

In the days leading up to my departure, conversation with Mark was strained. Almost as an afterthought, someone from NECOG Managua let us know that a delegation from the Partnership Office sponsoring us would be visiting while I was away. He was to meet up with them to travel with them for a few days and help with translation. Esther Smith, who was in charge of the Partnership Office in Michigan, did not hide her relief that I would not be along as well. Mark would accompany me to Managua for my departure so that he could meet the delegation when they arrived a day or two later, but he would not meet me when I returned. We would simply meet up at home in Santo Domingo again after the delegation had moved through. While nothing of my affair with Lennon or the evening of the terrible fight had been admitted or spoken of aloud, there was a tangible coldness between us. I was content to let it hang. I had moved my wedding rings to my right hand. I knew that he noticed but said nothing.

Lennon gave me a letter the day before I was to travel to Managua before heading to the States. He gripped me tightly, kissed me with tenderness, and solemnly instructed me not to open the letter until I was at least on the plane. Dora gave me a tape of songs from the radio that she had recorded for me to listen to while I was away. Many people seemed worried that I would not be coming back. I was more worried that it would be my last trip back to the States before committing myself forever to this land and its people.

My goodbyes with Mark at the airport were platonic to say the least. As I passed through the gates, I felt enormous relief. My steps quickened and my bag seemed lighter. I was excited to see so many friends and family, and to get away from the strain of my home situation for a few days. Nearly five months had passed since we'd left Detroit and I missed my family terribly. I smoked one more cigarette and got onto the plane.

The letter was burning a hole in my pocket, but as I settled into my seat, the older Nicaraguan gentleman next to me struck up a conversation. He had a very interesting story and was equally curious about me, and we ended up talking through nearly the entire two flights back to Detroit. I could hardly believe that eight hours of travel had passed when the pilot came on to tell us we were landing in Detroit. I was suddenly very nervous about seeing my family and felt uncharacteristically shy.

I was seated near the back of the plane and took my time getting off. Walking up the gangway felt like being in some space-aged tunnel. It dawned on me that I had been living a very rural and technology-free life in Santo Domingo. I began to wonder how foreign being "home" was going to feel. I caught sight of my parents peering hopefully and eagerly down the gangway. My father nearly knocked a couple of people over waving at me as he spotted me. We both began to cry with happiness.

The more sights and sounds I took in, the more overwhelmed I felt! Reverse culture shock is a difficult thing to experience. I felt very disoriented – things that were supposed to be familiar and feel like "home" now looked so foreign to me and felt uncomfortable. I quickly grew very tired and just wanted to sleep. I also realized that speaking English and only English felt like a big piece of me was missing. My parents tried to be sympathetic but I could tell that they just had no concept of what I was going through.

I crashed right after dinner. As I was reveling in the softness of their guest room bed and starting to drift off, I suddenly remembered

Lennon's letter and my eyes flew open. I jumped out of bed and rifled through my jeans' pockets to find it. The trip had been hard on it – it was crumpled up under my passport. I climbed back into bed and slowly unfolded it, wanting to savor every word. I knew I would read it again and again in the next five days before I returned to see its author in person. I smiled as I began to read it.

My dearest love Elena -

I hope that this letter finds you safe and in good health. I wonder if you waited until you got onto the plane or all the way to the United States before reading this, or if your curiosity won out sooner. In any case, know that I am thinking of you and eagerly awaiting your safe return to me. Enjoy your family while you are with them and please send them my best regards if you think it appropriate. But please come back. There are many here in Nicaragua who love you, whose lives you have touched, to whom you are very important. The first among them is me. Travel safely.

A million hugs and kisses and all my love,

Lennon Calderon

I reread it five or six times, then curled up like a cat after a sweet bowl of milk, and let sleep consume me.

Chapter 31

After the rehearsal dinner was over and everyone had left, I finally had a chance to be alone with Toni. I was dying to tell her about Lennon and my life in Santo Domingo. She had always been the wildest child among our circle of friends, and I wanted her perspective as well as her approval. I remembered from our college days that she had always sought our comfort that she wasn't a bad person when doing something she knew wasn't exactly the "right" thing to do. Well, the tables were now turned and I needed some reciprocation.

We settled in at her parents' house where we'd be spending the night. We poured ourselves a couple of glasses of wine and went up to her old bedroom. She had seen that my wedding ring wasn't on the correct hand almost as soon as I'd arrived earlier that day. Her look of concern mixed with suspicion had made me laugh at the time, but I wasn't feeling amused any more. I was very nervous about what she would say to me.

"So what's the deal with the rings?" she asked, barely having closed her bedroom door. Toni had never been one to mince words or stand on ceremony. It was one of the things I loved most about her. She watched me closely as she folded her lean, six-foot frame into a chair.

"Well, I've lost a lot of weight I guess and they don't fit well on my left hand anymore," I answered lamely, looking at my hands. "Funny how weight loss affects your hands differently." I had suddenly lost my nerve to come right out with everything.

She continued to stare me down as she sipped her wine and pondered the challenge of getting me to open up to her with the truth. She changed her tone to a soft one. "Honey, you know you can tell me anything. You've always been there for me and I hope the same is true in the other direction. Right now it would seem to me that you need a friend to confide in, so spill it. I'm not going to scold you or judge you. I just want to be here for you. What's going on?"

That was enough to convince me. True to the emotional roller coaster I felt like I was living on these days, I was suddenly buoyant and hopeful that she would see the same wonderful promise and romance of Lennon that I did. I brought out the letter and handed it to her. She looked at it for a moment.

"You're going to have to help me out here. My Spanish is good, but his writing is not. What's this word here?" I leaned over to her.

"Nicaraguan slang for the United States. Do you want me to read it to you?" She handed it back and I read it out loud.

When I looked up at her, she was still staring at me and was now shaking her head slowly back and forth. "Oh, boy," was all she said. A hint of a smile was playing at the corners of her mouth. "So it's not signed 'Mark' – there's a story here that I'm waiting to hear."

As I explained to her what had happened with my marriage to Mark, how I'd become attracted to Lennon and what led to our affair, I felt like I was trying to justify everything. Toni wasn't being judgmental; I was of myself. At the same time, I couldn't help feeling a little reckless and wanting to get back to Nicaragua so that I could be with Lennon again. The remorse about being unfaithful was real, but I firmly pushed it to the back of my mind. I had to in order to keep going. I again embellished the physical fight that Mark and I had. I needed to say out loud the reasons that I was telling myself for continuing to see Lennon.

When I had finished it all, Toni pondered what I had told her. She had asked some occasional questions during my story, but mostly had just let me talk. She looked sad.

"I always suspected that your marriage to Mark was doomed from the beginning. But I watched what happened to your friendship with Alexa when she tried to intervene before your wedding, and frankly I didn't have the courage to endanger our friendship like that. But Ellen, are you sure you know what you're doing? This guy sounds like he's playing you." She held up her hand as I started to protest. "But more than that, I think he could be dangerous. I think he could really hurt you."

"If you were paying attention, you'll remember that it was Mark that hit me – not Lennon!" I spat out. I was hurt that she wasn't giving me the carte blanche that I had been hoping for.

"I know, sweetie, I know. But I'm not just talking about physical hurting here. This guy sounds a little controlling. I'm just saying I want you to be careful. Look," she continued, reaching over to put her arms around me. "I don't want to fight with you! It's the night before my wedding and you've traveled halfway across the world to get here for it. I have always valued our friendship. So let's have another glass of wine and talk about other things."

We spent the next few hours doing just that, and I tried to forget the mild warning that she had given me. I firmly pushed away the little red flag waving madly at the back of my head. But when we finally collapsed into bed and turned out the lights, it was all I could see in the darkness.

My hair had grown considerably during the time we'd been in Nicaragua and I had not been brave enough to get it cut by someone locally. So one of the first things I did was head to the beauty shop where my mom got her hair cut to lop off a good seven inches of it. I felt like the new cut, a simple bob of one length that ended at my chin, was cute and carefree – fitting of my new emerging self. I was excited to go back to Santo Domingo to show it off to everyone, especially Lennon.

As I shopped for new clothes with my mom, I was amazed and delighted to discover that I had dropped considerably more weight that I had realized. When we arrived in Nicaragua, I had fit into a size 16 pretty comfortably. I was now buying size 10s and the scale said I had dropped 30 lbs. As we wandered through the stores, I kept grabbing the wrong size out of habit and my mom would have to remind me that I was now considerably smaller. Every time we passed our reflections, I stared in disbelief.

Toni was not the only one to notice the wedding rings shifting to my right hand – my father spotted the change right away. When he inquired what was going on, I tried the same evasive tactic I had tried on Toni, only to realize that it wasn't going to be any more effective. Conversation at the dinner table stopped as I squirmed under my family's scrutiny. Even my brother had come home for dinner, though we were by no means close. My father watched me as I struggled to find my way carefully through the minefields of possible explanations.

"Well," I managed finally. "You know things haven't been so great between me and Mark – I wrote you about that." I examined my plate to avoid my father's penetrating stare.

"Mm-hmm," was all he said after a moment.

"I don't know, Dad," I blurted, tossing my head back with an air of defiance. "What do you want me to say? Mark's not very nice sometimes." I regretted it as soon as the words were out of my mouth. Now all eyes were on me.

"What does that mean?" he said quietly, a hard edge creeping into his voice.

"Nothing," I said quickly. "Just that I don't feel like wearing a visible sign on my hand right now that is supposed to signify happiness and holy matrimony when what I feel like is that we have neither, okay? Can we just leave it at that, please?" I was looking at him now, pleading.

In that moment, my dad's eyes let me know that he understood something bigger was happening but would let me off the hook for explaining. For now.

I managed to get through the rest of the visit carefully avoiding the subject.

Chapter 32

The day after I got back to town, I was working in my office trying to catch up on whatever I might have missed while away in the States for most of a week. I was distracted, listening for the sound of Lennon's motorcycle to pull up. I hadn't seen him yet since returning.

Finally he pulled up around 10 a.m., an hour and a half after the office opened. He went into the main office first and I could hear him greeting everyone. After a few minutes, I heard his footsteps approaching my office. I quickly reached up and smoothed my hair, giddy with butterflies and excitement to see him again. He walked in and froze in the doorway.

"What did you do to your hair?" he asked icily, spacing out each word, indicating his displeasure.

"I cut it!" I answered with a bright smile, twirling my head and patting my hair, trying to be light-hearted to avoid an argument. "I think it looks cute! Don't you?" I displayed my concern at his disapproval on my face clearly.

"I can see that," he snapped. "What the hell were you thinking? I don't like short hair."

I was stunned into silence for a moment. "It's not really short, Lennon, it's more of a medium length," I was stammering. "Besides, it will grow! What's the big deal? I was hot."

He stepped closer to me, grabbing my wrists. "I don't like it when you make changes without talking to me first," he said softly, though the menace in his voice was clear. "Did you get another tattoo while you were there, too? Any other surprises I need to know about?" His grip on my wrists was tight.

"Ow, you're hurting me, Lennon," I whined softly. I broke out in a light sweat and felt like he could smell my fear. I had a small turtle tattooed on my shoulder that he didn't like. "No, I didn't do anything else... geez.... Let me go!" I was twisting my wrists now, trying to break free of his grip.

He held me a moment longer before flinging my hands away. Then he stood regarding me with a cold look in his eyes. "You've changed, Elena, you've changed." And he walked away.

I watched him go, rubbing my wrists and feeling desperate to chase after him, but I didn't want to make a scene. People in the office already watched us closely enough. I felt torn and confused. I instantly doubted that my hair looked as cute as I had thought it did, even though friends and family at home as well as everyone else I had seen back in Santo Domingo had complimented me on it. Then I felt self-righteous, like who the hell was he to tell me what to do in the first place; and then immediately chastised like a small child, worried that I had somehow disappointed him in an important way by not consulting him first. I mean, wasn't that what people who were important to each other were supposed to do?

7/7/97

Dear Folks at home -

Once again I'm back in Santo Domingo. In a lot of ways, this is positive; I missed our house, Flea, my friends and my job. I did not miss the rain or mud, which is well underway in earnest. I did not miss the roosters crowing at 3 a.m. or the bugs, which are also out in earnest. I missed the heat, speaking Spanish, the food, the pace of life, dancing to Latino music, quiet moments of appreciating nature, did I mention my friends? And, of course, Mark. (I think.)

The trip back was uneventful. I arrived in Managua and proceeded to Santo Domingo in the truck with Juan Carlos's wife, Juanita, and her brother. Thursday, I rested and unpacked. Dora took off for her hometown of Muelle where her very sick grandmother passed away on Sunday. Mark was gone with the delegation from Michigan in San Carlos on a river trip, and Lennon had gone to the campo for the day, so I made a quiet and somewhat lonely entrance into town.

Friday I went back to work where everyone seemed pleased that I came back. I had a meeting in one of the nearby colonies, Calero, with Lennon and his boss from Juigalpa, Daniel. While on the way back, it was decided that I would accompany them to Juigalpa for the weekend, with Patricia and the girls as well. Since I would have essentially been alone for the weekend, I went. We had a great time! I got to know both families and the city better. I also got to spend some time with just the two of them (the "Lennon's"), which is almost always fun! Things are going better between them and it was a pleasure this time. We missed the late bus on Sunday, so we actually didn't get back until Monday morning. We left in the first bus at 4 a.m. (ugh) and arrived here in town at 9 a.m.

Mark and the delegation arrived at 12:30 p.m. on the third flight of the day to Santo Domingo. There were 12 people in the delegation, including Mark and two translators from NECOG, Managua, so the third trip was made especially for them, as the plane holds only up to 15 people.

The visit went pretty well. I did not get along with Esther, as usual, and consequently did not feel free to express my concerns as elaborately as I would have liked. She and the other leader were even a bit defensive with Mark, the Chosen One, so we really didn't get any concrete answers to anything. We asked about money and were told that basically Esther needs to make some phone calls to get some stuff cleared up with the head guy in the States.

They also brought some cash with them to give us to cover set up fees (yay!), but left without giving it to us or telling us how much it is. I had food poisoning or something and was throwing up and running to the latrine all morning, so I didn't go to see them off and ask about it, and of course, Mark forgot. However, one of the committee members and a translator stayed behind for a later flight (they didn't all fit on the first one; it was a smaller plane), so I asked her about it and she promised to look into it and contact us from Managua today. Probably we will just have to get it next time we are in Managua from the office. Jane or Ana or Dan and Vicky will keep it safe for us, I'm sure.

As for the question about the University, they were less than excited, especially about me teaching. They also said we need to "re-evaluate our priorities here in Santo Domingo". They expressed concern that it might change our status as Mission Volunteers to be paid by an organization. We have a meeting today with the University folks, so we'll talk to them about all this. Mark is also writing a letter that we'll fax to the guy in charge in the States to clear up money questions for ourselves. Maybe someone will have some suggestions. Otherwise, it looks like we won't be teaching there. For my part, that's okay. For Mark, it's a tragedy, and since he wasn't there for this conversation with Esther, it's harder for him to take.

We will no longer be paying for e-mail access. The

decision should have been made months ago because I didn't realize that it would not change anything. Anyway, we will be using the $35/month for a fax budget here in NECOG to use the fax machine as means of rapid communication. Each fax costs between $5-6, so that will cover about seven calls per month. To send faxes to us, you must do it between the hours of 10 p.m. and 10 a.m. your time because it's only during this time that the fax machine will be able to receive direct faxes.

I find myself feeling more homesick in some ways than I felt before I came home. I don't feel like that has changed who I am as a person, though, but Dora and Lennon keep telling me that I "seem different". Maybe it's that they were doing the same things as normal while I was gone and the time passed slowly for them, whereas I was busy, busy, busy at home and, in some ways, didn't want to come back. I think that because I expressed regrets or reservations about coming back, at least so soon, along with expressing having missed them both lots, that now they think I've changed. That's not helping me feel any less homesick.

I also find myself more impatient in reassuring them that everything's fine over and over and over and over again. No one here has ever lived abroad and therefore can't understand how hard it is some days. They don't understand that in the morning when I wake up not feeling like speaking in Spanish, or like I can't understand any Spanish, there's not a damned thing I can do without staying in bed all day. Or days when I just want to go home, they don't understand why. Often they think they are responsible or it's because I'm miserable here when in reality, I just miss my family and friends whose language I speak and understand as well as they do their own and in whose culture I don't have to wonder if I'm doing or saying the right thing all the time.

Well, enough self-pity. For all I know this will make you all think I'm miserable here, too, and you'll start telling me it's time to come home. Do you see why I feel isolated sometimes? Most of the time it seems that no one here or there understands me. But I still love it here!

I came home to a painted house. The living room had been painted before I left, but Mark decided to surprise me with painting the kitchen as well. The only problem was that we had been talking before I left about switching houses (as many of you know), and this was an investment that makes us feel like we have to stay in the house to make it worthwhile, at least until fall in the States.

Flea forgot where he lived for a while. We were gone so much that he adopted a family with kids across the street; the one with the beautiful kids, Felicia and Julio. Well, Felicia likes to talk about us and is a part of the reason that I want to move. When I went to collect him, she was rude to me. I was as nice as possible for as long as I needed to be there getting him, and then I went on my merry way, and have yet to speak to her again. It's better that way.

Well, it's now Monday morning. We spoke with the University folks at our meeting on Thursday, and they really want us to teach. They are willing to write us the necessary documents to help change our status as well as help convince the church if that is what it takes. We sent a fax to the guy in charge of the partnership in the States, and are now awaiting a response since it's his decision and not Esther's.

I heard about big storms in Michigan that did a lot of damage, but details beyond that are sketchy, as we don't get a lot of international news out here. Any damage on the home front?

We will be going to Managua soon if things calm down there; right now there is a strike of the students going on because President Aleman is trying to change the Constitution without consulting anyone. He wants to change the policy that says the students get 6% of the national budget for the funding of the universities. Unfortunately for the peace and calm of Managua, the other businesses and everyone else are supposedly joining the strike today, which means more violence because of the solidarity. If it's calm, we'd like to go visit Dan and Vicky because we have next week off. We'll keep you posted.

That's about it. I love you all bunches and bunches. Marital problems continue as before, sometimes worse, but we manage to co-exist most of the time. I look forward to your first fax!!

Big hugs and kisses to all,

Ellen

Chapter 33

"You need to go back to Santa Gorda," Mireya's mother said to her flatly. "We left some suitcases at the house, and you have to go get them."

Mireya's eyes narrowed slightly as she looked at the older woman. She didn't want to walk several kilometers back to Santa Gorda through the heat and narrow path cut through the jungle to get the suitcases. She stood her ground silently.

Her mother glanced at her sharply. "Well, what are you waiting for, you lazy whore? I said go!" She waved her hand at Mireya, shooing her off like a fly. "Take your brother with you to help."

Mireya continued to stare at her mother in silence for a moment. She had ten siblings, three of which were brothers. Only one was old enough to go and help her carry suitcases.

Mireya turned away from her mother, and walked out into the small "yard" where her younger siblings were amusing themselves. Julio, her 10-year old brother, was hitting a small plant with a stick, imitating men chopping through the jungle with machetes. He looked up when Mireya came out.

"Let's go," she said quietly. He followed without question, always happy to follow his 19-year old sister, especially away from home.

They had been walking for about 20 minutes when Mireya spotted soldiers coming towards them on the narrow path. Her breath caught and her eyes darted around quickly looking for a place to hide. She grabbed Julio's hand and tried to yank him into the brush at the side of the road, but the soldiers saw them.

"Halt!" yelled one of them. "Stop!"

Mireya froze. They were Contras, and Contras carried guns. With Sandinistas moving through the area as well, they wouldn't hesitate to shoot. Her mind was racing and she strengthened her grip on Julio's hand as she slowly stood up. He was half-hiding behind her.

The soldiers had run the short distance to where they had been trying to leave the path, and were panting as they reached Mireya and Julio, guns trained on them.

"Where are you going, girl?" asked one of the three men

gruffly.

Mireya stared at the guns silently, her heart pounding so hard she was afraid it would come out of her chest. She was afraid to speak, frozen with fear.

One of the other men jabbed the one who had spoken with his elbow and said, "Maybe she's a Sandinista, boss." He snickered.

Mireya looked up sharply and found her voice, though it trembled as she spoke. "No, we're not Sandinistas. You asked our family to move further into the jungle to keep us safe from the fighting, and we have forgotten some of our suitcases. My little brother and I are just going to collect them."

The first one spoke again. "I don't think so. I think you're Sandinistan informers, trying to learn of our position so that you can go tell them where we are!" With that, he took a step closer to Mireya and jabbed at her chest with his weapon.

A small shriek escaped her lips as the second man came around behind her and the third man grabbed Julio away from her.

The first man moved the gun up from her chest to her forehead. With the second man holding her from behind, he pressed the barrel into her head. She shut her eyes, tears immediately streaming silently down her face, and began to pray.

"Dear Mother of God, bless my soul and forgive –"

"Shut up!" the first man hissed at her. "Someone is coming!"

A man on horseback came trotting down the path. The first man held his gun towards the approaching figure while the second man continued to hold Mireya, and the third still held Julio.

The man on horseback shouted a greeting to the soldiers. They shouted back, calling him Captain. Mireya couldn't see his face because of the angle of the sun, but her heart sank at the realization that he knew her captors.

"Who do we have here?" he asked as he swung down from his horse. The first man stepped aside so that the Captain could see Mireya. She looked up at his face and realized that she knew him. He had always smiled at her when riding his horse through the small colony where Mireya had returned to live with her family a few months before. She had no interest in him and had not smiled back, but he had never been unkind to her. Her hopes began to cautiously rise.

"Captain, it is good to see you again," she said tentatively. "My brother and I were just on our way to our family's home to retrieve some forgotten bags of clothing. Won't you please allow us to pass?"

He smiled at her. "Ah, yes, Señorita Mireya, I remember you. You have not long returned home from Sandanistan country, have you?" His smile was in place, but his eyes were cold.

Mireya broke out in a cold sweat. "No, no, well, yes, Captain," she stammered. "I am not with the Sandanistas, but you are correct that I have recently returned to my family's home and that I was living in an area where there were a lot of Sandanistas before, sir." She paused, looking him directly in the eye. "I am not a Sandanista. Please let us pass," she said quietly.

He chuckled softly. "I'm afraid I can't do that, sweetheart." He turned to his men and said, "I'll take her with me. You bring her brother. Let's go back to camp."

With that, he firmly took Mireya's arm and led her to his horse where he swung her up before climbing easily up himself. She grabbed the horse's mane to keep from falling off as they trotted back down the path. She glanced over her shoulder in time to see the third man give Julio a little shove forward, and her brother's scowl.

Mireya and her captors arrived at the base camp. The Captain had freely held her around the waist as they rode. She didn't feel she was in a position to stop him, even as his touch made her skin crawl. Julio didn't look happy, but he wasn't visibly injured either.

After the flurry of activity their arrival caused had settled down, it was starting to get dark. Mireya had taken hold of Julio's hand again and not let go. She rubbed one arm with her free hand while she looked around, trying to figure out if they were going to sleep there. Her mind felt numb, and fear kept coming in waves. She was relatively sure that the Captain wasn't going to kill them, but simultaneously sure that some of the others would do just that, given half a chance.

There were low, squat tents the color of dirt scattered among the trees that made up the encampment. The Captain appeared out of one of them, and beckoned Mireya over. She kept a strong grip on Julio's hand as she walked towards him.

"You're going to sleep in here, Mireya." He stepped aside, holding the flap of the tent aside for her and Julio to duck inside. She could make out a bedroll in the dim light taking up most of the ground. She crawled onto it gratefully, suddenly realizing how exhausted she was, and pulled Julio down with her. The Captain was peering inside at them, and he smiled.

"No, sweetheart, little Julio is going to sleep in another tent." Mireya suddenly felt panic seize her.

"No!" she exclaimed. "He can sleep with me! Please let him stay with me!" She was pleading now, terrified of what might happen to him without her.

The Captain's smile faltered a little. "I was hoping you might sleep with me," he said softly. "After all, I did save your life today, didn't I?"

Mireya felt nausea creep up from her stomach. She froze, unsure what to do in this impossible situation. After a moment, she felt herself dumbly nod. Julio had been looking back and forth between them, trapped. Now he faced her, eyes wide with shock and fear. She patted his hand, then looked up at the Captain.

"No harm will come to him if I stay here with you, right, Captain?" she spoke softly, trying to keep her voice even.

The Captain's full smile was back. "Of course not, sweet Mireya, of course not!" He reached down to help Julio up and out of the tent. The flap closed behind them and Mireya was suddenly shrouded in dusk. She was shaking and tried to take a deep breath to calm down. She did not want to sleep with the Captain, but feared what would happen to her and Julio both if she didn't comply.

The tent flap suddenly opened again and the Captain came in, smiling broadly. As he sat down beside her and began to undress her, she closed her eyes and kept repeating silently, "I will go home again. I will go home again. I will go home again."

After three weeks in the Contra encampment, Mireya was getting used to the coming and going of soldiers. She felt fairly safe, as the "Captain's woman", which is how the others referred to her. Julio was very subdued and quiet most of the time, and she constantly grilled him about whether anyone was bothering him. He insisted no one was, but some days Mireya found herself wondering.

One day, while the Captain was away in another region to the North, the soldiers who had first captured Mireya and Julio came and rounded them up roughly, saying that it was time to go. Mireya's hopes rose for a moment that they were finally going to let them go home. However, as they headed out to the south, it became clear that this was not the case.

"Where are we going?" Mireya asked, fear returning to her stomach.

The soldier gave her a little shove forward. "There are some people who want to see you down in Rama," he said gruffly. "They aren't as convinced as our Captain that you are innocent of connections with the Sandinistas."

Terror exploded in her stomach and she was sure she was going to vomit. As she leaned over, the soldier gave her another shove, more roughly this time. That was enough to push her over the edge, and she fell to her knees, heaving into the brush. When she had finished, the soldier pulled her to her feet and pushed her forward with the butt of his gun.

She took hold of Julio's hand as he looked up at her with concern. She glanced at him grimly, her jaw set, and nodded once. They didn't speak.

The walk to Rama took several days. They slept in the jungle without cover of anything but the trees each night. The soldiers took turns watching them and keeping guard. Mireya especially was overwhelmed with exhaustion and could barely stay awake while walking, let alone once they had stopped for the night.

Once they reached the headquarters in Rama, a group of Contra senior officers interviewed Maria at length. They wanted to know why she had come back to the region where her family lived and why she had been away. She explained over and over again that she'd left to get away from her family, and that Esteli had just seemed like a nice place to live. She also explained that she'd come back home after having a baby on her own, and getting tired of struggling alone as an 18-year old. So she'd returned home out of desperation. The baby had become sick and died from pneumonia less than a year later.

She explained how her family was cooperating with the Contras, providing them with food and shelter as requested. She told them how her family had recently moved further into the dense jungle communities at the order of the Contra soldiers, and that she had been returning to collect forgotten suitcases when she and her brother had been taken into custody. She refrained from using the word "hostage" for fear that it would show a level of non-compliance.

After several days of waiting, word came to her that the men in charge did not believe her story. They claimed to have proof that she was working as a spy for the Sandanistan Army. They were planning her execution.

Mireya rocked and wept as quietly as she could, gripping Julio tightly. The young boy shuddered with fear. They spent the night like that, awaiting death in the morning. There was no chance that they could get away. As the night wore on, Mireya found herself in a daze, muttering softly as she talked to her dead daughter, telling her that she would soon join her.

In the early dawn light, a man came to unlock their heavily guarded cell, and Mireya found she was out of tears. The man was silhouetted against the light, and she could not make out his face. He approached her, kneeling down to look at her, and she did not even have the will to resist or turn away.

"Mireya," he said softly. "It's time to go."

She startled out of her daze as she recognized the voice of her Captain. She threw her arms around his neck and pleaded for him to save her from execution. He picked her up and carried her out of the cell, Julio following closely. He put them both up onto his horse, which was waiting outside in the courtyard.

"Commandante," he said to one of the officials who had interrogated Mireya. "This woman is my prisoner, and I am taking her back with me. I will vouch for her credibility that she does not work for the Sandanistas. If she is found to be engaged in any activities that are not in our best interests, I will execute her myself."

With that, he took the reins of his horse and led it out of the courtyard. No one stopped or challenged them.

It was all Mireya could do to keep from falling off of the horse with relief.

Chapter 34

The road up into Santa Gorda was not passable by any means but on foot. It was just one of the realities of the rainy season in rural Nicaragua – expect a lot of mud, seemingly impassable roads, and life to go on anyway. As we stood at a *venta* having coffee before beginning our trek up the mountain, I watched locals maneuver with ease through the muddy path that the road had become. They made it look easy enough – no one was even really getting very dirty. There were 7 kilometers of mountain road between the *colonia* and us. The guys were saying it shouldn't take us more than a couple of hours to get there on foot. I was used to riding with Lennon on his motorcycle up this road. That usually only took about 30 minutes. As I continued to watch people come and go with apparent ease, I tried to feel confident. The morning sun was shining brightly and I entertained a fantasy that it would dry the road before we started up.

"The trick is to walk on the ridges," Pastor Miguel said softly. I turned and smiled at him. He was looking at me with his usual look mixed with brotherly affection and a hint of mischief. "The horses make holes and the buses make tracks in the mud. You have to look for the ridges of both to walk on."

"I'm not so sure...I think I missed this day of training," I answered lightly, turning back to watch the road again. There was a woman, probably in her late 40's, with two small children coming down the road. They moved at what seemed to be lightening quick speed. They all wore knee-high rubber boots and there wasn't a spot of mud on their clothing. The boots looked as if they'd been worn on a regular dirt road after a light rain, in other words, barely muddy. I found myself thinking of Mireya and how many times she had likely made this same trek on foot.

There were five of us going up that day. Santa Gorda was one of the furthest *colonias* NECOG served. Even in the dry season it took nearly two hours to reach from Santo Domingo, up winding roads to the top of a mountain. It had no electricity or running water. We were going all together to fulfill a multitude of roles at one time. Gathering the community was tough – farming up there was an even more demanding prospect than in other *colonias* due to the landscape, and farmers didn't easily take a day off to gather. Pastor Miguel and a man from the colonia where we were having coffee were going to talk to the Peace and Reconciliation Commission representatives about rumblings they'd heard that a small group was rearming. One of the local community leaders had come down to meet and escort us back up. Lennon was going to check on two of his projects that had been started six months before, and I was going to see if I could get a viable brigade started. We carried packs and hammocks for sleeping. We would be spending the night before hiking back down.

It was time to head out. We all wore jeans and boots of some sort. I had on my regular Nicaraguan military boots that I wore everywhere, as did Pastor Miguel and one of the locals. Lennon and the other local wore the knee-high rubber variety. As we started up the steep hill, I tried to concentrate on finding the ridges and not getting left behind. As usual, I was amazed at how quickly and agilely the natives moved over the mud, seeming to float on it almost, as if it were a regular dry road.

It took us nearly four hours instead of the two they had anticipated. I knew I was slowing them down somewhat, but the road was also much worse than expected. And only the two locals were really fit enough for a rapid climb.

It was well after two p.m. when we reached the village. We had been expected at noon. There was a crowd of about 40 or 50 people gathered waiting for us and visiting cheerfully. The concept of time was relative in Nicaragua, and the further you were from a city, the more relative it became. No one seemed surprised or angry that we had kept them waiting for so long. Several people came over to greet us warmly as we approached, and instructions to begin serving lunch were shouted. I was exhausted and starving after the long hike but tried to smile and be gracious as people came to greet me shyly. Finally someone put a chair under me and I almost collapsed into it.

Lunch refreshed all of us. Lennon sat across the table and down a couple of seats from me where he could watch me and make eye contact without being too overt. He kept winking and flirting with me, the confrontation about my hair long forgotten. It made me feel giddy. After lunch we found the room where we'd be staying – we were all together in one room of someone's house. We strung up our hammocks and left our bags.

The meetings of the afternoon progressed as if we had arrived on time, with no regard to time. As darkness settled over the mountain, candles were brought out and lit, and the meetings kept going. It was exciting to be part of it. I watched the people listen intently and respond with the honesty and lack of pretension that I had come to recognize as a trait of the people who lived in the rural communities. I loved sitting there and taking it all in. I felt like I was part of something important.

I also felt like I was camping. It was hard to get my mind around the fact that people lived here every day. It was like being transported back to the days of the Western settlers I had read about in history books. The only thing that was different was their style of dress. Clothing in rural Nicaragua came from the second-hand donations of the USA.

When we finally said goodnight to everyone and were heading back to our bunks, the guys put out all candles and flashlights, and we all climbed into our hammocks to sleep. My body was exhausted from the physical exertion of climbing but my mind was still racing. Lennon was in a hammock across the room. It was torture knowing he was so close but so inaccessible. Besides, my period was ending anyway, and our relationship wasn't about snuggling. I closed my eyes and tried to get comfortable. We all slept in our clothes.

As I listened to the breathing around me settle in deeper, I began to feel sleepy, too. Just then, a hand gently touched my leg and I gasped. Before I could yell, another hand was over my mouth and a whisper came in my ear, "It's me! Keep quiet!" I stopped struggling and reached out to find a familiar form beside my hammock. He leaned over and hugged me, nuzzling my neck.

Without a word, he unzipped my jeans and began tugging on them. I pulled his ear close to my mouth. "My period is just ending."

"I have a cloth. It will be fine."

I let him undress me in the pitch dark. I wondered how he had found my hammock so easily. It was so dark that I couldn't even make out his form in front of me. I stopped wondering as he climbed carefully into my hammock. Now I knew why he had checked and re-checked the knots in the ropes holding it up earlier. I smiled.

We both held our breath in the final moment, squeezing each other tightly. I felt tears come to my eyes; I wanted him so badly, for more than just a night. I was heartbroken when he pulled away a moment later.

"Can't you stay with me for a while?" I whispered in his ear. Tears were rolling down my face. I was suddenly overcome with emotion.

"Let me get cleaned up and then I'll come back, I promise," he whispered back. He kissed me softly and climbed out. I lay contented but aching for him. I waited for what seemed like an eternity but he did not return. As I finally drifted off to sleep, I wondered if I had just dreamed it all.

The next morning, I awoke early to the sound of roosters and women making breakfast nearby. There was blood on my hammock. It looked like Lennon's "cloth" had been my hammock. My face burned as I quickly untied my hammock and balled it up in my bag before the guys seemed to notice.

Lennon didn't seem to want to let me get close enough to talk to him for a minute. I kept trying to casually approach him, and each time he'd move just as casually away towards someone else. We all sat down at a large table to eat breakfast with our hosts. Lennon sat at the other end from me, engrossed in conversation with one of the local leaders.

Breakfast consisted of *gayo pinto* and *chicharones*. I didn't know what those were, but they had obviously been deep fried in a lot of grease. I tasted one of the small chunks tentatively; some part of a pig. They weren't bad, and everyone was watching me to see what I'd do, so I ate a few. I smiled and nodded appreciatively at our hostesses. They seemed satisfied.

After tying up some loose ends and saying goodbye to everyone, we headed back down the mountain to San Carlito. We planned to arrive in time for lunch, and then head back to the office by late afternoon. In spite of Lennon's behavior, my spirits were high. I figured having made it up the mountain, going back down would be a piece of cake. The sun was already bright, it was a beautiful day, and Pastor Miguel was hiking near me making plenty of conversation.

Hiking down was going much more quickly than hiking up had gone. We were about an hour into it when my stomach began to cramp and make angry noises. I knew I was going to be sick from one end or the other. I begged off into the bushes as the guys eyed me warily. I thought I saw a trace of amusement on some faces.

The diarrhea hit hard, but I was thankful that I wasn't vomiting. When it seemed like I had it all out of my system, I rejoined our crew a little weaker but ready to move on. Pastor Miguel seemed concerned and asked if I needed anything. I laughed and asked him if he had a ride for me to take the rest of the way down. As it happened, one of the local men accompanying us knew the farmers whose land we were passing. Their house was only another kilometer down the road. When we got there, before I realized what was happening, he went inside and asked if we could borrow a horse for the *gringa* to ride down the mountain!

I immediately protested and started apologizing profusely. I was making it through the mud on foot alright, but I had watched every horse that had passed us by and was not eager to get up onto a beast that was having more trouble than I was keeping its footing in the slick mud. I had not seen anyone but very small children on horseback – the rest of the time, the horses were being led or even pushed through the mud.

I was starting to panic, thinking I was losing this polite argument and was going to have to become rude and just refuse when Lennon stepped in. He quietly explained to the man and his farmer friend that I was afraid of heights and more likely to spook the horse, and hurt it and myself if I was riding. They were still watching me suspiciously, but seemed to accept his argument. I was grateful to him and gave him a quick smile to show that. He looked away. I was hurt but determined to hide it.

We were on the final descent overlooking San Carlito. I had managed to stay fairly clean. Not as much so as my Nicaraguan counterparts, but I figured I wasn't doing too badly for a *gringa* on her first trip through the stuff. As I was congratulating myself in my head and enjoying the beautiful view of the town below us, I missed a step and went crashing down.

I slid on my belly through the thick, red, muddy clay. I screamed out, the sound echoing down into the town. The toe of my boot had gotten caught in a tree root that was half buried in mud and was still stuck there as I went down. Not only was there no traction to be had, but I was also in serious pain. There would be no graceful recovery from this one!

Pastor Miguel and Lennon were immediately at my side, pulling me back in the direction I had slid so as to untangle my foot without breaking my ankle. I couldn't stop the tears that began to flow – it felt as if someone had ripped the big toe on my left foot clean off. They managed to get me on my feet again and I gingerly tested the weight on my foot. That toe was in a lot of pain. On top of that, my boot was completely stuck under the root. It was going to have to come off to get it out.

They helped me ease my foot out of the stuck boot, and then freed it, too. I wanted to look at my toe right there, but was afraid to leave my boot off for more than a few seconds. If there was swelling, getting it back on wouldn't be pretty and we still had a couple of kilometers to go before reaching the town. There was no other option but to walk.

I got the boot back on and limped along, Miguel right at my side with his hand on my arm, and Lennon not too far ahead in front of me.

In case I slipped again, he could break my fall. The rest of the trip down was messy. I was not able to avoid the sinkholes like I had before falling, so I went into mud up to my knees several times. I was completely coated in heavy mud up to my thighs and all down the front of me by the time we reached the bottom.

Pastor Miguel discreetly asked one of the local leaders he knew who had a house right at the bottom of the mountain if I could use a room to change clothes. I thanked them both profusely and ducked inside. I had a cleaner shirt – the one I had worn the day before – in my pack, but no clean jeans. At least with a clean shirt I felt somewhat better. I washed my face and arms outside at their laundry tub to get the majority of the dirt off. I redid my hair into a fresh ponytail and tucked it under a baseball hat that I always carried in my pack. I felt a million times better.

On the ride back, Lennon and I sat in the back of the NECOG truck while Pastor Miguel drove with a local woman who needed to go into Santo Domingo. I knew Lennon would sit back there. I had told them both that my leg needed to be stretched out so I climbed into the back stiffly, too. He was quiet until I spoke to him, looking at the passing landscape and humming under his breath.

"So did I dream last night or what?"

He looked at me with surprise. "What do you mean?"

I just stared at him. "What do I mean?" I laughed. "I mean that someone came to me in my hammock and had sex with me last night. That person sure sounded, smelled and tasted like you. And there was blood smeared on my hammock this morning. But the person who came to me last night said they would come back. And you sure didn't do that." I was glaring at him.

"I dropped the cloth I had brought and couldn't find it, so I had to use your hammock," he said lamely, looking away again. "Sorry."

"Why didn't you come back?" The longing I had felt for him the night before was turning to anger.

"I thought I heard one of the guys getting up so I went to my hammock and then just fell asleep," he answered smoothly, still not looking at me.

I was at a loss for words. Before I could think of any, Pastor Miguel stopped to pick up some people walking towards Santo Domingo. They piled in the back with us. We rode the rest of the way home in silence.

Chapter 35

7/15/97, Managua

Dear Mom and Dad,

HAPPY BIRTHDAY TO YOU, DADDY!!

It sounds like you had a restful day and weekend. Did you take out the present I brought you and look at it again?

We arrived in Managua yesterday about 6 p.m. Unfortunately, no one's phone lines are working very well right now, so we had to wait to come to the NECOG, Managua office this morning to send e-mail.

We are staying with Dan and Vicky until tomorrow morning, and then we are going to the beach for a couple of days. The Frenchies from Santo Domingo invited us to go along; it will be a cheap holiday - they buy the food here to cook, and take hammocks to sleep in. It's safe, don't worry. Anyway, I thought a break in the sun and surf would do me some good since rain is all we've been having back in town. Also...

Mark and I are not doing so well. We had a long talk the day after his birthday (the 9th, Wednesday) about how our marriage is in trouble, which he at least recognized. I told him the biggest problem I have with him is his lack of responsibility and initiative, which not only are a problem at work but one at home as well, when I have to do all the work around the house if I want it done that day. He's famous for saying, "I'll do it later", but then later never comes. We talked about what we could do, all amiably enough. I told him I thought responsibility was something that he would have to learn the hard way, by being on his own. He said as much as he would not like to be away from me, that he thinks maybe I am right.

Well, if we were in the States, at this point I would look for another place to live (it would take him too long to find one), we would divide up our stuff and be separated for a while. However, we can't do that here. Therefore, we don't know what we are going to do. Basically we are just trying to live peacefully for the moment. I'm trying to set up separate space for myself in the house so that I don't have to live in his mess, nor clean it up.

I've moved most of my clothes and stuff into the smaller bedroom where I'm now sleeping. I'm sleeping in the hammock, which is actually really comfy! It closes up around me like a built-in mosquito net. Mark has the bed. Frankly, I think I got the better deal.

So anyway, we leave for the beach tomorrow morning. We'll be back on Friday in the afternoon some time (we don't know the bus schedule yet), and head back to Santo Domingo on the 3:30 a.m. bus Sunday morning. I'll try to call you before we head back.

Love,

Ellen

Chapter 36

We were back in San Carlito a couple of weeks later. I didn't have any real brigade there, but Lennon needed to go and asked me to come with him. We hadn't really spoken much since the trip there a couple of weeks before, so I accepted. I figured maybe he'd have something interesting to say. For my part, I was beginning to think this relationship needed to come to an end. I was starting to feel used.

He talked about mundane things on the ride out there, telling me about school and his upcoming exam. I had graduated from college two years before coming to Nicaragua. Listening to him talk, I missed my friends and the bubble of college life. Even though his experience with the university was nothing like mine had been, it still made me nostalgic.

We went around and visited a few people in San Carlito, winding up eventually at a house I didn't recognize. A friend of Lennon's, one of the local leaders, stepped outside without a shirt on. I knew this wasn't his house, but he invited us inside. It became apparent that his mistress lived there. His wife and young children lived in another house across the *colonia*. I suddenly felt dirty, like I was now part of this community of the unfaithful who led double lives and broke the hearts and spirits of those who loved them most. My face burned as I slowly realized that I had been part of it for quite a while. My discomfort seemed to go unnoticed by Lennon and his friend.

We visited with the guy for a little while, the two of them drinking beer while I looked around the room and let my mind wander. Finally Lennon stood to leave and we said goodbye.

"You could have been a little nicer," he said frowning at me. "What, are you on your period again or something?"

I recoiled as if he had slapped me. "What the hell is that supposed to mean? And how could you think that would ever be an appropriate comment to make? You can't talk to me like that!" I started to turn and walk away from him towards his bike. He grabbed my arm hard and spun me back around to face him.

"I'll talk to you however I want," he growled, glaring at me. "And if you think you're the only woman I have, you're fooling yourself. So watch it or I'll dump you before you know what hit you."

I was stunned. Had I heard him right? "You have other women?" I stammered. "But you've always said I was the first! The only!" I suddenly felt very, very foolish. And very, very angry.

He barked out a harsh laugh. "You really are stupid, aren't you? Of course you aren't the first. How do you think I know so much about sneaking around without getting caught? About how to behave in any circumstance? About when it's okay for you to be close to me and when it's not? No, *amor*, you aren't the first. You're not even the only one. I have women in half the *colonias* we travel to. Haven't you ever wondered where I go when I leave you talking with your silly brigades, or with Albert in Carabas?" He laughed that harsh laugh again.

I was having trouble catching my breath. I thought I would be sick to my stomach. I had to get away from him, from this Lennon that I didn't know. I turned away again. Again he grabbed my arm and spun me back around, this time, not letting me go.

"Where are you going, *gringita fea*?" His tone was softer now, almost conciliatory. "We have appearances to keep up. You will stay with me." He was looking into my eyes as though he was trying to hypnotize me. I looked away and tried to break free. Tears were forming in my eyes and his hand was going to leave a bruise. I struggled not to cry.

"Obviously you have no more use for me," I said with genuine sadness, not looking at him. "Let's just go back to Santo Domingo and forget this ever happened – all of it. You can have your other women and keep Patricia in the dark, and I'll move on. Let's just be done with it." I choked on the last sentence.

He let go of my arm and laughed more softly, more like the Lennon I knew. "I'm just joking, *amor*! Did you think all that was serious? Come on, now. Come here," he smiled, holding out his arms to me. "It was just a joke! I would never be unfaithful to you. Of course you are the only one. Come here!" He was beckoning now with his hands, wanting me to come into his arms of my own free will.

I was now thoroughly confused and didn't know what the hell to think. I looked at him. Confusion, sadness, fear, shame and hope all washed over me simultaneously. I wondered for a split second if he might be mentally ill. I found myself slowly moving towards his embrace.

"That's right. Come to me," he murmured, patting my hair and holding me close. "Now let's go home. We can stop along the way and I'll show you that you are the only one for me."

I stared at him dumbly. It was all I could do at that point. I followed him to the bike and obediently climbed on the back. We sped off through the hills towards town. When we cleared the areas where most of the houses were, he slowed down, scanning the dense forest at the side of the road.

My heart was pounding and my hands shook. I was so confused – angry and hurt, and yet still desperate to win his affection. I felt foolish, and yet unable to stop myself from following his lead.

He found a spot that he liked, and pulled the motorcycle off of the road into the bushes a little bit. It was mostly hidden from the view of anyone passing by that wasn't looking. Only someone on foot would have easily noticed it.

He took my hand roughly and led me into the trees a little ways. We came to an old tree stump and he let go of my hand, coming around behind me. I just stood there, looking into the forest. Tears began to roll down my face and I felt paralyzed. Part of my spirit felt broken, and I was helpless to do anything but wait.

I heard his belt and zipper, then felt him tug down my jeans. I didn't stop him but I didn't help him either. There is no way that he could have possibly felt I wanted or enjoyed anything that happened next. When it was over, I threw up in the bushes while he wiped himself on leaves and walked out of the trees, leaving me there to get my clothes arranged and clean myself up.

I stood for a minute, leaning on the stump, tears blurring my vision, and tried to clench my jaw against the nausea. He started the motorcycle and I panicked, suddenly sure that he would leave me there alone.

I yanked up my jeans, running back out to the road as I did. "Don't you leave me here, Lennon!" I could hear the fear in my own voice.

He laughed and I heard cruelty. "Now how would that look, *gringa fea*, if I came back without you?" He paused, his face pinched in a mean mask. "You know, you really are ugly."

I thought I was beyond numb at that point, but that remark cut through me like a razor. I just stared at him, unable to believe how the day had unfolded. At the same time, I was unable to believe I had been so incredibly blinded for so long.

My face burned and I looked down at the ground in what I hoped was a submissive enough look that he would just think I was pathetic. I was counting on that being the end of our interaction, and just wanted to get back to town.

I climbed onto the bike behind him, grasping the metal rack for stability, and hung on as he rocketed off down the road. I closed my eyes, breathed deeply, and didn't let myself think about what had just happened. I felt dirty, cheap, and every bit as ugly as he said.

Mireya was waiting for me at the NECOG office when we got back. She was usually home with her kids by this point in the day and looked out of context to me. Seeing her jarred me from my state of numbness, and I immediately went to her and asked what was wrong.

"I had a bad feeling about you," she whispered to me quietly, looking past me at Lennon who was going back into the office. "I was cooking dinner for the kids and just had a bad feeling that you were in danger. Are you okay, my daughter?" She looked up at me with eyes filled with concern.

"I'm fine, Mireya, I'm fine," I said to soothe her. "Are you turning psychic on me now?" She smiled a little. After a pause, I said, "Can I come back to the house with you? I need to talk and I don't want to go home yet."

"Yes, of course," she said, taking my arm through hers. "I will make you some dinner and you will tell me what happened." She paused, and then added coyly, "and I'll tell you about my other visions", squeezing my arm. We both laughed.

It was quite a walk to get to Mireya's house. She lived in a section of town with hills and hidden streets that were unfamiliar to me. It was almost completely dark by the time we arrived. Her three children came scampering eagerly out to greet us. It was only the second time I had been to her house before. The two daughters, one 12 and one five, grabbed my hands while their brother, eight, pouted that he couldn't get a part to hold onto, too. I chuckled with affection at his sad face and held out the arm attached to the 12-year old for him to fit under. His pout quickly changed to a broad grin.

Even though she clucked at me the whole time about how I was going to get sick and die from it, I was insistent that Mireya let me bathe before dinner. I had to wash the slime of the day off of me. I felt like my skin was crawling. I threw my underwear into her trash pit, and borrowed clean clothes from her.

After settling the kids down and having dinner together, they fought over spots on the sofa to watch a program on Mireya's tiny black and white TV set while we moved to her front porch to talk. I told her what had happened out in San Carlito. I was vague and left out details when telling her about the stop at the side of the road, but I'm pretty sure she guessed. She listened without interruption.

When I had finished and was lighting another cigarette, she sighed. "Oh, Elena, I knew this guy would be bad news. And I knew something terrible had happened out there! I just had a feeling." She was rocking gently in an ancient rocking chair and looking up at the night sky. "You have to end it," she said, finally looking directly at me. "You have to end it," she repeated.

I didn't answer her, just took another drag on my cigarette and flicked it out into her yard. "I am sure that you are right. This has gone on long enough. And now he's trying to deliberately hurt me or play mind games with me or something. I mean, who thinks that kind of thing is a joke? Ever?" I was still angry, but a part of me wasn't ready to end the relationship.

"It's just that I've learned so much from being with him," I said softly, leaning back against the wall. "At the beginning, he made me feel beautiful and sexy and smart – all the things Marco doesn't! And even though the circumstances of our relationship are wrong – and I know that, Mireya, I know that – I felt like he respected me. Somehow that has helped me learn to respect myself a little bit. That's hard to walk away from." I leaned forward and lit another cigarette.

"And yet, look how much you smoke these days!" she exclaimed. "He's causing you stress and to be angry and hurting you and playing with your head as well as all those other things you named! I don't know, Elena, but from where I sit, he's doing you far more harm than good."

I tried to absorb what she had said and sort out all the thousands of feelings and thoughts racing through me. We sat like that for a while, the sound of a Columbian soap opera in the background. Finally I rose to go. I needed to get home and clear my head. I vaguely wondered if Mark was worried about where I was.

I said goodnight to the kids, who seemed genuinely sad to see me go, then walked with Mireya back towards the other side of town. She insisted on walking with me, that it wasn't safe for me to be out alone. When I asked who was going to walk her back home after that, she gave me an impatient glance and said, "I'm not a tall, white gringa whose head is worth a lot of ransom money." I just laughed. She was so motherly and protective. It felt nice.

I did not sleep well that night. I tossed and turned, finding it hard to get comfortable. I couldn't seem to shut my brain off and it raced, replaying over and over again the scenes with Lennon in San Carlito, and in the woods. As I finally fell into sleep, that scenes became mixed with Mireya's warnings. She stood beside us, shouting, like a referee at a soccer game. The place where Lennon kept grabbing my arm bled thickly every time he grabbed at me. I watched the dark red drips roll down my arm and hit the ground in dull splats.

Chapter 37

I awoke at dawn with a pounding headache and got up right away. I put on some water for coffee before heading out to the latrine. I hated the ice cold shower, but since I was too lazy to heat up bucket after bucket of warm water to bathe, as Mireya sometimes did for me when I was sick, I took a deep breath and braced myself as I stepped into it. Miraculously, I had found the Nicaraguans to be right when they said a shower (meaning a cold one) would cure a headache. It seemed counterintuitive, but it never failed.

I drank my coffee, smoked my first cigarette of the day, and listened to the news on the radios of our neighbors as I reheated some *gayo pinto* for breakfast. When Mark came down, grunting a greeting on his way out to the latrine, I went upstairs and dressed. We both finished our respective morning routines and heading out walking to the office together. He had seen me come home with Mireya the night before and hadn't shown any curiosity about where I had been. I didn't volunteer any details.

As we passed by Dora's house on the way, I noticed it was still closed up. Mark saw me looking and asked, "So where did your buddy go?"

I shook my head. "She went back to Muelle for her grandmother's funeral, but I don't think she ever came back." It wasn't all that uncommon for people to just up and leave for another town. Dora hadn't had a job in a very long time, so I wasn't surprised that she left to be with family. Our friendship had been strained since the fateful Mother's Day party. Mark and I walked on in silence.

When we got to the office, he went inside to get a few things and headed off to one of the schools. He was walking away when Lennon pulled up on his motorcycle. I wasn't ready to see him yet. The dream from the night before was still fresh in my mind, as was the exchange we had had on the side of the mountain in San Carlito. I was trying to put what happened in the woods completely out of my mind.

I told Alejandra that I'd be in my office working on my monthly reports if anyone needed me. I was walking out the back door of the office as Lennon headed in the front.

"Good morning, *gringita fea*," he called in a mocking tone. "Good morning, everyone."

"Good morning, Lennon," I replied over my shoulder without

turning around.

Once I settled into working on the monthly reports, I became absorbed and forgot about him for a while. I actually enjoyed the process of reviewing what I had done in the previous month and evaluating my progress. It gave me a sense of accomplishment as well as direction for how I needed to spend time differently in the coming month. I was looking up a descriptive verb that was eluding me and didn't hear him come in. All of the sudden, he was in front of me, half sitting on my desk. He wore a smirk on his face.

"So what's your problem today?" he asked mildly, swinging his leg and kicking my desk.

"I don't have one. You? Stop kicking my desk, please."

He looked at me for a moment as if deciding something. "How did you sleep?" he asked after a moment, seeming to make up his mind.

"Just fine. You?" I didn't meet his eye and instead went back to scanning the dictionary.

"Really well. Patricia wanted to reconcile our latest argument so I had some help getting to sleep, if you know what I mean." He winked at me, as I looked up, unable to conceal the hurt his comment had intentionally caused. There was a mean look in his eyes.

"You know what, Lennon, I don't think this is going to work anymore. Don't get me wrong – I will probably always have feelings for you, but it just seems that we've been doing more hurting of each other lately than anything else. I think it's time for us to both move on."

I watched the meanness change to genuine surprise as I spoke. Then his face became closed off, as it had almost always been when I first met him. I thought then that he just had a really difficult face to read, but as I watched it change, I realized that he could intentionally drop a curtain over it to conceal his emotions at any time. This realization caused me a moment's hesitation as I considered the fact that this meant he had allowed me inside of himself perhaps more than I had thought. He saw the uncertainty on my face and pounced.

"Fine. It's over. Don't talk to me anymore and don't ask me to give you any more rides to the *colonias*. You're on your own. Good luck." He got up and walked swiftly out.

A big part of me was hugely relieved that it was over. I let out the breath I hadn't been aware I was holding and leaned back in my chair. I thought about going home to see Mireya for a second, but decided that letting him see me walk by the office to leave would give him more satisfaction than I wanted. I shook my head to clear it and resumed working on my reports.

Mark came back right before lunch and stopped in our office to see if I wanted to walk home together. I was surprised that so much time had already passed and more surprised at his invitation. It was as if he knew something had happened that morning with Lennon to move him out of the picture. I smiled at him and grabbed my bag. We headed off together. I made a point of laughing loudly at something he said as we passed the main office in hopes that Lennon would see that he wasn't the only one capable of giving the appearance of returning unfazed to the arms of his spouse. Mark gave me a strange look but didn't comment.

Chapter 38

Writing those monthly reports and planning out the next month's activities was generally something that took most of the final week of the month. I actually didn't take that long to write mine, but then it had to be reviewed by Juan Carlos, who always gave it to the Social Promoters to look over for some reason, and then I had to revise it based on their "suggestions". I found after a few months that if I just took the whole week to write it and turned it in at the end of the week, there weren't any revisions to make.

Later that week, I was working alone in the office designated for Mark and me when Lennon came in again. I heard him approach this time, stopping to make coffee in the little supply room adjacent. Mark was over in the main building working on Alejandra's computer with her. After he made his coffee, he strolled into the office stirring his cup. Since he was so big on formality and greetings, I decided to ignore him until he formally greeted me. As I studied the page in front of me and made a show of writing something on it, he watched me and stirred his coffee without saying anything. After a minute or so, he left. I had the distinct feeling that he was toying with me. It made me angry.

The following Monday was another day in the office. Again Mark was out somewhere and I was preparing letters to go to all of my colonias informing them of the days I planned to visit. Since Lennon had told me I couldn't ride with him anymore, I had checked Eduardo's schedule against mine to see if I could ride with him to the other colonias. There were only going to be a few times that worked out, so I had resigned myself to experiencing the Soviet-made Cold War era trucks, called "IFA trucks", that passed as public transportation, taking people without private means to and from the colonias every day.

Lennon came in through the coffee room without stopping and walked right into my office. Without a word he came over to me, grabbed my arm and pulled me out of my chair. He pinned me up against the wall and started kissing me aggressively. I tried to push him away and tell him to stop but he was much stronger than me. I finally slapped him lightly across the face, more to get his attention than to hurt him. He stopped and looked at me with a very cold and mean look in his eyes.

"Lennon, what are you doing?" I sputtered.

"No woman tells me it's over. I tell you when it's over and I'm not done with you yet," he growled.

"Well, I'm sorry, but it is over, Lennon," I snapped back at him. "Maybe you should have thought of that when you were saying all those terrible things to me in San Carlito!"

He started kissing me again forcefully. There was no love or tenderness behind it. I tried to push him away again but this time he held me up against the wall tightly. I couldn't get my head away from him. I began to feel afraid of him.

He started pulling at my jeans, trying to unzip them. He was standing directly in front of me, pinning me to the wall with his body. His legs were slightly spread apart from the effort of keeping me pinned. I suddenly felt sure that he might try to rape me again. That realization was enough to summon a hidden reserve of strength. I brought my knee up hard into his crotch.

As he doubled over and yelled in pain, I shoved him aside as hard as I could, and started to go around my desk towards the front door of the office. I was caught in a nightmare – one where I couldn't make my legs move fast enough to get away from my attacker. The chair tipped over and I stumbled to the ground on top of it, cracking my side against its rungs. Terror brought me to my feet quickly and I shoved the chair aside. Lennon was starting to regain his feet and come towards me. In desperation, I slid across the desk and opened the door just as he grabbed my arm but it was too late. There was a group of people coming up the steps towards the office next to mine and they could see him. He turned quickly and walked out the back door.

I instantly felt ashamed for some reason, like I deserved his attack, so I tried to smile at the people and said good morning. Once they went next door, I collapsed onto the floor and sobbed. After only a moment, I began to be afraid that Lennon might return or that someone else would come in and make me explain why I was such a mess, so I grabbed my bag and left as casually as I could muster. It never occurred to me to tell Juan Carlos or anyone at the office what had happened. There was no question in my mind that they would not believe me, so I fled.

Mark wasn't home for lunch when I got there, so I poured out my heart to Mireya. She did her best to console me. Now that the danger had passed, I realized I was more furious that he had tried to rape me again than anything else. We were still talking about it when Mark came in. He gave me a curious look but didn't ask what was going on. He sat down at the table with Mireya and me.

He watched me push my food around on my plate and fume in

silence for a few minutes as he chewed. "You wanna tell me what happened?" he asked in English.

"It's not polite to speak the language our friends don't understand," I replied in Spanish, not looking at him. "But no, you probably don't want to hear it anyway."

"Try me." This time he spoke in Spanish.

"Fine. Lennon came into our office today and tried to rape me." My eyes flashed with anger as I looked up at him.

He paused in his chewing for a moment, then looked away and muttered something under his breath that I didn't hear. Mireya did though, and she sucked in her breath. "Marco!" she breathed.

"What did you say?" I demanded in English.

He looked me square in the eye and said, "I said, you flirt too much. Besides, you probably misinterpreted what he was doing. He doesn't strike me as the violent type." He calmly went back to his food.

My mouth went completely dry and my cheeks flushed a hot, deep scarlet red. As I slowly stood up and grabbed a cigarette from the pack on the ledge behind me, I growled at him, "Neither do you." I walked out with Mireya calling after me.

10/2/97

Dear Folks at home -

To speak frankly and to the point, today was pretty horrible and discouraging. To say it most directly, today <u>sucked</u>.

Juan Carlos, Lennon and Eduardo are quite possibly the biggest assholes that I've ever met. If I wander too much from this point, just refer back to this central theme; they are bad people. I don't have the computer right now (hence the handwritten letter), so I can't refer back to what I told you in previous letters, but I think I communicated that I got fed up trying to coordinate my schedule of meetings in the *campo* with the boys, and so, with Juan Carlos's initial support, I went looking for ways to go with other people or in the public transport. Then he changed his tune and said that I wasn't working as "part of the team of NECOG".

Throughout the month of September Lennon was gone or I was, and so when I went out to the *campo* it was exclusively with Eduardo or with a ride to a colony of Lennon's. I think this must have bent his (Lennon's) little nose out of shape or something because he's not being very nice now, to put it diplomatically. (It's a skill that I'm starting to pick up here, believe it or not.)

The last two days we've all (except Mark) been writing a two-month report on our activities in August/September since we didn't do one last month. My part was to write about the inventory of the tree nurseries and the visits, meetings and seminars with the Ecological Brigades. Juan Carlos said that I should collaborate with the boys on this. Fine. I tried yesterday to ask Lennon some things and he blew me off. I also asked them both if they would be going out to the *campo* this week. They both said no, not until next week. Fine. I figured I'd write what I had and then drag the information out of them today. This morning they both took off for the *campo*. Not only did I not have the chance to get info from them, but also they both knew that I needed to go where they went to finish gathering data. Did they ask if they could get it for me or pass a note for me or anything of the sort? **No.** Did they give me their info before leaving? Ha. Did they even tell me that they were going? Not a chance. I found out as I heard the motorcycles pulling out. Very nice, boys.

Fine. I finished my reports with what I had, and I made sure that Juan Carlos knew what had happened. The asshole had the nerve to shrug and say, "Well, they had work to do." Like I don't?! Seems like that's what he was trying to say to me. Oh, if I only had a motorcycle or truck...

The icing on the proverbial cake in retrospect was that yesterday Mark and I saw a memo that Juan Carlos is sending to Juigalpa asking for a motorcycle for his "personal work", that the truck isn't enough. Don't you love it? I know I sure laughed in merriment and glee.

You know if this was an isolated incident, I could let it go, but after seven months of this bullshit, it gets a little harder to keep shrugging it off. I had a breakdown this morning in the office that no one seemed to notice except Mark, and then again at lunch when I was telling Mireya what happened. She's so sweet and sensitive that she began to cry when I did. She said she really feels my frustration with these macho pigs and hates standing by and watching them treating me this way. She was very supportive and after a while, I felt better. It really is a sad situation. I hate living like this.

We also have come to a decision about the whole hassle of getting a toilet that I'm afraid is going to make you prefer another Hammock and Breakfast in the event that you make it down here. For various reasons, it's just not working out. Number one, no privacy; it would be in our kitchen, no way around it. Number two, expense; the landlord won't pay for the whole thing. Number three, hassle of getting the damned thing here and installed; it has to be brought from Managua, the floor (tile) would have to be all broken up and re-installed, and an extremely deep hole dug (that also falls under expense).

The truth of the matter is other outhouses aren't nearly as offensive as ours. So when I went to tell them that we aren't going to do it, he agreed to improve the latrine.

First, he's going to put a better, longer tube in to go out through the ceiling (as opposed to ending inside as it does now). Second, there's some substance (lime or something) that you can add every few months to keep the smell down; he's going to buy it and put it in. Third, he's going to replace the "throne" with its four corners of cement with one of wood with round corners and smoothed out (can you imagine splinters in your butt?? Not a pleasant thought.), and we may take your suggestion that I foolishly discarded as silly and get a toilet seat with a lid to put on top of that. In the end, it will be a much better and way easier solution that will make us happy and hopefully won't make you cancel your trip.

That's about it. Don't worry about me too much. If the situation gets too bad, we can always pull out at the last minute and come home after one year. But don't get your hopes up; I hate to do it because it means they win.

Love you lots,

Ellen

Chapter 39

I first met Pedro and Joaquin at the French doctors' house. They seemed to attract a wide array of interesting characters at their home, and always made everyone feel very welcome. They were nothing like the French people I knew in Paris; they were much more laid back, totally in love with each other, the country and their work, and had embraced life in the *campo* without losing their ability to see a con coming from a mile away.

We were having dinner at their house one night when Pedro showed up. He reminded me very much of my brother in feature and dress, except for being about a foot shorter. His playful quick wit was not something I had seen much of in these parts and it caught me off guard at first. By the end of the evening, I found myself really looking forward to the next time we'd meet. Mark seemed skeptical of him from the start, regardless of how much the Frenchies seemed to trust and like him. I think he was just jealous that Pedro was flirting with me.

Not long after, I met Joaquin, and quickly realized that the two of them were rarely separated. They began visiting me at NECOG, and dropping by the house on weekends. Pedro was getting married soon to the only midwife in town, Carlita. She was a good ten years older than him and had been married and had children before – not an uncommon situation in Santo Domingo. She ran the only Women's Clinic in town and treated lots of patients for women's health. She, too, is quite bright but much quieter than Pedro. They seem to be a good pair. We were invited to their wedding – an intimate affair held at their home. It was a lot of fun. I got some great pictures from the evening of Pedro and Joaquin acting like a comedy team, and of all of us together.

Carlita offered to have a look at my lingering problems with my big toe that began when I took that fall coming down the mountain from Santa Gorda. I was convinced that it was just an ingrown toenail gone awry, but agreed to let her examine me. She said that it had become infected and had me take some antibiotics. She also said that the nail needed to be lifted to prevent it from growing back into my toe, as well as to give the infection some room to breathe. This was done by slowly shoving a tiny piece of gauze under my toenail all the way down to the cuticle. It was pretty painful and left me unable to wear anything but open-toed loose sandals. It got easier with each time she changed the gauze strip, but there was no anesthesia involved.

As I sat in my office planning an upcoming project with the school kids in Santa Estelita for the following day, Lennon appeared in my doorway. He stayed in the doorway, stirring his coffee to make it a nice espresso as he watched me. He glanced towards the front door of my office, which I now always kept open since that day. I had also moved the desks so that when I sat in my chair, I could be seen from the street. I didn't want to be ambushed again.

"Lennon. Can I help you with something?" I tried to keep my voice casual. The truth was my heart still skipped a beat in fear when I saw him, as much as I hated myself for it.

"Are you now sleeping with those two bastards you're always hanging around with?" I don't know if he was trying to keep his voice nonchalant or not, but the jealousy came through clearly. I decided for my own safety not to bait him.

"Not that it's any business of yours, but no. I've decided that infidelity is not for me." I watched him closely, trying to read what he would do next.

"Oh, I bet you are. I bet you fuck them both at the same time – one in your ass and one in your mouth. I bet you –"

"Get the fuck out of my office now, you son of a bitch!" I screamed at him as I leaped to my feet. "If you ever come back in here or talk to me again, I'll kill you!" I hurled a book across the room at him as he ducked laughing out of the doorway.

Alejandra and Pastor Miguel came running from next door. "Elena, are you okay? What's the matter?" said Alejandra, worry written all over her face. Pastor Miguel just looked around sharply and caught a glimpse of Lennon as he tried to duck out the back of the coffee room and go next door. He looked back at me with his jaw set tightly.

"Elena, are you okay? Do you want me to work in here with you for a while?" His tone was grim. He tended to be very protective of me.

"No, I'm sorry, you guys. I'm fine," I answered, trying to keep my voice steady as I hid my shaking hands in my lap. "Just a stupid misunderstanding. I think I'm going to go home for an early lunch." I got up and grabbed my backpack.

As I headed out into the street that managed to be both muddy and dusty at the same time, I shook my head and thought, "What a day to be wearing white jeans." That, plus the emotion of the encounter with Lennon made me laugh out loud.

"Hey, crazy *gringita*, what are you laughing about?" I heard someone call out from down the street behind me. I turned and saw Pedro and Joaquin coming towards me. "Wait up!" they shouted and started racing each other towards me. I laughed as they blatantly try to keep each other from reaching me first. They were closer than brothers.

As they walked with me towards home, joking and warmly playing with me as usual, they noticed that I seemed troubled. Pedro finally touched my arm and said softly, "Hey, what's going on? You've barely cracked a smile at our foolishness today."

"Oh, I had an unpleasant run-in with Lennon in my office a few minutes ago. It was nothing."

They exchanged a look over my head. "It doesn't look like nothing! Tell us what happened. Do we need to beat him up and leave him for dead in a dark alley?"

"No, no, nothing that serious. I'm sure a good kick in the shins would take care of it." I smiled at them both. "Besides, he won't bother me with the two of you around." I linked an arm through each of theirs and we strutted off together towards my house.

10/26/97

Dear folks at home -

Greetings from the land of rain, rain and more rain! We are feeling a little bit wet here in the tropics this week. It's really good for us, and it means I will have a busy day on Tuesday out in San Carlito helping transplant little trees from nurseries to the ground, and the farmers will have better weather for planting corn, which is what everyone is in the midst of doing right now.

This week was... good and bad. I managed to avoid seeing Juan Carlos and the boys all the way until Thursday afternoon! I was in the *campo* Monday. As I said in the last letter, they were gone Tuesday. I was in the *campo* all day Wednesday and most of the day Thursday. Friday, I was subjected to their presence only part of the time, too, so all in all it was a pretty good week in that respect!

The first community I visited on Wednesday was Las Bestias and the men were all planting corn. Also, the leader, Julio, had forgotten I was coming that day (this is typical of him) and hadn't notified anyone else either! Needless to say, there was no meeting of the Brigade.

So I went to the school to see how the plants were doing that I transplanted with the students about a month ago. Unfortunately, they almost all died. This is not the kids' fault because a few did survive and are doing well, and since school is only in the morning and they were to be watered in the late afternoon (less sun then), a student who lives close by was coming over to do the watering and watered all of them pretty much equally.

I have my theory about what happened: Julio had planted his tree nursery directly in the ground instead of in the bags. When we went to get the plants out of the ground, they were very close together and I think the roots were tangled. Well, he thought I was just being a wimp about pulling them up, so he ripped several of them out of the ground. He did it with a handful of earth surrounding the roots so he thought he was protecting them, but wouldn't listen to me about needing to be a little more careful. Apparently Eduardo (a personal friend of his and the Social Promoter of this community) had tainted my credibility with him and told him that I had never done this before and was implying that there wasn't much need to listen to me, especially since I'm "just a woman". End result: 27 baby trees were killed. Is it a coincidence that four survived and I had managed to carefully pull up four or five from the ground?

In the end, I got Julio to admit somewhat begrudgingly that maybe the next time we should try it my way.

So I went onto the next colony - El Sol. I was about three hours early having not had either activity I was planning to have in Las Bestias, but Juana de la Paz (or Pacita, as I call her) welcomed me into her home anyway and laughed knowingly at the story of Julio's forgetfulness about the meeting. She already knew what had happened to the tree nursery there; after all, this is a small zone. She was equally disappointed that he wouldn't listen to me back when it happened, and shared my sorrow at having participated in the death of 27 saplings.

She's a Brigade person in El Sol and quickly becoming a good friend. Unfortunately she may be moving to her family's farm (about a 30 minute walk from the village) to manage it and have a small income. She has three children, ages eight down to two years, that she has to manage alone since her husband drowned a couple of years ago, before the youngest child was even born. She is 27 years old. If she moves, she will be outside of the boundaries where I work, but I am going to find a way to include her still.

She fed me hot enchiladas that she was making a ton of to sell in the market that day. Enchiladas Nica-style are made of dough of ground corn, with a little bit of onion, green pepper, salt and a touch of chili. The dough is patted by hand out into a flat circle, like a tortilla, then a handful of a pre-cooked rice mixture with a hint of ground beef, onion, green pepper and vinegar is put in the center and the tortilla folded over into a pocket. The pocket is deep-fried for about two minutes, and voila. It is not very healthy, but they can be made very cheaply (they are sold for one Córdoba apiece) and when you are starving, you don't worry about a little bit of grease. It's also extremely tasty if you eat them fresh and hot!

After sitting with her and chatting until I was expected at the school, we went in search of the other Brigade member (there are only two right now in this community - also common as we reorganize) who had not shown up at the appointed hour. We finally found him, went to the school and made our presence known, only to find out that he had never gone to inform the teacher that we were coming and they were taking an exam! Pacita and I were disgusted and chewed him out. He was very embarrassed at having forgotten his duties and bought us what they call ice cream, literally translated, but it's not. It's either milk diluted in half with water, fruit added and frozen, or juice with fruit and frozen. They are frozen in little sandwich bag size baggies, and sold two for one Córdoba. I am fond of the pineapple juice ones. It's very tasty and hits the spot on a sweltering day, as Wednesday was.

Anyway, after having a brief talk with the students and setting a date to return to go clean up the river and reforest the riverfront, we left. Roberto was still feeling bad, so we were treated to a pop this time. We had a meeting together to plan the next visit for a Sunday when we would have better luck getting folks together for a town meeting, and then I headed back.

Thursday, I went to San Carlito only to find that the leader there hadn't told anyone about the meeting either! Last time I couldn't make it and my note to excuse myself and cancel the meeting had arrived the day after the meeting was supposed to have been held. I had talked with him to plan the make-up visit, but he apparently thought I wouldn't come again because when I arrived at the pre-school teacher's house, we went looking for him and he was out on his farm working, and no one else was around, nor knew of the meeting for that day.

This is a common problem that I have with the Brigades - either people don't show up, don't remember that I'm coming, or never receive the note in the first place. I am going to have a talk with them at the seminar on Thursday and Friday (the final one of the year). Since I now have to spend from my own pocket to travel, we need to all do a better job of coordinating. I seem to be the "darling" of the communities where I work, so I'm really hoping that I have enough leverage to pull this off!

This morning we went to the Baptist church to hear our co-worker and friend Pastor Miguel preach. He doesn't have his own church anymore and was invited to preach at the one in town today. We went to support him. He was very good; he's not a crazy screaming evangelist like most that we have encountered on previous occasions.

Flea is fine. Everyone comments on how big he is, but I still think he's a shrimp compared to the cats that reside in the Patnaude household. He's very vocal, affectionate, and right now is sleeping in one of his favorite places - the third shelf of the bookcase. He no longer gets stuck up in trees as he did when he first came to us, and has Mireya completely won over. Mark is still reluctant, but Flea doesn't give up hope of someday sitting on his lap again (it happened once for about two minutes a couple of months ago).

Speaking of Mark, he's fine. He's been very busy getting together this month's edition of the *Messenger*, and it will go to press at the end of the week. He did a supplement edition, mostly for the locals, I think, about the issue of autonomy of the schools. Classes continue for him, but only three nights a week now (he's combined his two English teachers/students together into one class). He could be a little more supportive of my daily struggles against the macho freaks of NECOG...

I am working on creating quite the trip itinerary for you when you visit in December! I'll send it next time when we have a few more details.

Lots of love, hugs and kisses,

Ellen

Chapter 40

Santa Estelita! Who knew how excited I could get about a far-off rural community in Nicaragua. Even though it required a 5-kilometer walk over a stretch of crushed rock and hard red clay that the locals called a road…it still would be an adventure. Farm horses used to heavy labor had trouble slogging through the mud during the rainy season and most people journeyed on foot as I did. The *campesinos* made the trip in well under an hour – I would be proud of myself if I made it in two.

It crossed my mind that trekking alone as an American woman in an undeveloped country might not be the brightest idea but I was determined to show everybody how independent I was. *Hell, back in the States, I'd walk the streets of Detroit any night of the week, and I never would have even given it a second thought!*

Besides, I was the one who ignored my family and friends' warnings against coming here anyway.

And wasn't it me who stood up to the bossy NPCA Church bitch who tried to keep me off the mission staff?

And just because I'm the only woman, the men here leer at me and treat me like an object. I'm gonna prove I can stand up to the macho attitudes that surround me!

When I reached Santa Estelita, I felt great. A deep sense of accomplishment and optimism settled over me as I walked into the village center. Dominica was watching for me out her classroom door, and when she saw me, she smiled broadly and waved me over. I was going to be playing some games with the kids in the school in hopes of raising their environmental awareness. If it worked here, I was going to use it with other *colonias* to get more people involved in the work.

I was feeling nervous as I walked up to the open classroom door and 40 pairs of eyes turned my way to look me over with somber expressions. I saw a couple of smiles, which I readily returned, but mostly my glances around the room were met with the solemn expressions I had come to expect from most people. People in general, but especially kids, just didn't seem to know what to make of the tall, denim and t-shirt-clad *gringa* who entered their presence.

Dominica quickly rescued me by announcing to the class that we'd all be going outside to learn about our environment from the "Director of Reforestation with NECOG". The official-ness of the title seemed over the top, but the need to credential was something else to which I was becoming accustomed. I tried to keep my head up and look nonchalant as the kids began filing past me out the door.

Dominica and I exchanged warm greetings before following the kids outside. In addition to being a teacher, she was the Director/Principal of the school, so she immediately took charge of getting all of the other classrooms to come outside and I quickly realized that we were going to do a school-wide event! I was glad that I had more sets of materials than I would really have needed for just one class with me. The kids responded to her with obvious respect as she shouted instructions at them.

With Dominica's help, I gave the kids instructions for how to play a couple of different games designed to increase their awareness about the environment in their community and ways to protect it. One game in particular was very popular. Each group of 3-4 students was given the name of an animal and instructed to make the sounds and movements of that animal. One-third of the students were assigned to be trees, and one-sixth were assigned to be water. The tree students were interspersed among the animal students, and the water students wove through the middle in a long, snaking line. Then the animal students had to try to get to the water. The message was clear – some animals would have to die to maintain balance in the ecosystem. But more would die if we continued harming the few resources that they had naturally available to them by polluting their water with chemicals and trash, and burning down more and more of their trees.

Soon they were laughing and running around, having a great time. They were not used to playing games as part of their educational process but they responded to it very well. Consequently, they were very excited to take the next step and talk about how to change their behavior in their community in regards to disposing of trash, in particular. When it was time to dismiss them for the day, many lingered around, asking me if we could play again.

Dominica took me home to her modest three-room house. Actually, there were four rooms, but two were closed off by curtains from the rest of the main room. She had two small children of her own and no husband at home – a fairly common household arrangement. Her parents lived next door. She prepared a simple and wonderful supper for us all – *gayo pinto*, fresh tomatoes and cucumbers (which she was careful to tell me had been washed well and peeled to protect me from getting a parasite), and tortillas. After supper, she helped her kids with their homework as I wrote notes from the day and wrote in my journal. I would be going to Santo Tomas the next day – a colonia even further into the mountains – before returning to Santo Domingo that night.

So, we all fell into bed by nine o'clock—I was exhausted. Still I glowed with anticipation in a way that I hadn't experienced in a long time. I imagined striding into the office when I finally got back, clean from head to toe, even after two days out in the very muddy *campo*. I knew the guys would be expecting to razz me about my filthy clothes and how I was whining about something terrible that had gone wrong. I pictured the looks of shock that would cross their faces as I breezed in, fresh as a daisy and coolly asked the secretary if there had been any messages while I was away. Smiling at the thought, I finally drifted off into a deep sleep.

"Arghh! SHIT!!!!"

A sharp pain stabbed my gut. I hurtled out of the narrow bed, doubled over and sprinted for the rickety outhouse behind Dominica's home. I vomited over and over. Just when I thought it had stopped, I felt a stream of hot liquid going down my leg, so I spun around and plopped myself down on the hard and scratchy stone toilet. My head drooped and I leaned against the rough wood wall, fully spent. This continued all morning.

I could hear people muttering outside of the latrine, but couldn't tell if they were concerned about me or if I was annoying them. It was a shared latrine after all...for two households.

On one of my trips back to the house, I stumbled over my own feet, catching my balance just before I fell. Dominica was standing in the back doorway, arms crossed, watching me.

"Elena," she called softly, alarm on her face. "Is everything all right?"

"Yes, Dominica," I said lamely. "Everything's just fine." I chuckled under my breath as the sheer falsehood of my statement struck me.

Dominica watched me closely, her dark eyes narrowing. She smiled tentatively, unsure of the joke. "You've been sick to your stomach?"

I nodded, came to a stop by the doorway and leaned against the rough planks of the outside wall. They felt cool on my burning face. I closed my eyes. I was going over everything I had to eat and drink the day before, trying to pinpoint what could have made me sick.

"You haven't been sick?" I opened my eyes quickly, hoping someone else was sick so I could understand what was wrong.

Dominica shook her head. "I was careful to wash the tomatoes and cucumbers we had last night. I even peeled them." She paused, a guilty look on her face, her eyes averting. "I hope you don't have a parasite," she practically whispered.

"No, no," I said, waving my hand, dismissing her worry. "I'm sure it's just... well, I don't know what it is, but I'm sure it will pass. Probably something I ate and too much sun yesterday. I don't know," I moved towards the doorway and Dominica quickly stepped aside. I headed for the bed.

She brought me bottled water and soda crackers, and I willed myself to get up and get dressed. I felt determined to make it to the next community where I was expected later that day. That meant I had to get back to San Eduardo so that I could catch a bus there in time for my meeting with the *brigada*.

Dominica was worried about me trying to make it back to San Eduardo on foot and she tried to convince me to stay longer at her house, at least until I felt better. I lied and said that I was really feeling much better. For some reason, I was determined to cling to the fantasy of a triumphant return to the office.

She watched quietly as I gathered my things together and used all my strength to put on a show of improved health. She told me that there were two women who would be walking back to San Eduardo with a couple of small children and that I should walk with them, if I insisted on going. I grudgingly agreed, confident that I could certainly keep up with a couple of older women and small children.

We set off a short time later, the women eyeing me with suspicion and the children just staring with big round eyes. I smiled at them, and they scampered on ahead laughing. I shook myself, trying to clear my head and convince those watching that I was up to this walk. It was mid-morning.

We hadn't been walking for more than 15 minutes when I had to stop and squat. I went off the road a little ways into the bushes. The women walked a short distance ahead and then stopped to wait for me, shouting to the children to stay with them. I laughed and shook my head at how stupid I had been to think that keeping up with the group would somehow be easy.

After the third stop, the women were clearly annoyed. I had managed to shuffle along in sight of them for a while, but finally decided to just wave them on ahead. I knew it was going to take me a long time to get back to San Eduardo, but I still felt confident that I would make it eventually.

My "companions" had been out of sight for only a short time when my eyes suddenly felt like they were on fire, and I got very lightheaded. Then I puked again. I stumbled and fell to my knees, teetering on all fours. I panicked. I realized that I was all alone on a very long road, and quite sick.

On this stretch between Santa Estelita and San Eduardo, I became aware that I could see only a desolate landscape. Even the squat, lean-to type shacks that people made as homes were absent. In this rugged area, there were patches of scrub trees and bushes littering some open fields, and endless sky – and most importantly, there was nobody in sight.

A breeze rustling the trees and bushes at the sides of the road took on a menacing quality as I imagined bandits hiding there. They would not believe their luck at catching a sickly American woman alone unable to defend herself against rape and kidnapping. I felt my temperature rise and the gentle breeze turned into a cold wind.

The road had been reduced to a slippery, viscous topography that grabbed hold of anything that sunk into it with such force as to suck the boots off of people's feet. Animals that managed to navigate the conditions often lost their footing, sinking deep up to their knees, leaving behind holes in the mud that would fill with rainwater. This would mix with the mud, feces and bugs, creating a cloudy soup. At one point I became so dehydrated that I actually cupped a handful of that cloudy soup, and drank it.

A few minutes later, I regretted doing so as it came rushing back up.

Soon my heavy jeans and boots were completely covered in mud from stumbling, falling and limping along. My chills turned back to burning heat and I felt a desperate need to shed clothing. I peeled off the light cotton long-sleeved shirt I wore to protect me from the sun's rays, down to just the tank top that I wore underneath. As I opened my small knapsack to stuff the shirt in, I saw the light cotton pants that I had worn for sleeping, and inspiration struck.

I sat down on the side of the road and clumsily stripped off my boots and jeans, slipping into my sleeping pants instead. I was so relieved to be out of them that I stuffed the jeans haphazardly into the sack, left the boots sitting in the muck and continued my walk barefoot. At least I was enjoying the warm mud between my toes but I completely forgot about all the dangers being barefoot posed – stepping on any number of sharp objects like rocks, branches, and glass, etc., for one. Another very real danger was coming across a snake. There were five kinds of snakes in the area, all poisonous. In fact, I had heard of five people who had died during the past six months from untreated snakebites. But I didn't care anymore.

I stumbled on. I had no concept of how much time passed. I occasionally gagged or had to stop to squat, but mostly I kept moving. My progress was extremely slow. I started to babble and began to cry when I realized that the sun was not going to stop beating down on me. In a burst of profanity, I shook my fist up at the sun, screaming at it to let up. Then I covered my face with my hands, smearing mud, dirt and grime all over it. This was the last straw. I staggered over to the side of the road and landed hard on my rear end. I was openly sobbing. At some point I fell backwards into the weeds and passed out.

I awakened to the sound of young voices talking softly. I lifted my head slightly and forced one eye open into a squint to see a huge gray-white horse standing about five feet from me with a very startled looking pair of boys of about 10 or 11 years old on its bare back. As soon as I saw them, I opened the other eye and tried to ask them to please help me. I was reaching my hand out towards them when one of them kicked the horse hard and took off at a gallop.

I was now sure that I was going to die on this damned road. The wheels in my fevered brain didn't seem to want to turn and I plunged into despair, unable to think of any alternative to just lying there. I had no strength left. I closed my eyes and slipped once more into oblivion.

The same horse returned at a gallop but with a man in his 30's on its back this time. He got down and walked quickly over to me. I tried to shield the sun from my eyes to see him. He took my arm and gently tried to prop me up. He was talking softly to me, but I couldn't understand a word. I also had no strength left, so he basically picked me up and hoisted me onto the back of the horse somehow.

He pointed to his feet and seemed to be asking me where my shoes were. I just shook my head that I didn't know, so he took my backpack and put it on his own back, climbed up behind me and we started slowly riding towards San Eduardo. Something about the whole thing revived me slightly and I began to feel embarrassed – for how dirty I was, for losing my shoes, for deciding to try the walk in the first place. It took us only about 10 minutes to get into San Eduardo. I felt even more embarrassed at how close I had been to getting there.

I managed to tell him I needed to get back to Santo Domingo, now abandoning all hopes of making it out to the other community. He took me to the bus stop where coincidentally the same two women and kids from Santa Estelita were waiting. Their jaws opened in shock when they saw me, and all conversation ceased as we approached. I was an awful sight to behold. The man climbed down, lifted me down and sat me on the side of the road. He bought me a bottle of water and some more soda crackers from the *venta* right next to the bus stop. He asked me if I would be all right to get back home. I nodded dumbly, too consumed in my own shame and embarrassment to even speak. He touched my hand, then climbed onto his horse and rode off. I never got his name, and I never saw him again.

Chapter 41

The bus ride back to Santo Domingo was short in comparison to everything else I had been through that day. By the time we arrived in the busy market square, I was feeling somewhat better physically, but sunken further into my humiliation. Long gone were the visions I had so foolishly had the night before of walking, chin held high in pride, into the NECOG office to show what a capable, independent, invincible woman I was to my machista enemies. I shook my head at the image as I looked out the window.

I could not bring myself to walk back to our house in my current state. I was barefoot, though I did have a pair of flip-flops in my backpack, and covered from head to toe quite literally in mud. My pride could not bear the humiliation. The stares I had endured on the bus ride had been too much already.

I looked for a taxi to flag down as soon as I stepped off the bus. It was just my luck that there were none in sight! My infected toe was hurting so badly by this point that I could hardly walk anymore. I limped in my flip-flops through the market square, feeling every pair of eyes on me, until I got out to the main street and could flag a taxi.

Once home, I realized that I was a full day earlier than Mireya or anyone else was expecting me to be home from Santo Tomas. There was no electricity or water, nor did I have any energy to do anything, so I simply stripped off all my clothes, climbed into my hammock and slept.

I was awakened by the sound of Mark's heavy footsteps on the stairs. He knocked lightly on the door to my little room, which was closed. It was now dark outside.

"Yeah, come on in, Mark," I said, trying to sit up. I was very, very stiff and had a pounding headache.

"Hey, when did you get back?" he asked softly, opening the door and looking in at me with concern. "I thought you weren't coming back for another day or so."

I laughed a little. "Geez, I'm glad I wasn't relying on you to know if I went missing or something!" I looked at him, still smiling. He looked puzzled. I decided I didn't want to pursue his lack of understanding or attention to my schedule, so I went on. "Well, I got a little bug or something in Santa Estelita and wasn't feeling well enough to go to the other *colonias*, so I just decided to come home." I laid back again in the hammock, my headache getting the better of me.

Mark just looked at me for a moment. "Well, do you need anything? You look pretty dirty. Is there anything I can do?" This last offer was made in a half-hearted offhand sort of way, and I just laughed again. I couldn't believe how far apart we'd drifted.

"No, thanks, I appreciate it, but really I just want to sleep some more. Thanks anyway." I rolled onto my side and pulled the hammock up around me again, blocking him from my view. After a moment, I heard him softly shut the door and go back down the stairs.

I couldn't explain the hot tears rolling down my face, so I chose to ignore them and go back to sleep.

Something smelled wonderful when I awoke next. The sun was bright and Flea was curled up in the crook of my legs. I felt much better, but very grimy and dirty. I stretched, disturbing Flea from his slumber, and luxuriated in the cocoon of my hammock.

I could hear Mireya pouring large quantities of water into the storage tub. I smiled; she must be preparing a warm bath for me. It was enough to make me want to sit up. Before I did, I heard voices talking softly. I couldn't make out what they were saying, but then Mireya laughed, and I knew Pedro and Joaquin must be there, too.

I got up slowly, testing whether my headache had gone or not. It was still there, but not nearly as much as before. My stomach growled loudly and my bladder felt like it might explode.

I grabbed clean shorts and a t-shirt, and grabbed my towel as I headed down the stairs. Pedro popped his head around the corner of the kitchen doorway from his chair in time to see me coming down.

"Hey, beautiful! We were wondering if we were going to have to come and wake you up!" He smiled all the way up into his eyes, looking genuinely happy to see me. As I came into the kitchen and he could see me better, his smile froze. Mireya gasped.

"Oh, my God, are you alright, *gringita*?" Pedro had jumped up out of his chair. Mireya's hands went up to her face and she came rushing over to me.

"Marco told me you were back early and that you weren't feeling well and looked a mess, but I didn't realize that it was this bad! Are you hurt, my child?" She was poking me and squeezing me like a fruit in the market, testing to see if I yelped in pain.

I smiled at them both instead. "I'm fine, you two old women! Stop worrying. I'm fine. I had a bit of trouble on the road from Santa Estelita.

I decided to come home instead of going further into the campo, that's all." I headed for the latrine. As I glanced over my shoulder, I could see Mireya had her hands on her hips now, looking at me like a mother looks at a naughty child who's just been caught in a lie.

When I came back from the latrine, she was back to filling the tub with hot water. The two of them were speaking in hushed tones. They both stopped as soon as I came up the back steps. I stopped at the top of the steps.

"What?" I said, returning their stares. "What's wrong?"

Pedro spoke first. "Elenita, something bad obviously happened to you out there. What was it? You really look terrible, like you were in a fight or something! I think Doña Mireya here is worried that someone tried to kidnap you. Tell us what happened!" Mireya was still glaring at me.

I laughed, and then winced a little as my stomach cramped up. I was clearly still sick, in spite of having slept for most of the previous 24 hours. Mireya rushed over to my side, taking my arm and led me back to sit down, clucking at me the whole time.

"I knew something terrible happened! What was it? You need to sit down! Did someone hurt you? Were you sick? Your color is very, very bad. And how did you get so dirty?"

I had to laugh again at her interrogation, the warmth of her love washing over me. "Mireya, mamita, I'm fine. I ate something bad I think, and it made me sick. I was probably not very smart to leave Santa Estelita, but I think I had quite a high fever and wasn't thinking clearly."

I proceeded to tell them the story of what had happened, leaving nothing out. By the time I finished, Mireya was wiping tears from her cheeks at how close I had come to dying. Telling them about the experience was sobering for me as well, but also made me feel even more ashamed that pride had dictated my actions.

Instead of letting me dwell on it, Mireya waved her arms at Pedro, kicking him out amid half-hearted protests, so that I could take my bath. He promised that he would return later in the day, waving as he left.

The bath was wonderfully, deliciously hot and soothing. I took my time, continuously pouring the warm water over my head and down my body until all of the heat was gone from it. Mireya had prepared a huge batch of *gayo pinto*, sweet plantains, *cuajada* and eggs, and I dove right in, famished.

Chapter 42

11/18/97

Dear Folks at home -

Last week's outings into the campo went fine. Tuesday I gave a talk and had a long meeting with the Brigade of Calero. Wednesday I went to Victoria and finally met with the community leader that has been eluding me all this time. We had a very productive lunch meeting, talked with a few folks around town, talked with the young people's Ecological Brigade that we formed in the school a few months back, and set up a town meeting to elect a new Brigade of adults because, in reality, none exists right now. We talked about many problems that the Brigades have and reasons why they don't function at times. I feel like I learned a lot and made a good ally in the community.

Thursday I went to Los Arces and stayed overnight since there wasn't another bus back out until morning. One of my Brigade leaders put me up at his home. They were very nice. I got home from Los Arces at 9:30 Friday morning, took a shower, packed my stuff, and took off with Mark, Pedro and Joaquin for the mountains.

We took a bus to Punto de Encuentros, which is a fairly close colony (only about 30 minutes by bus) and then hoofed it in on a road leading up into the mountains. We walked it in about two hours, with a half hour rest. We arrived at the home of a long-time family friend of Joaquin, an old guy in his 70's who makes that walk in 30 minutes flat. He was on his way out to catch a bus to town for the weekend and was sad to not spend time with us, but we promised that we would come back another time to spend some time with him.

Anyway, he has a wooden one-room shack that is attached to another two-room shack where a family of five lives. This isn't as bad as it might sound - you have to understand that most people spend the majority of their time outside, so the rooms are really just for sleeping and holding a few belongings. Even the kitchen area is outside, so very little is actually done inside of the house.

There were three sturdy trees in a triangle, so we strung

the four hammocks across them and made a little camp with a small fir in the middle. Mark and Joaquin were double-decker in their hammocks. We all slept great the first night, apart from Pedro's snoring and being cold (the wind is strong across that little mountain top where we were and it was darned chilly). (We could also hear howler monkeys in the distance, which didn't bother the Nicas or the unflappable country American boy, but which made this city girl's ears perk up a bit...)

The second day we went to the river to swim and walked for a long time through the river (it was a wide stream but very shallow and we walked for about 30 minutes. We probably only went about a mile, but it was very rocky and VERY slippery.). We finally came upon an absolutely magnificent waterfall that looked like something out of a fairy tale or picture book. We played, washed and horsed around for a couple hours there, and then headed back.

Joaquin didn't feel like going all the way back through the river, though, so about halfway back we started up the bank on one side and cut our way through the wilderness with the machete (being very careful to look for snakes: there weren't any!) and up a fairly steep hill.

We finally made it out and back, all needing to bathe again and nap. The only down side was the downpour that hit us in the middle of the night on the second night. I've never seen people move so fast or untie knots so fast! We got the hammocks and everything into Don Juan's shack (the old guy) and then just strung them up in there and slept through. It was a lot of fun!

The rest of the time we just lazed around, eating oranges, four different types of bananas, raw sugar cane, drinking coffee and water from the nearby mountain stream, and joking around. It was so great and so relaxing that we all agreed we would do it again before Christmas.

On the way back, we hauled ass (excuse the expression, but it really does fit), making the hike out in one hour flat with no rest. Since my toe was absolutely killing me, it was quite a feat for me! We made it in time to catch the truck back to town at 9 a.m. It was full, so we climbed up on top and I had the most comfortable ride I've had yet on one of those hulking things!

I think I'll try to ride on top all the time! We got back to town about 9:30 a.m., had breakfast with Carlita at her and Pedro's house, and then went home and crashed for a few hours.

I felt great Monday morning, aside from the fact that I had to go to NECOG to work. I went to see Carlita for a treatment on my infected toenail. She has been "curing" me. She puts a thin strip of gauze under my nail all the way down to the cuticle. She slowly shoves it in there with the tip of some surgical scissors. Can you all say "ouch" together? No anesthetic, no nothing. I'm getting pretty good at this pain endurance thing.

I went back today and Pedro cleaned it for me, saying that it already is doing much better than yesterday. I think they are going to take it out tomorrow. If not, I'll be wearing my sandals out to San Carlito for my meeting Thursday because I can't even look at my combat boots without feeling pain! I cancelled all other trips out to the campo this week (Monday, today and tomorrow) but I really need to go on Thursday. However, if it's too bad, I just won't.

Now it's late and I'm tired so I'm going to bed. I'll keep you posted on the nail situation as with everything else. Flea sends his greetings, and Mark is grumpier than ever...

Lots of love, hugs and kisses to all the diligent readers of my boring weekly prattling...

Ellen

Chapter 43

12/11/97

Dear folks at home -

Sorry for the long silence from the tropics - things have been crazy, sad, happy, painful and just generally really busy for the last couple of weeks.

The situation with Mark has not improved. The only change is that I keep realizing more and more things that make me feel like the action of getting married was not the right decision. I was the one in a hurry to get married, and I think maybe we decided to do it because of Nicaragua. That was a hard realization to come to and it still is painful to think about, but the more I think about it, the more truth it holds.

We were at a retreat for all of the mission workers for the National Protestant Church of America (NPCA) in Central America from the 6th-11th (we got back this morning on the plane). While we were there, I talked to a friend who works in Managua and who is a psychologist. She said that she hears me saying that I feel empty, like I have given to the relationship without getting much back. She also agreed with me that it sounds like we have always been very good friends, which is true, but that sometimes it doesn't work out to marry your best friend if you need more than friendship from your spouse, such as passion and romance.

I haven't made any decisions yet but the more I think about it, the more convinced I become that I deserve to be happy and if Mark can't do that, then maybe I am better off without him as my spouse.

This causes me despair, anguish and a deep feeling of guilt for entering into such a holy and serious contract as marriage. I am beginning to feel like maybe I needed to be about 25 years old before I would have been ready to begin considering marriage! Why, oh why, did I not listen to the many friends who tried to warn me? Why was I in such a hurry?

On to other things before we all get too depressed! During this retreat I showed my toe to a couple of the NPCA home-based folks. They took one look at it and sent me straight to the hospital to have it looked at by an actual doctor there in Managua, where things are supposed to be better. HHHAAAAA!!!!! Since it was red and swollen again, I went. Pedro had come into town to visit his mom who is sick and to take some heavy purchases we had made back for us on the bus since we knew we would be flying. I met up with him and found out that his mom had gone back to their hometown not far from Santo Domingo the day before, so I invited him to go with me to the hospital so that I wouldn't have to go alone. He did, and I was glad.

After examining me, they found that the infection was back and had spread under my toenail to the other side. You can guess what's coming, at least partially - they removed my entire toenail from a little bit beyond the bottom cuticle on up. HOWEVER, down here in the wonderful country of Nicaragua, folks must be of a hardier stock than this little white girl. They stuck a needle in my toe with a pretense of giving me anesthetic, but less than one minute (literally) later, as I'm laying on the gurney trying to calm myself and waiting for the numbness to kick in, the doctor grabbed my foot with one hand and my toenail with his torture instrument in the other, and yanked.

Now, I've lost some weight, but I'm proud to say that it took three nurses to keep me from decking that f*cking doctor. I sat bolt upright and screamed. It was quite possibly the most painful thing that has ever happened to me, and I almost passed out from the pain. Instead, I cried from sheer agony, fear and desire to be almost anywhere but there.

As soon as I moved, any anesthetic that had been there wore off, and I was certainly glad that Pedro was there because I could hardly walk. Afterwards he wouldn't let me go back out to the retreat center by myself as I couldn't walk alone and was still in tears from the pain. He got us a taxi and we zoomed off. He was invited to stay after we got there, and ended up just spending the night and went back to Managua at 4:45 a.m. with us.

So now I have to cancel all of my meetings in the communities until the New Year, and I am essentially off for Christmas vacation! That is nice since there is a lot to do to get ready for Christmas and, more importantly, for your arrival. I have six meetings that I am going to miss and the majority were lunches or get-togethers to celebrate the end of the year. I sent Joaquin to Carabas to cancel that meeting and pay for the luncheon since they killed the chicken for it at dawn this morning and it was all set to go before I ever got back from Managua. The rest I will cancel by way of radio announcements and notes to each community tomorrow.

The retreat was wonderful. I really needed to be with other missionaries to hear their stories of struggle to realize that I am not alone. I often feel alienated, even from Mark, and rely much more heavily on Mireya, Pedro and Joaquin to take me through the hardest times.

Anyway, Mark pretty much ignored me throughout the retreat, and I returned the favor, so it was nice to be with others who were reaching out. The three themes were Disparity, Koinonia (fellowship, basically), and Hope. We had excellent discussions every day in both small and large groups (there were about 35 of us in total with the missionaries plus US-based folks). Mark, being the passionate one, just thought it was "all right". Well, to each his own.

More soon. I love you all.

Ellen

Pedro accompanied me to a couple of the *colonias* in the days that followed. He was masterful at relating to the campesinos with whom I worked. They instantly liked him and laughed at his jokes. His presence seemed to deepen my own relationship with them as well. We had a great time together. I hadn't laughed so hard in a very long time... so I didn't see it coming.

After one particularly intense trip to the *campo*, I suddenly realized that I was in danger of going down the same road with Pedro that I had been on with Lennon. To make matters worse, I was seeing Carlita on a regular basis to treat my infected toe. Facing her once I realized Pedro's intentions was making me feel worse than the slime I often scraped off of my boots after a muddy day in the *campo*. I finally sat down and wrote Pedro a letter, to tell him how I was feeling and to make it clear that our friendship could not progress any further.

I started out in what I had learned to be very typical Nicaraguan *campesino* fashion – with the positive. I printed on small notebook paper, and the first side of the page got filled up with all that positive stuff – how much our friendship meant to me, how wonderful I found him to be, how grateful I was to him for his attention and gestures, as they had helped me to be transformed into someone who was finally starting to see myself as valuable and attractive.

Then I flipped the page, and started writing about all the reasons why it could go no further. I acknowledged both of our marriages as well as the fact that we both seemed to feel that each of our own marriages was flawed, but held them up as bonds and commitments that we needed to honor for as long as we each were in them. I ended by expressing my sincere wishes that we remain friends, but was clear that we should spend a lot less time together.

I found Pedro the next day in the market and gave him that letter. I told him that I needed him to read it and try to understand. He looked worried, but took it and nodded his head that he understood. We parted without speaking further. I felt as if a small weight had been lifted.

Chapter 44

The following morning, I was up early cleaning house. It was a Saturday so Mireya wasn't going to be coming, but I somehow felt so relieved and energized by having done what I was sure was the right thing in writing that letter that I awoke early, in high spirits and ready to start the day. I had made a pot of coffee, had my first cigarette, and was listening to the local radio station, getting ready to mop the floors, when I heard quick, heavy footsteps approaching the front door gate. I turned and looked up, ready to smile at one of the neighbor kids running past, and found myself looking at Carlita. She held up her hand, which she was shaking at me, and which held the letter I had given Pedro the day before. My heart was instantly in my throat and my knees threatened to give out as I walked quickly to turn off the radio and let her in.

"What the hell is this about, Elena?" she demanded, her voice shaking with anger and hurt. "What the hell is this?" she repeated, her voice a little more shrill. She paused, then continued seeing my stunned silence. "Where's Marco? He needs to come down here and see this. Marco!" she took a couple of steps towards the stairs, yelling his name.

"Don't go up there, Carlita," I said, finally finding my voice. "Marco is still sleeping. What's going on? Where did you get that?"

She looked at me as if she couldn't believe I was actually asking. She took a step back towards me, shaking the letter at me once again, making no attempt to keep her voice quiet. I cringed as she yelled at me, "What the hell is going on between you and my husband? Who do you think you are? We just got married, for God's sake! You were at our wedding! How could you do this?!" Her voice became more and more shrill with each question. I shrank back, horrified that this was happening, and terrified of who might be listening.

Mark appeared at the top of the stairs, rubbing his eyes, and came down quickly. "What's going on?" he asked, trying not to yawn. Carlita repeated her accusations and handed him the letter to read, asking if he had any idea what I had been doing with her husband.

I started backpedaling as quickly as I could. "Carlita, it's not what you think, I swear. This letter was my attempt to put a stop to things before they went any farther. I didn't want you or Marco to get hurt. Did you read both sides of the letter?" My heart was thumping loudly in my chest as I tried to appear calm and reasonable. She simply stared at me, rage and disgust all over her face. Mark was trying to make sense of the letter in his sleepy state while watching Carlita like he was waiting to see if she was going to physically attack me. I wondered briefly if he would do anything to stop her.

Carlita turned and snatched the letter back out of Mark's hand, turned back and called me a very nasty name, then slammed out of our front gate door, leaving the two of us in stunned silence. "Look, it's not what you think," I stammered when I finally found my voice. Mark turned and went back upstairs without a word.

Later that day, Joaquin came by and asked me to go for a walk with him. Mark was sitting in the living room strumming his guitar and just stared coldly at both of us as I left with him. He took me to a mutual friend's house where Pedro was waiting. I launched myself at him as soon as I saw him, fists beating down, yelling.

"How you could you be so stupid!?! What have you done?! How could you let her find that letter!" He was holding up his arms to protect his face from my attack and laughing while Joaquin tried to grab me and restrain me from behind. Our host looked on like a deer caught in headlights at the scene unfolding in his one-room hut.

"Calm down, Elena," said Pedro. "It's not that bad! I forgot it in my pants pocket last night and she found it this morning when she took them to wash. I didn't know she was going to wash today. She usually leaves it for the *empleada*." He was smiling at me, trying to get me to calm down. It wasn't working.

"Look," he went on. "We need to tell Carlita and Marco that the four of us are going to have dinner together and sort this out like mature adults." I started to interrupt him, incredulous that he could even suggest such a stupid idea, but he held up his hands. "All we need to do is sit down and explain that I developed feelings for you, but that it has gone no further and will not go any further. We just need to reassure them both that our marriages, while obviously suffering a bit, are both still intact and that we plan to keep them that way."

He paused to gauge my reaction as I stared at him. It had never in a million years occurred to me to handle the situation this way, but with both he and Joaquin nodding their heads that it was a good idea, I found myself starting to wonder if I'd hit my head somewhere. I lit a cigarette and looked for a seat in our friend's extremely messy and cluttered hut. There wasn't one to be had, so I leaned up against a table and looked at all three of them. They were watching me expectantly.

"What exactly do you plan to gain from this supper out?" I asked. "I can't even imagine that either of them would agree to it in the first place!"

He repeated his basic idea for what we would say, and somehow convinced me that it was worth a try. I left to walk home alone, steering a very wide berth around the Women's Clinic, pondering if it could actually work. When I got home, I found Mark working on something on the computer.

"Hey, look, I need to talk to you a second," I said, waiting for him to look at me. He didn't, but I rushed on anyway. "Look, that was an ugly incident this morning with Carlita, and I'm very, very sorry that you woke up to that. Actually, I'm very sorry that it happened at all, but especially that it was what started your day." I waited to see if he would react, but he just stared at me coldly, so I rushed on again.

"Listen, I think it would be a good idea for the four of us to sit down together and simply talk about this as civilized adults. I wrote the stupid letter to prevent the relationship from going any further – not to promise to leave you or asking him to leave Carlita, but rather to stymie his efforts before it went any further down a dangerous path." I paused again and lit a cigarette. Mark continued to stare at me coldly, making no reaction. "So look, would you be willing to come to dinner with me and meet up with the two of them and talk about this?"

I stood waiting, one hand on my hip, the other holding my cigarette, watching him closely. After a moment, he muttered, "I'll think about it," and turned back to his computer. It was all he was going to give me then, so I said, "Great," and walked into the kitchen.

The dinner was set for a couple of days later. We met up at El Ranchon, a nice restaurant at the far edge of town. I felt giddy and nervous and terrified all at the same time. Pedro seemed to feel the same way and we both kept giggling, even though we knew it was completely inappropriate. Neither of us seemed to be able to help it. Carlita and Mark both tried not to look humiliated.

Pedro took the lead, trying to explain that we had developed a friendship that was in danger of turning into something more, but that I had had the good sense to stop it before it did. He tried to make it sound like they should actually be grateful to me instead of angry, especially Carlita. The more he talked, the more the terror in my gut subsided and the giddy nervousness took over, causing me to chain smoke and laugh at inappropriate moments even more. I was mortified at my own behavior but felt like I had no control over it. I felt dizzy, like I was having an out-of-body experience. My face felt like it was on fire throughout the evening.

At one point, everyone seemed to be waiting for me to say something, so I said the first thing that came to my mind. I leaned over and pinched Pedro' cheek, and said, "What can I say? I just love this little man!" I laughed, sounding hysterical to even my own ears, then added, "But we've done the right thing here. We've put an end to it before something happens that we all regret."

When we left the restaurant, my giddiness had not subsided, but I felt cautiously optimistic that we had headed off a disaster on several fronts. Mark didn't have much to say, other than that he felt totally humiliated by the experience. I chalked it up to what had been going on between us as much as anything that had happened at dinner, and didn't think anything of it after that.

Chapter 45

After that night, Pedro left my life almost as quickly as he had entered it. Neither of us felt it would be a good idea to continue being seen together in public or private. Strangely, I didn't feel much anxiety or sadness over our parting. Instead, I mostly felt relief.

The emotion that hit me hardest was loneliness. I had become accustomed to the near constant companionship of at least Pedro, if not Joaquin as well, and they both stopped coming around very suddenly after that dinner. While I realized that it was for the best, it didn't help make the adjustment any easier.

Mark was out one evening a week or so later teaching a night class and I was at home puttering in the kitchen, feeling sorry for myself, when there was a voice at the door.

"Hello?" came the soft, deep and playful tones. "Anybody in there?"

I immediately recognized Joaquin's voice and became suspicious. My heart skipped a beat in mild fear, wondering if Pedro was with him. Being home alone – it just all would look so bad. I came around the corner frowning and found myself face to face with just Joaquin. "Oh, hi," I said, my brow still furrowed.

He laughed softly. "Can I come in or shall I state my business first?" He furrowed his brow, mocking me playfully. The door wasn't locked but he was respecting the boundary.

"No, no, of course, come in!" I stammered, embarrassed by my momentary fear and suspicion. I moved towards the door as he unlatched it and let himself in. "How have you been?"

"Fine, fine. You? How are you holding up these days?" his voice seemed to hold genuine interest and concern.

"Oh, I'm fine," I smiled. "I miss you guys, though. I miss just hanging out with you both, actually." I blushed slightly as I said it. I think it was the first time I'd ever really been alone with Joaquin. These days I was extremely conscious of every nuance of that one-on-one dynamic and it made me extra sensitive.

"Well, that's why I'm here, *gringita*," he smiled back at me, lighting a cigarette he had taken from the pack on my bookshelf. "I feel like going dancing and I figured you could use some company, so go upstairs, put on something pretty, and do me the honor of coming with me." His smile was confident and warm. I could not detect any sarcasm or mischief, though I watched him closely for a moment.

"Alright," I said finally, my spirits lifting immediately. "I'll be right back!"

I ran up the steps to my bedroom, thinking already of what to wear. I didn't want to dress too casually because I would feel unattractive and un-feminine around the other women there. At the same time, I didn't want to select something that could possibly convey the message to Joaquin or anyone else that I was moving on to another "conquest". By this point, I could no longer accurately judge how much people suspected about my love life. I just knew that rumors abounded about both Lennon and Pedro and me. I also had known for many months that Mark and I lived our lives in a fish bowl with the rest of the world continuously looking in. As I considered all of this, I began to doubt the wisdom of going out in public at all. I stood still for a long moment.

"Hey, *gringita*, did you fall asleep up there? Come on – let's get going!" Joaquin's voice floated up the stairs to me, jarring me from my trance.

I went to the edge of the stairs and peered over at him. "Are you sure this is a good idea? I don't know what people are saying about me these days," I said in hushed tones.

His smile and playful manner vanished as he considered me for a moment. "Elena, you are a beautiful woman who also happens to be very intelligent and unafraid to speak her mind. Regardless of what so-called sins you may have committed, there will always be people who will feel sufficiently intimidated by your mere existence and boldness who will talk. Do not concern yourself with them. They are small and petty. Now go get ready and let's go!" Except for his last directive, there was a sincerity and gentleness to his voice that I hadn't seen before from him. I was moved and reassured by his words, so I cracked a big grin and demanded he pass me a cigarette and stop rushing me.

He laughed, lit one for me, and passed it up to me, a twinkle in his eye.

I settled on a mauve pair of flowing linen pants I had always loved, paired with a tan linen top and sandals. I put on a little bit of face powder and mascara, ran a brush through my hair, and bounced down the stairs five minutes later. I watched closely for his reaction while trying to appear unaware that he was looking me over.

"Do I pass inspection?" I asked lightly as I moved around the kitchen and living room gathering my things.

He laughed. "Definitely, *gringita*, definitely," was all he said.

Throughout the evening of loud music and dancing at a disco where I had not been before, I felt slightly uncomfortable. Part of me was busy worrying the whole time about seeing people that knew me and who would wonder what I was doing out with Joaquin. Another part was worried about how I was supposed to be acting with Joaquin – was this a date? Why did he keep watching me with that slightly amused look on his face? I was starting to feel a little like I was being hunted.

Joaquin danced with me plenty, but he also danced with other women and seemed to have no objection to me dancing with other men, which I did. I had always loved to dance but had never enjoyed it as much as I did in Nicaragua. The beat of the salsa and meringue and coastal Caribbean music was infectious and made it impossible for me to sit or stand still. I didn't feel particularly adept, but felt I was holding my own. I came to realize that Joaquin did not agree.

We were dancing to a coastal number together when he began to laugh heartily. "Come on, gringita, I know you can do better than that!" he shouted over the deafening music. He put his hands on my hips and began to move them for me. "From your waist! Move your hips! Hold your shoulders still!" he commanded as I tried to follow his lead. He laughed again. "Just relax and let the music penetrate your soul!"

I was honestly trying as hard as I could to follow him, and that, he explained when we took a break to grab a drink a few minutes later, was exactly the problem.

"You have to just relax your body, feel the music and let your body respond to it," he said, that twinkle back in his eye. "You are trying too hard and that comes out as rigidity in your movements."

I was blushing deeply, not sure how to respond to this man. After spending the evening with him, I was suddenly aware of his looks for what seemed like the first time. He was taller than me, closer to Mark's nearly six-foot frame. He had a mop of somewhat unruly, longer dark curls and a broad face that was lit up completely by a very white toothy grin. Dancing with him had been an intimate, almost sexual, experience and I was now acutely aware of how our bodies fit together. All of this left me feeling at a loss for words to respond to him.

I took another swig of my beer and nodded at him, as if I had just been carefully considering his suggestions as opposed to considering *him*. I hoped the heat from the disco would make my burning cheeks seem less noticeable.

He seemed to take on teaching me how to dance "properly" as his mission and I found myself dancing with him non-stop for the rest of the evening. Even the slow dances he felt I needed to be "re-educated" about how to dance properly. I was no longer worrying about what other people might be thinking. Instead I was worrying about what might be happening between us. His face betrayed nothing but I was certain that I was being lured in.

We walked back slowly towards my house late into the wee hours of the morning. At my door, he took my hand in a most gentlemanly format and kissed it.

"Thank you for accompanying me this evening, Señora," he said softly, watching me from dark, veiled eyes.

"The pleasure was mine," I responded, mimicking his exaggerated formality. We bowed slightly to one another, laughing softly. I waited for him to walk away, enchanted by the moment.

"Aren't you going to open your door?" he asked.

My smile froze on my face and I was instantly suspicious of what he wanted in return for this evening out. "Uh, yeah, I am," I stammered, the enchantment vanished. "But Marco is asleep upstairs, so I'm not sure you should come in..." I finished lamely.

He stared at me for a brief moment before his face crumpled into stifled laughter. "Oh, *gringita*, I'm not trying to bed you!" he said, gasping for breath. "Don't get me wrong – you are beautiful and I like you very much, but not all men in Santo Domingo are the same! I just wanted to make sure you got into the house safely before I departed." His laughter died off as he finished speaking, a warm smile in its place.

I flushed deeply once again and turned to fumble with my key in the lock. "Of course," I said briskly, my back to him. "I was just saying that in case you wanted to come in to talk or something. I didn't think you had any other intentions." I made my voice sound as incredulous as I could to cover my embarrassment. I finally got the doors opened and turned back to him.

He was watching me with an almost tender look on his face. "Good night, then, *gringita*," he said softly, and turned and walked into the darkness. I watched him go until I could no longer hear his footsteps on the gravel road.

Chapter 46

When Joaquin kissed me for the first time a week later, I did not hesitate. Joaquin didn't talk about Pedro and I didn't ask about him. It just went without saying between us that he was a topic and a person to be avoided. Those two just seemed to always be aware of exactly where the other one was, and we never ran into Pedro. Not once.

By that point, I was feeling pretty good about myself on some levels. My relationship with Mark had settled into pretty peaceful co-existence; he didn't bother me and I didn't bother him. I still felt anger and sadness when I looked at him. I was so tired of feeling guilty around him, so I avoided him as much as possible. Between having separate bedrooms, separate work lives, separate friends, and separate schedules, it wasn't hard to do.

I would watch Joaquin from a distance, walking past slowly, as he played basketball on the court in the central park in town. It was conveniently located along my walking route to and from the office, so I began timing my comings and goings to when I thought he might be there. Shirt off, sweating and dark skin gleaming in the afternoon sun – well, he was a beautiful sight to behold.

I spent more and more time at Mireya's house. She still came to our house everyday during the week to be our *empleada*, but many evenings and most weekends I was at her house. We often went out dancing with Joaquin. He always made a point of showing her tremendous respect and flattery. She laughed a lot when he was around, but also smacked him playfully if he did something overtly affectionate towards me in public. She was very motherly and conscious of keeping our private lives private.

Mireya was the one person who consistently showed me in her quiet ways that she loved me without judgment or conditions. She clucked over me like a mother hen; watched out for me; took care of me when I was sad or happy or sick. She made me believe that she thought I was beautiful and smart and good; that I could gain wisdom from my experiences; and that I didn't need to walk around with my shoulders hunched and my gaze to the ground. She made me believe that I deserved to be happy, and was the one person around me that allowed me to rest from my internal battles with guilt, shame and depression.

She almost made me believe that I was a good person, and that that meant bad things wouldn't happen to me anymore.

Almost.

Chapter 47

I was engrossed in thoughts of Joaquin and our plans for Christmas Eve, humming as I mopped the floor in the kitchen. We would be going to mass with Mireya and the kids, then I was going to attempt to oven-roast a chicken without a real oven and serve everyone dinner. I smiled faintly as I wondered how it would turn out. It was two days away.

The phone rang, breaking my concentration and causing me to frown. Since it rang so infrequently, I was unaccustomed to its sound. Mark was playing his bass guitar in the front room sitting right next to the phone. I looked up to see if he would answer it but couldn't see him from where I was mopping.

"You gonna get that?" I half-yelled, not bothering to hide the irritation in my voice. In a lower voice, I muttered, "Some of us are busy actually doing something productive."

Mark made that sound he made under his breath when he wanted to make sure I knew he was exasperated with me. "Sheesh", was how it always came out sounding to my ears. He got up to answer the phone. His every move grated on me these days.

"*¿Bueno?*" After a pause, he said, "Oh, hi! Wow, how are you?" Another pause, then, "Yeah, she's here, too....No, we only have one phone, but I can put it on speaker phone if you want to talk to us at the same time. Hold on." He put his hand over the receiver and looked into the kitchen where I had stopped mopping and was watching him. "It's the head guy from NPCA", he said, a note of mild surprise in his voice. "And he wants to talk to both of us."

I put down my mop and walked into the front room. Mark put the phone on speaker mode and replaced the receiver. "You there?" he asked.

"Yup, I'm here. How are you, Ellen?" came the grainy voice through the crackling connection.

"I'm fine; you?" I replied. I was instantly nervous – something was wrong.

"I'm fine. There are actually a couple of other people on the line with me – Jane Sims, Esther Smith, and Ana Ruiz from the Managua office. We have something serious we need to discuss with you both."

My nervousness instantly turned to cold fear. I frowned and looked over at Mark. He looked equally startled."We've received a fax from a woman called Carlita in Santo Domingo that we need to discuss with you... um... How is your marriage doing?" he asked.

I was desperately searching my guilty mind and soul for a clue as to what this could be. Mark just looked perplexed. After a moment of silence, I managed, "It's...fine, I guess. Why do you ask?" Fear was pounding through my ears. I broke out in a sweat.

"Well, this note we got faxed to us is a letter that you wrote, Ellen, to a man named Pedro? He's apparently married to someone else, yet this letter from you has some pretty serious.... amorous, shall we say, feelings expressed in it. We're concerned about your marriage and wondering what's going on", he said with obvious discomfort.

"What?! How the hell did you get that letter?" I demanded before I could stop myself. Mark's hand came up and gripped my arm hard. I looked at him. His brow was furrowed and he was shaking his head at me. His jaw was set. I felt like my legs were going to give out.

"Well, as I said, we received it via fax. It appears to have some rather damaging language in it. We are concerned first and foremost about the health and state of your marriage, and are calling to talk about whether it is still a good idea to extend your contract for a second year."

Mark had buried his face in his hands but at the mention of our contract being in jeopardy, his head shot up quickly and he frowned at the phone. "That's a bit drastic, don't you think?"

"Yeah," I chimed in. "That letter was one big misunderstanding. There is nothing going on, first of all, and second of all, that letter is dated more than a month back. The situation has already been addressed and we've all moved on." Mark was cracking his knuckles and twisting his hands in a nervous gesture. I gently laid mine over his to stop the noise before continuing, "Besides, we've become quite involved at the local Catholic Church, and have decided to pursue counseling with the priest we've come to know." I was staring hard at Mark as I stretched the truth beyond thin on the counseling bit.

He nodded his head at the phone and said, "Yeah, what she says is true. What you are looking at is a snapshot of time. Everyone has moved on here from that moment, including us." He looked so serious that I wondered for a moment if he realized I had just committed us to counseling.

The head guy was the first to respond to us. "All of that sounds good and makes sense, but we need to take some time and do an evaluation of the situation among ourselves. We'll let you know tomorrow what our decision is."

"Hold on a second! Who exactly is going to be evaluating this situation? Who among you is even in Nicaragua, let alone in Santo Domingo or has been for months? On what basis are you going to better evaluate this situation than what we tell you?" Panic was rising in both my face and my voice as I tried to keep from yelling into the phone. Mark once again put his hand on my arm but this time I shook it off without looking at him.

"No, honestly, she's right," he added, jumping in before I could do more harm than good. "Don't make the mistake of suspending our work when we are just beginning to make real progress based on some note." While he sounded calmer than I did, his voice at least carried more force than it had before. I could barely contain my hysteria.

"Well, sometimes a more objective analysis is necessary than what those on the inside can give us," came the sickeningly sweet voice of Esther. With that, I jumped to my feet and began pacing around the room. If the one person who had had it in for me from the beginning was going to be actively swaying others to her line of thinking, I knew we had no chance. My fear and panic turned to boiling rage and hatred in a flash. I lit a cigarette and continued pacing.

"We appreciate your concerns, Mark and Ellen," came the head guy's voice once again. "We'll certainly take everything you've said into consideration. If you can excuse us now, we'll let you get back to your day. Everyone else, please stay on the line so that we can begin our conversation. Thanks again, Mark and Ellen. Blessings to you both. We'll be in touch tomorrow."

A chorus of goodbyes followed and then Mark clicked off the line. He turned to look at me with a mixture of rage and pain on his face. I instantly was consumed by my guilt and reached out towards him. "Mark..." I began, tears welling up in my eyes. "I'm so sorry!"

He got up and stormed out the front door without bothering to close it behind him.

Eventually Joaquin had come by and knew right away something was very, very wrong. He coaxed me into telling him about the call and Mark's reaction. The letter he already knew about. His reaction was much stronger than I anticipated. He was outraged at the Church, at Juan Carlos, who he was certain had facilitated the whole thing, and at our own powerlessness. He wanted to go out somewhere together, but I really couldn't face anyone. I didn't even want to walk all the way across town to see Mireya. I knew she would want to know what was going on, but I worried about upsetting her without knowing for sure what was going to happen.

Finally Joaquin decided to head out without me. He couldn't sit still. I made him promise not to tell Mireya anything, or anyone else for that matter. While he was still visibly angry, he solemnly agreed. He gripped me in a tight hug and kissed me in a way that communicated his worry, fear and anger better than if he had used words. I watched him go before heading upstairs.

After the call was over and Mark had left, I had sat for a long time, smoking and thinking. I toyed with the idea of calling my parents to tell them what was going on, but was embarrassed by the whole situation and feeling very much at fault for all of it. I spent a lot of time cursing Pedro instead. I spent even more cursing myself.

I was already tucked into my hammock reading with Flea curled up on my legs when Mark came home that night. I listened to him throw his shoes off and start up the stairs, realizing that he was drunk. I glanced up at the door to my little room, checking to make sure it was bolted. I sat up a little, disturbing Flea from his half-slumber.

Mark fumbled around in the main bedroom on the other side of my wall, found his way to bed and collapsed without speaking to me. Soon his breathing was even and I relaxed. I patted Flea on the head and he settled back down.

As I lay in the hammock listening to Mark's breathing and Flea's purring and the sounds of Santo Domingo at night, I felt consumed by sadness and regret for decisions ill-made in the midst of passion, stupidity and naivety. The tears burned my cheeks and choked my throat. I closed my eyes and begged whoever might be listening for forgiveness and mercy. Somehow I was doubtful, even in that moment, that anyone had heard.

Chapter 48

We were like caged animals the following day. What should have been a relatively happy time of preparations for Christmas Eve the following day, and my parents' upcoming visit the day after Christmas, was spent in tension. Neither of us could leave the house for fear that we would miss the call and one final opportunity to persuade the powers that be to give us another chance. Every time one of us would go to the outhouse, we would silently search the other's face upon return for some sign that the call had come already and breathe relief at the shaking of a head.

I went through an entire pack of cigarettes before lunch and couldn't bring myself to eat at all. While I was terrified of what the decision might be, I couldn't quite bring myself to believe that they would actually bring us home based on such shaky information. The whole thing was very surreal.

The phone finally rang around 2 p.m. We both raced for it, then stood watching it ring, not able to bring ourselves to pick it up.

Mark finally lifted the receiver slowly. "¿Bueno?" he said cautiously. Then, "Yes, she's here, too. Let me put you on speaker." Then, "Okay, we're both here."

Greetings were exchanged all around. It was the same group as the day before. My knees were suddenly so weak I had to sit down. I silently grabbed a chair from the kitchen as Mark sank into a hammock chair.

"This has been a very difficult decision for all of us to come to," the head guy started out. I put my hand over my mouth to contain the scream I felt creeping up. I just knew what they were going to say. "We carefully weighed what the letter said, what your responses and explanations were, what our collective experience in mission work has been, and finally, the wishes of your sponsoring Partnership Office. With all factors combined, we are forced to say that we will not be extending your contract for a second year. It is time for you both to return home."

I gasped and squeezed my eyes shut as if to bury my head in the sand and pretend it wasn't real. Mark heaved a deep sigh and said quietly, "You're making a really big mistake."

The head guy went on to say that we needed to book flights home by the end of January, only one month away; that marriage counseling would be required for us upon our return in order to receive our final three meager paychecks; and that they had decided it wasn't necessary to cancel my parents' planned trip in the coming days. I was too numb to respond to anything. I got up and went to the kitchen for a cigarette, leaving Mark to finish the call.

My brain felt like it was working in slow motion. I stared out the back door for a moment waiting for some emotion to grip me. Nothing did. I felt compelled to be near people who loved me, so I headed out the door and ran most of the way to Mireya's house.

Chapter 49

Christmas was a subdued affair. It was strange to be in such a hot, humid and lush green climate celebrating the holiday that I had always celebrated with hopes of snow. We had all agreed to go forward with our plans of celebration and try not to dwell on the recent bad news. Even Mark was making an effort to keep things light.

The main celebration of Christmas comes on Christmas Eve day and evening in Nicaragua. I had had a dress made for myself for the occasion – it was brown with small blue flowers all over it. The cut was more fitted than I was used to, but Mireya assured me that it was far better than all of the other dresses I had brought with me, all of which were long and flowing and loose-fitting to hide a multitude of sins. This dress was form fitting. The compliments I received from everyone, especially Joaquin, made me blush.

I attempted a roasted chicken dinner, borrowing the oven from our neighbor-landlords, and in spite of taking about three more hours than it would have in an oven in the States, it came out very well. It was much richer than what Joaquin and Mireya were used to, and even my stomach was rejecting it after only a few bites. But it was a taste of home.

We all went out dancing at the *discoteca* that night and drank a lot. Joaquin and I made no attempts to be discreet – we danced together all night. I was too consumed with sadness as the reality of our departure began to sink in to care what anyone else was thinking. I figured that anyone who was watching had already made an assumption about me, and nothing I did from that point was going to change anything, including our fate. As we danced slow dances together, Joaquin held me very close to him. My throat ached and burned and my eyes stung with suppressed tears. Periodically he would whisper to me that he loved me, making it harder to keep my composure. I couldn't even look at Mireya.

The next day was Christmas and was uneventful. Mark and I did not exchange gifts. He sat in his hammock chair most of the day playing his guitar while I packed a few things to take to Managua. I would be leaving the following morning to pick up my parents from the airport. I had already made it clear that Mark shouldn't come with me.

The next morning I was waiting with Mireya and Joaquin by the crude dirt strip that served as Santo Domingo's airport and runway. I watched people periodically moving slowly across it as a cut through from Zona Tres to the main part of town. Many of them carried baskets on their heads filled with goods to sell in the market place. After nearly a year, I was now used to moving at such an unhurried pace myself.

I thought about the arrival of my parents and again checked my watch then the horizon. There was no sign of the little 12-seat airplane that was supposed to have arrived an hour before. I mumbled to Mireya that I was going to be late getting to Managua and started over to the little one-room stone building that served as the airport. The young guy working as the ticket agent, air traffic controller and runway clearer was on the radio as I approached the doorway.

"*Si, Señor*, I understand," he said into the hand-held microphone. After a scratchy response from the other end that I couldn't make out, he said, "No, I'll let them know. I only have a few today anyway." I was starting to get a bad feeling. He turned to me and said, "Elena, I'm sorry, but the plane isn't going to come today. You'll have to wait until tomorrow."

"Tomorrow? But my parents are arriving in Managua from the United States today! Why isn't the plane coming?" I knew it was futile to even discuss it, but I couldn't help myself.

"They just aren't going to make it," he replied, startled that I would even ask for an explanation. "They'll be here tomorrow morning," he repeated. "Do you want to go then?"

"I'll have to let you know. I need to get to Managua today." I turned and walked back towards Mireya and Joaquin to tell them the news. I was trying not to panic. "The plane's not coming today." They didn't even ask why; just nodded their resignation. It was a level of acceptance for the maddening that I had not yet mastered even after nearly a year. The additional stress of my parents' arrival made it even harder to accept. My panic level continued to rise.

"What am I going to do?!" I exploded. They both looked startled. "My parents are arriving in Managua in a few hours and they're counting on me being there to meet them!" I nervously lit a cigarette. "Is there another bus leaving for Managua yet today?"

"No, honey, not until late tonight – the Express," answered Joaquin, looking relieved to be able to offer some useful information to me. "And you really shouldn't ride that alone."

With nothing left to do, I stomped off my frustration in the dirt and we headed back to my house to pass the rest of the day making phone calls to Managua to arrange for Ana to meet my parents, and Vicky and Dan Johnson to house them overnight until I could get there the following morning. My frustration and stress level, anticipating their disappointment, was a bitter taste in my mouth. I attempted to rid myself of it by chain smoking.

The following morning I repeated the routine of getting to the airstrip with a pit of dread in my stomach. There was a terrible feeling of deja vu as the same handful of people gathered to patiently wait and see if the plane would grace us with its presence. I stood scowling with Mireya and Joaquin until we saw the young man from the office run out to the airstrip to clear it of horses, cattle and people so that the little plane could land. Only once I was on board waving goodbye to them out the little window did I finally relax. I closed my eyes for the take-off as always, not wanting to see the mountainside rushing towards us as the little engine strained to gather enough momentum to clear it. Within minutes we were airborne and within an hour we were in Managua.

Instead of me meeting my parents' flight at the airport, they were there to meet mine! I was fretting far more than they were about the whole situation, but it didn't help me feel calmer. I felt guilty for any disappointment with my mother.

We had decided to drive Ana's Suburban truck out to Santo Domingo and back. Neither of my parents was crazy about flying in little planes, especially having heard me describe the journey in detail on several occasions. So the following morning we packed up and headed out together. The ride went smoothly until I hit a pothole while driving too fast over one of the more deserted sections of the road to Santo Domingo. As my dad got out to examine the damage, I began to realize just how dangerous it could be for us if the wrong people discovered us, or if no one came by at all. I was trying to decide which one would be worse when a jeep full of German college students came by and helped us get the tire changed. I'm not sure if the alternative scenarios had been playing through my parents' minds, but I decided not to find out. We went on and reached Santo Domingo just after nightfall.

My mother was having trouble adjusting to the humidity and sweating profusely as we sat around visiting that night. I marveled at how acclimatized to many things I had become as I reached for a sweatshirt. It was unusually cool that evening – only around 75 degrees. We were at the kitchen table having dinner – my parents, me, Mark, Mireya and Joaquin. The back door was open to let any breeze that might be moving come through for my poor mother. There was a sudden movement from the doorway and something smacked Mark in the face and stuck there.

"What the fuck is it?!" he yelled, jumping up and overturning his chair. "Get it off me!" He was swatting furiously at his face. Joaquin stood to help him but by then, whatever it was had flown off and out the door again. My dad was laughing hysterically while the rest of us were too stunned to react.

"That was a really rare beetle that is all but extinct now," said Joaquin softly as everyone sat down again. Mark was still wiping his face. "I wish you hadn't slapped at it that way; I would have loved to look at it. You don't see them much anymore."

Mark shot him a dark look and said sarcastically, "Well, perhaps if I had your poise and grace I could have just sat there as it attacked me."

"Hey, no need to get nasty, guys," I said in English. "It's over now. Are you okay, Mark?"

My dad was still laughing. The whole thing seemed to have hit a funny bone in him. Pretty soon, watching the tears stream from his eyes, we were all laughing, too. Even Mark managed a small smile. That just made my dad laugh harder. Soon the tension that had built up since their arrival drained away and we finished our meal at ease.

During the few days that we were in Santo Domingo, we spent a lot of time with Joaquin, Mireya and her three kids. My parents said over and over again how they had a strong sense of deja-vu walking around the town, meeting many of the people I had described in my lengthy letters home and seeing many of the sights I had both described and occasionally sent photos of. I basked in the warmth of their approval of the place I had come to love as my home.

The subject of our impending departure was a topic we all silently agreed to avoid. Instead we splashed and played in Rio d'Oro, went to the market, played with Mireya's kids, dined out at restaurants, and even went to the discoteca on New Year's Eve. My mother wondered out loud if she could handle the long road trip back to Managua with the humidity and potholed roads. We agreed to fly instead, asking Joaquin and his friend Jorge to drive Ana's Suburban back and meet us at the airport so that we could then all travel out together to the Pacific Coast for a few days at the beach.

The journey went smoothly until we reached Managua and reunited.

Chapter 50

We were finally all piled into the Suburban, ready to head to the beach. Jorge was driving with Joaquin, Mireya and my dad crowded up front next to him. My mom, Mark, Estelita, the two smaller children and me were packed into the back seat. We reached the edges of Managua and were turning onto the road leading towards the coast when they flagged us down. The officer was standing in the middle of the road and there was no way Jorge could go around him without running him down.

We pulled over to the side of the road and the car was abuzz with chatter about what was going on, including questions in English from my parents for whom this was a totally new experience. Joaquin turned and gently asked everyone to please be quiet in English. As the officer approached, strutting casually, Jorge rolled down the window.

The officer asked him to come out of the vehicle, which he did, with Joaquin following closely behind. The three of them huddled by the front wheel and I found myself wondering what they were conspiring about. I had lost the ability to completely trust anyone, especially a man, following my ordeal with Lennon. I watched through narrowed eyes as Joaquin shook his head in apparent disgust and walked back towards the driver's door. He opened the door and leaned over the seat, obviously uncomfortable.

"Elena, they are telling us that our infraction is that Jorge turned without using his turn signal and then didn't wait long enough before merging into the center lane of traffic," he said in Spanish.

"What?! This is bullshit!" I replied. "He wants to gouge us because he saw my dad in the front seat!" My anger was hot and immediate. My mom was elbowing me, quietly asking what was going on.

"I know, *amor*, you're right. But the bottom line is that he's saying for C$150, we can pay the fine right now and go on our way. He's taken Jorge's license and isn't going to give it back until we pay or settle this in court."

A string of curses escaped my mouth as my mom's elbow hit me with more urgency. I explained the situation in English. Mark was stony silent. My parents agreed that we should just pay the fine and get going. C$150 was about U$15 at that time, which to them was nothing. To me, after a year of living on poverty wages, it was steep. My dad pulled a wad of money out of his pocket, peeled off the correct amount, and handed it to Joaquin.

Anger was burning in my stomach as I watched Joaquin walk back to the officer and smooth things over. After a minute, we were on our way again. I couldn't contain my anger and let forth with another string of curses and insults for the corrupt police force of Nicaragua. My mom's hand went gently onto my arm.

"Please don't let this ruin the beginning of the second half of our vacation together," she said in the tone she always used to try and appease me. "It's paid, it's over, we're on our way to the beach, and look at the beautiful scenery here! Ron, what are those trees over there?" With that she turned and pointed out the window.

As my family and friends tried to communicate through broken English and Spanish fragments, laughing the whole time, I quietly tried to shake my anger loose. I soon joined in the conversation and as Managua faded behind us, slowly began to relax.

We spent three days between two beautiful beaches and touring various sights in Masaya. My parents got one room at the hotel for themselves and me and Mark, and one for Mireya and her kids. Joaquin and Jorge stayed with a friend in town. I ended up sleeping with Mireya and her kids.

We had all just eaten a fabulous and rich seafood dinner at a restaurant on the beach one night, and were taking a walk in a long string along the water. It was dark but the sky was filled with moonlight and stars. It was hard to imagine a more peaceful or beautiful place. I fell into step with my mom as everyone spread out, walking and playing at their own pace.

"Ellen, I just want you to be careful," she said, after I had asked what she thought of Joaquin. "He seems like a very good guy, but I know you are vulnerable right now with all that's happening with Mark. I just want you to think clearly and be sure you aren't setting yourself up to get hurt even more than you already have been."

I began a sincere and rigorous defense of Joaquin's character, which died on my lips with a steady look from my mom. It was as if she knew about my moment of doubt back on the road with the police officer. My face flushed in the darkness and I looked away. "Thanks, mom, I will," was all I said. She didn't bring up our obvious relationship again.

As the week came to an end, Joaquin told me that he had a

girlfriend that lived in La Santa, a town we'd pass along the way back. He claimed that they had been together for a few years but hadn't seen each other in a long time. He wanted us to drop him and Jorge off there so that he could end the relationship with her and have some closure.

Anger, confusion and hurt consumed me as I stared at him. It was my worst nightmare coming true – there was someone else! I was doomed to always be the other woman; changing hands as I passed from man to man. I felt dirty and began to walk away. He put his hand gently but firmly onto my arm.

"Elena, wait." He waited for me to stop and look at him. "I could have lied. I could have said that I was just going to visit a friend or so that Jorge could see a girl, but I chose to tell you the truth. Isn't that worth anything to you?"

I felt like I was in the middle of a bad soap opera unable to escape. I tried to smile and shrug it off. "You can do whatever you want, Joaquin. After all, I'm the one who's still married, right? Who am I to judge?"

"Amor, don't be like that. You know I love you and want to be with you. That's why I need to do this. Don't be mad." He had a desperate look on his face. I wondered if it was real or manufactured for this occasion. I forced myself to keep smiling and nodded my head.

"I know," I said, patting his arm reassuringly. "I'm not mad." With one more smile that I hoped was convincing, I turned and walked away, numbness replacing anger as I struggled to figure out what was real and who was just playing me anymore.

The parting with my parents at the airport was very emotional. Mireya and her three kids were all in tears, which made my dad cry, too. My mom just kept cooing and patting everyone. I, too, was tearful, but for a different reason. I just couldn't shake a bad feeling that something terrible was going to happen to them on their trip home. I whispered my concern to Mark, who just looked at me coldly and said I was having a bad case of separation anxiety. I laughed out loud at his complete lack of empathy. But after all, what did I expect?

As we traveled back to Santo Domingo on the 16-hour hot and dusty bus ride, I had plenty of time to think about all that was happening. My parents called to say that they made it home just fine. Mark had been right – separation anxiety was at work in me, but not in the way he thought. I was filled with anxiety and stress at the thought of disengaging myself from my life in Santo Domingo and leaving it all.

I found myself often wondering what I was going home to. Sometimes I would startle myself and people on the street by being so deep in thought about it that I would suddenly ask out loud, "And for what?" in a fierce tone in Spanish. I'm sure there were more than a few who thought that *la gringita fea* was going crazy.

The reality of the phone call and its implications for my life in Nicaragua began to take hold. I was enraged with Pedro, the National Church, Esther, the head guy, Juan Carlos and anyone else tangentially related to the situation for allowing it to happen in the first place, including anger at myself for ever writing the stupid letter. I was also overwhelmed with sadness and guilt that I was going to have to leave this life and really had no one to blame other than myself.

I focused on the rage and began planning what I was going to do when I got back to town. How was I going to break the news to all of my brigades? They would be furious with Juan Carlos for facilitating the damaging communication. They would see it as a culmination of all the other hell he had put me through to try and frustrate me into going home. Having been my guardians during the worst of it, their fierce protectiveness of me would not allow them to see it any other way.

There was so much to do – making plane reservations, packing up our house, trying to wrap up a year's worth of planned work in less than a month, saying goodbye to everyone... I was quickly overwhelmed by it all and fell into a restless sleep as the bus bumped slowly along.

Chapter 51

I sent the first batch of letters to the *colonias* the day after our return to Santo Domingo. I took out my calendar, saw where I had already planned to visit that month, and filled in the rest of the days with visits to the rest of the colonias, combining them wherever possible. The letters simply said that I needed to have an urgent meeting with all members of the Ecological Brigades and the date when I would be in town. I went to the market and gave the letters to the drivers of the IFA transport trucks to take to the *colonias'* leaders for me.

Juan Carlos feigned surprise when I walked into his office and told him that we'd be leaving. I knew that he had been consulted in the process of making the decision and when I confronted him about it, he just laughed.

"I guess you caught me, *gringita*," he laughed. "Or wait, were you the one caught?" He laughed harder at his own joke. I stared him down with my worst scowl but it only seemed to make him laugh harder. I finally turned and left him still chuckling.

He called a staff meeting later that day and announced in a very somber tone that our contract had unexpectedly come to an end after only one year instead of the planned two. Alejandra burst into tears and hugged me tight, while Lennon and Eduardo looked genuinely shocked. Pastor Miguel turned away, kicking at the dirt. I concentrated on what a phony Juan Carlos was to keep myself from joining Alejandra in her reaction. Somehow hearing it spoken out loud like that in an announcement suddenly made it much more real.

Word quickly spread around town. The reaction from those with whom we each worked was one of shock and sadness at the loss of a second year to really cement into habit what we'd practiced in our separate jobs. Padre Nacho and the girls in the choir were confused and deeply saddened as well. Padre Nacho's face quickly turned to dark anger when I told him what had happened in the privacy of his counseling room. He swore quietly at Juan Carlos's betrayal.

"It's one thing to come after you himself to try and frustrate you into going home," he said, lighting yet another cigarette. "But to aid someone else in distorting a situation outside of his realm... well, that's just low. I expected more from him." He paused, contemplating the burning ash. "I always knew he was slippery but I didn't realize that he had no honor."

I felt more eyes on me than usual in public places but the words from Padre Nacho and other friends and allies kept me from hanging my head in shame. I began to believe that it wasn't my fault at all; that I was merely a pawn in Juan Carlos's game.

Joaquin and Mireya insisted on accompanying me to some of the *colonias*. Their rationale was to spend as much time with me as possible, as well as to keep me safe since the abruptness of the visits had not allowed for arranged accompaniment from each *colonia* by a *brigadista*. I felt braver and stronger with them along.

Mireya had always dressed in a very typical fashion for women who worked as housekeepers – knee-length skirts, simple blouses or newer t-shirts tucked in, sensible shoes. Going to the *colonias*, she wore pants but also less sensible shoes and fancier blouses. Next to her in my jeans, work boots and tank tops, I felt like a slob.

We went to Calero one day and were heading back on the IFA truck through Punto de Encuentros, the very first *colonia* I had visited so many months ago with Lennon. The IFA was very crowded and hot, and I was bothered by the enclosed smells of body odor and chickens. At one of the stops, Joaquin suggested we climb up onto the top of the IFA to ride in more comfort. Even though I had really enjoyed riding up on top just a few weeks back when we'd gone camping out in the mountains, I hadn't done it since then. Mireya and I both hesitated, but with Joaquin's reassurances that we would be fine, we climbed up. There were already some men sitting up there who looked surprised to see two women, least of all a *gringa*, climbing up, but they quickly recovered enough to give us a hand.

We settled in and were starting to get used to the ride from up top. Joaquin was facing me and Mireya, holding onto our hands. We had our backs turned to watch the scenery go by from behind while he faced front. All of the sudden he shouted, "Duck!" and did so himself quickly.

I managed to get out of the way in time to see Mireya knocked flat by a branch. She screamed and Joaquin grabbed her with both hands to keep her from falling over the side of the 20-foot tall truck. My stomach turned to jelly.

"Oh, my God, Mireya, are you okay?" I yelled. The men began banging on the top of the truck and yelling at the driver to stop. There was blood running down Mireya's face. She looked dazed.

"What was that?" she asked softly, then reached her hand up to feel her face. As she pulled fingers sticky with blood back, she screamed again and began to sob. "Oh, I'm going to die!" she moaned as Joaquin took a handkerchief and began cleaning her face.

"No, you're not, Doña Mireya," Joaquin said gently but firmly. "Your head just got itself a little cut on it, and heads bleed a lot." He continued talking to her in a soothing voice while gently cleaning her face. He made her keep looking at him while instructing me to move behind her to keep her from falling. She was starting to swoon.

I quickly got behind her and braced her with my legs. I was a good six or seven inches taller than she was but I didn't realize how small she really was until I sat with her like that. I pulled my water bottle out of my backpack and handed it to her to take a drink. She did in a daze, and then handed it to Joaquin who used some of it to continue cleaning her face.

The IFA had stopped and a small crowd gathered and looked up at us, watching. Mireya caught a glimpse of everyone looking at her and panicked again. When she started crying again, her head started bleeding more. It was quickly becoming a vicious cycle.

Joaquin and I decided that we needed to get her down and into the main part of the truck. It was quite an ordeal, but we managed with some help from some of the men on top and below. We got her onto a bench at the edge of the truck and looked more closely at her head. There was a small cut where her hair met her forehead – less than a half an inch long. I was instantly relieved but Mireya could not be consoled. She started screaming at Joaquin that it was all his fault for making her go up there. I couldn't believe how rattled she was by the whole thing.

I joined Joaquin in trying to calm her down as the IFA driver was now growing impatient to get back on the road. The crowds were still gathered, watching her as they murmured among themselves. The driver started up the truck again and people quickly began piling in. I was soon wishing we were back up on top, but kept my seat next to Mireya and my arm firmly wrapped around her shoulders. Her crying subsided to sniffling and I found myself comforting her as I would a child. It was a new dimension of our relationship. Always before it had been me in need of comfort or rescue. I was shaken now more by her need of my comfort than I had been by the accident.

Out in the *colonias*, the brigades were reacting to the news that I would be leaving at the end of January much as I had expected. They were outraged. I tried to describe as diplomatically as possible what had happened. Everyone speculated that Juan Carlos must have played a role in facilitating either the communication with the National Church, or encouraging the decision to pull us out, or both. I found myself encouraged to downplay my own role in this mess and emphasize Juan Carlos's, fed by their anger and disappointment that I would be leaving. Among the expletives and angry words directed at NECOG and Juan Carlos, there were profound expressions of how powerfully our time together had impacted them.

I soon realized that I would not be able to visit all of the *colonias* before our departure date. While I was disappointed in this, I resigned myself to scheduling visits in the closest *colonias*. It was quickly suggested by someone that we should have one big final meeting of everyone, all the brigades, together in Santo Domingo. They wanted an opportunity to say goodbye, to review and celebrate what they had done so far, and to get some ideas from me of how to continue the work without me.

As I sent radio announcements and hand-written messages out to all of the *colonias* informing them of the big meeting, Juan Carlos, Lennon and Eduardo began paying very close attention to what I was doing. They heard the radio announcements, no doubt, but I hadn't gotten permission or sought their approval to have the meeting. A friend and colleague from another NGO had arranged for me to be able to use a large pavilion at his organization's facility for it, and since I had had no budget to work with for a long time, I saw no need to include them in my planning. Juan Carlos sent Eduardo to try and feel out the situation first.

"*Gringita*, so how about this big meeting you're planning?" he said with his sickeningly sweet smile that I had come to loathe. "Do you think anyone will come? I could help you spread the word if you want."

"No, thanks, Eduardo," I replied, returning his smile with an iciness I hoped he wasn't too dim to mistake for authenticity. "I think we've got it under control."

"We? Oh, so are you back on good terms with Lennon now? Is he helping you plan this? You know, we can never tell what's going on with you two..." he intentionally let his voice trail off, the smile turning suggestive. I wanted to punch him.

"No," I said as lightly as possible, not wanting to let him get under my skin. "I have built brigades in each of the *colonias*, and each one has a captain or co-captains. They are doing just fine helping with the organization. Thanks for your concern though. And be sure to thank Juan Carlos for his for me, too." I turned and walked out of the office, leaving Eduardo with his mouth slightly gaping open. The stupid expression on his face was fitting for my feelings towards him.

Lennon had the sense by then to stay as far away from me as possible. If there were other people present, common Nicaraguan courtesy required him to acknowledge me in greeting, which he did as nonchalantly as possible. His face was always a mask of unreadable thought. Ever since our final confrontation a few months back, he had not tried to talk with me again. I always looked his way as coldly as possible to make sure he didn't see any invitation from me to change that.

Meanwhile I was spending as much time with Mireya and Joaquin as possible. Joaquin wanted to go camping up in the mountains at his uncle's place one more time before we left. We planned a trip one weekend with one other friend.

Mireya wanted to go with us, but she really didn't like roughing it and didn't want to leave the kids. Mark wasn't invited. We packed hammocks to sleep in and a few things each in a backpack, caught the IFA out to Punto de Encuentros, and hiked into the hills. It was even more beautiful and lush than I had remembered it. We spent time at the waterfall and stream, diving off the rocks and swimming in the deep pool below, hiking around the hills, and sleeping. Joaquin and I had agreed not to make our other friend uncomfortable by being overly affectionate, but it was a hard agreement to keep. I was constantly fighting off a wave of nausea at the thought of leaving him. I felt almost like I was on death row – I could see the end coming, felt powerless to stop it, and dreaded it every day. It was hard in that state of mind to keep myself from clinging to him.

When we came back, Mireya and her kids met us at the bus. She had clearly missed us and felt badly that she hadn't gone. The kids were climbing all over us. Mireya seemed to be feeling a little jealous that I was spending so much time with Joaquin. She fussed at me more than usual.

1/16/98

Dear Folks at home -

Greetings from the tropics for one of the last times... How sad it is to think that I won't be here for much more time. Today, I'm heading to the campo as I have done every day for the past week and a half. For that reason, I have not had time to write to you. I don't know what the problem is with the communication - I still have not received your fax. This poor communication system has always been frustrating, but it's ever more so right now because I have so little time left and I need to be in communication with y'all to make this transition a little easier.

The situation with Mark is the same. We sleep separately still, with me in the hammock in the small back room, and him in the bed. Sometimes I ask for the bed if my back gets to bother me too much, and sometimes he is kind enough to let me sleep there and he in the hammock. We don't argue; just co-exist. He is slightly more responsible, but that is not the only problem. I maintain an open mind about the counseling, but I am not holding my breath.

Joaquin and Mireya are stuck to my side and we pass the majority of our time together. Mireya even went to the *campo* with me yesterday, and the two of them will go with me today. We are going to Santa Estelita and San Eduardo, and I didn't want to make the trip alone again since I almost died last time I went alone. The road is mostly dry this time, but I think that incident psychologically damaged me. We'll be leaving shortly.

I have had success in my visits to the communities in all but one so far. All of the Brigades are very upset that I'm leaving and all have promised to bring letters of recommendation in the hopes of clearing my name back home with the church as well as maintaining hope that I may return to work with them again some day, and that the letters will help me to get a job here independently. I have planned a final meeting with everyone here in town for the 23rd. I am inviting all the Brigades and, at their request, the staff of NECOG. Several Brigades are upset with Juan Carlos and "the boys" for their treatment of me as well as their neglect of the communities, and several are preparing speeches. I promised them a time slot to have their say. I think it's important not only because it will prove to the staff that they were wrong about me and my work in the colonies, but because the Brigades need to work with NECOG after I go and I think it's important that they have a chance to air their true feelings. It will be a moment of truth.

I'll be in touch soon. Keep trying to send your fax.

Lots of love, hugs and greetings to all...

Ellen

Chapter 52

The week before the big meeting with the brigades was to happen, Juan Carlos had Alejandra come and get me from my office. I was working on an outline for the meeting and deeply lost in concentration. When she knocked softly on the door, I almost jumped out of my skin. We both laughed.

"Elenita, Juan Carlos wants to see you for a minute," she said when we'd recovered, still smiling.

My smile disappeared instantly. "What does he want?" I asked defensively, remaining in my seat.

"I'm not sure," Alejandra said, her own smile faltering a bit. She hated the tension between us and couldn't imagine being as confrontational and bold with Juan Carlos as she had seen me be. "He didn't say. He just asked me to come and find you."

"Okay, I'm coming. Sorry, Alejandra, I wasn't trying to jump at you."

"I know, Elenita," she said quickly. She paused as I got to my feet, then, "You know we're all going to miss you a lot around here. Not just me, but the men, too."

I barked a harsh laugh. "I doubt that you will miss me in the same ways, Alejandra," I said, smiling at her. She laughed a little nervously as I followed her out of the office.

I felt butterflies in my stomach as I walked up the steps to Juan Carlos's office and knocked on his door. He yelled to come in through the closed door, and I pushed it open.

The air conditioning was blasting as usual and hit me like a wall of icy air. I had never been a fan of air conditioning, and had become totally unaccustomed to it while in Santo Domingo. It took me a moment to adjust my breathing. Goose bumps broke out on my arms. I crossed them quickly.

"You wanted to see me, boss?" I asked casually, trying to hide my nervousness.

Juan Carlos just looked at me for a moment, scrutinizing my face. I tried to hold my gaze steady under his. Suddenly he went from stock still to leaping onto his feet. I couldn't stop myself from taking a step back. He laughed. "*Gringita*, I hear you're planning a meeting with my ecological brigades."

"*Your* brigades, boss?" I snorted before I could stop myself. "I'm pretty sure I'm the one who got them working and has had them working all year. When did they become yours?"

"Well, you work for me here at NECOG. Until you leave, everyone you work with and everything you do technically belongs to me and this organization." He took a step closer, looking at me with menace. "I just want to make sure we're clear on that, *gringita*," his voice soft. "I own the work done out here." He paused to stare at me coldly, then shifted his stance just as suddenly to a playful one. His voice returned to its normal jolly pitch. "So what are we doing at this meeting?"

It took me a second to swallow and regain my voice. Ever since the attacks from Lennon, I had become very aware of every man's physical presence in my proximity. I was sure he was intentionally intimidating me but I was also pretty sure he wouldn't be stupid enough to physically attack me.

"I was just working on the agenda for the meeting," I said, trying to keep my voice strong. I shifted on my feet as he went back to his chair behind the desk and leaned way back in it. He had not asked me to sit down, which would have been subtle in the States, but in Nicaragua was a clear message of disrespect. "Were you planning to attend?"

He laughed. "Of course! I wouldn't miss it for anything." He leaned forward and began shuffling the papers around on his desk. He looked up again as if surprised that I was still there. "Is there something else? Anything you'd like to tell me?" His expression was a mask of innocence.

"N-no..." I stammered, unable to catch myself. "I'll be going then." I turned and started for the door closest to my office. It was on the other side of the room from where I had entered from the main office.

"No, please use the other door," he said quickly from behind me. "I wouldn't want anyone to think that you were in here for an extended period of time." He paused as I headed for the other door, then continued, "You know, your reputation and all..."

I whirled around ready to jump over his desk and attack him. He burst out laughing loudly, holding his stomach and wiping his eyes. I fought with all my being the urge to respond or hit him. Instead, I turned quickly back to the door, slamming it with all my force behind me. Because of the stupid air conditioning, it shut with a very unsatisfactory "whoosh" that no one else heard. I could hear Juan Carlos laughing harder inside.

Tears stung my eyes as I stormed through the main office and back to my own. Once there, I picked up the papers I had been working on, stuffed them in my backpack and slammed out of my own office heading for Mireya's house.

1/20/97

Dear Folks at home -

Well, here I am again. I have had no success getting your last fax through, nor have I received the one that you were trying to send last week. I'm not sure why I'm bothering to write and try again. I must be an eternal optimist.

Joaquin, Mireya and I walked about 12 km on Friday with our trip in and out of Santa Estelita. Going into the mountains to camp, we walked 6 km on Saturday. Since we left early in the a.m. and were a bit rushed, we didn't have enough food, so Joaquin and I ran (literally) most of the way back to town looking for all the stuff we needed, and then again most of the way back (yet another 6 km). Counting the walking we did in town looking for all the stuff we needed, we walked about 20 km in total on Saturday.

On Sunday, we climbed the highest mountain around, which Joaquin says was at an altitude of 8000 meters, and we could see everything. We went back to the beautiful waterfall where we went the first time, and then walked all the way back. It was another good 18 km. I slept really, really well on Sunday night when we finally made it back into town at 6:30 p.m.

My last trip out to the campo was yesterday. Overall, I feel like I was pretty successful in the visits. I have several promised letters of recommendation, but if I get a half dozen, I will be overjoyed. I know the folks here are sincere, but most are fairly uneducated as far as formal schooling goes, and it's a major project to write a letter, so I'm trying not to get my hopes up too high. Maybe I'll be pleasantly surprised.

I did have some good news when I went to borrow materials from a friend at another NGO today. The engineer that loaned me the stuff is a friend of ours and he was telling me that they want to work with my Brigades. That means that maybe this fear that I share with the Brigades that they will be left unattended won't come to pass. He's going to come to the meeting on Friday and talk to them, so hopefully something good will come out of this. Also, he told me that in this year and the one to come, there are a lot of projects in agriculture and environment coming to the zone and that everyone will be looking to hire, so maybe if I decided to come back I would be able to find a job that pays well. He said he would be the first to recommend me for one of the jobs if it came to that. I know that probably doesn't make you too happy to hear, but we will talk more about it when I get home.

So everything is all set for our final days - in terms of work, I have a ton and it's all cut out for me. The house needs to begin to get packed up, but I can't do it right now and thinking that Mark will even think about it before Sunday night is a joke. I plan to start spending my evenings packing, but it's so hard to figure out where to start. I seem to remember having the same problem when we packed up our apartment. Could it be that I just really hate packing up and leaving places?

I'll see you all very soon...

Much love, hugs and kisses to all,

Ellen

Chapter 53

The night before the big meeting, I had decided to sleep at Mireya's house. Our house was mostly packed by then, as we would be departing in only a couple of days. As the time approached for leaving, I spent every moment possible with Mireya and Joaquin.

The landlords' daughter next door to where we lived had unexpectedly decided to have a dress made for me as a going-away present. I picked it up that day and was modeling it for Mireya. It was quite fitted – more so than the brown dress I had made, and more so than anything else I'd ever worn. Of course, I was slimmer than I had ever been in my adult life, but still quite unused to showing off my curves. It was made of a lightweight fabric that hung very nicely. It was red with big white splashes of flowers on it. The neckline scooped quite low and the straps were thin at the shoulders. The rest of it was fitted closely to my body and hung down to mid-calf. There was a slit up the back.

As I looked in the mirror and spun slowly around, I had to admit that I was impressed. I hadn't realized how much weight I'd lost until I put that dress on. Paired with very high-heeled strappy white sandals that were a gift from Mireya, I felt like a model. Mireya and the kids whistled and murmured their approval watching me.

We stayed up late that night, talking softly on Mireya's double bed as the kids slept on the other side of the partitioned wall. I got up to go have one more cigarette before going to sleep. Mireya was drifting off but I still felt restless and thought that if I just had one more smoke, I'd calm down enough to sleep. She insisted that I stay inside the house to smoke – she didn't want me opening the doors. I sat in the darkness listening to the sounds of Santo Domingo – the discoteca in the distance, crickets, salamanders, bats, countless other insects and creatures that I couldn't name, people talking and laughing softly as they stumbled through the streets to get home, a glass breaking somewhere.

The reality of leaving this place was washing over me in waves these days and I was often fighting back tears. My melancholy took me through random events, good and bad, of the past year and I stayed up to finish my pack of cigarettes, listening as the sounds of Mireya's even breathing were added to the others.

Finally I got up and felt my way carefully back towards her bedroom. As I got to the doorway, I remembered that there was a cloth curtain there but forgot about the narrow piece of wood along the doorframe at the bottom. My bare foot caught in it and I went flying forward, landing hard on my knee on the unforgiving ceramic tile floor. I sucked in my breath and clenched my jaw, gripping the doorframe to keep from yelling out. Pain was shooting through my entire leg and I wondered if something was broken. I was panting, trying to keep from crying out and Mireya heard me, startled awake.

"Oh, my God, Elena, are you okay? What happened?" she whispered, her voice thick with sleep and worry. "Where are you? Can you get to the light?" She was fumbling through the dark herself to reach it even as she asked.

"No," I managed to pant, the pain getting worse by the second. "I think I might have broken something. I tripped on the doorway. I forgot it was there." I was whisper-yelling it all, still trying to keep from letting out the scream ripping at my throat. "Don't turn on the light – you'll wake up the kids. I'll be okay. I just need to sit for a minute."

"The kids won't wake up and we need to take a look at you," she answered briskly, the sleep now gone from her voice. "What did you hurt?" The light was on and she was kneeling over me, gently but firmly prying my hands away from my knee.

It was swelling up and already turning colors beyond the red of the impact. I tried to move it and could, so I figured it would just be a nasty bruise. My hands and one elbow were also starting to sting. We could see they were scraped but nothing was bleeding.

Mireya helped me get up onto the bed. Ice was not a household item since very few people even had refrigerators then, and I was out of cigarettes, so there was nothing else to be done until morning when the ventas opened and both items could be purchased. After regaining my breath, the pain dulled to a steady throbbing and I fell into a restless sleep, Mireya's hand on my head.

1/21/98

Dear Ron and Charlotte,

I am sorry I have not been able to connect to you by phone, but I've been able to keep up with some of your comings and goings through Mark's parents.

I just want both of you to know that Ellen, Mark and all of you are in our thoughts and prayers during these times of transition. We of the Partnership Committee feel deep care and concern for Ellen and Mark as well as our NECOG partners and the whole situation of this relationship.

I thought both of you would be interested in the draft letter we probably will use to inform the congregations below . I hope we have expressed ourselves thoughtfully enough that Ellen and Mark will have the space and time they need to work on what is important for them.

There is a good chance that several from the Partnership Committee will be on hand to greet them as they return home. I'll look forward to seeing you then.

In the meantime if there is anything we can do for you, please do not hesitate to call on me or members of the Partnership Committee.

In Peace,
Esther Smith

1/98

Dear Friends and Colleagues in Ministry:

The Mission Partnership Committee of the Partnership Office wishes to share some recent news with you. Mark and Ellen Hendricks are returning to the United States for personal reasons at the completion of their one-year service commitment. They will arrive in the United States at the end of January. Through the years of the partnership relationship with NECOG, the Mission Partnership Committee has appreciated your congregations' support in delegations, with extra commitment giving through other gifts, hosting visitors from Nicaragua, and scheduling mission programs about this Partnership Office mission project.

We are deeply grateful for Mark and Ellen and the shared relationship with Worldwide Ministries of the NPCA and NECOG that created the opportunity for their ministry partnership with NECOG. They have been energetic and dedicated in their work with our NECOG partners - teaching English, creating newsletters, and working on significant reforestation projects in several small villages.

As they rest and reconnect with family and friends, they will also spend time reflecting on the year's experiences, preparing for a re-entry retreat at the end of March sponsored by the denomination for all returning service workers, and assessing further directions in their lives. We will not schedule any programming during this time of re-entry and resettling. We will keep you informed of these opportunities as they arise....

Again, we thank you for all your support. And we hope for your prayers for Nicaragua and for the small green shoots of peace and reconciliation being nurtured through our Mission Partnership journey.

In Service to Christ,

Jane Smith, Co-moderator

Mary Jones, Co-moderator

Chapter 54

The next day I awoke early to the sounds of women in nearby houses coughing out the sleep from their lungs, roosters crowing in their random, cranky ways, and a throbbing in my knee that made me think I would not be able to move.

Mireya was already up and I could smell coffee along with rice and beans cooking in her little lean-to kitchen near the house. The kids were getting up, arguing softly among themselves as they rubbed sleep from their eyes. Mireya scolded one of them for something. These were the sounds I would miss; these were the sounds of everyday Nicaraguan life that had surrounded me for the past year. I was overcome suddenly with emotion and a hot tear slid down my cheek. I quickly wiped it away. I needed to go to the bathroom, which was going to require that I get my stiff knee moving.

I sat up slowly, testing my knee gently. It would move with some effort but I couldn't stop the groan that escaped. Immediately Mireya yelled for the kids to come and help me get up. They came bursting through the curtain as though they'd been waiting there all along, and I was once again surprised by the muscle strength that covered their small frames.

It took quite a while to get to the outhouse, get a shower and get dressed. I was still too modest to let any of them help me much, but I finally emerged from Mireya's room in the brown dress I'd worn at Christmas. We'd decided that the red one was too flashy for a work gathering. I noticed that the brown one hung off my frame more than it had only a few weeks before; I'd lost more weight with the stress of leaving looming over me all the time.

By the time I reached the meeting place, many members of the brigades had arrived. I had asked Mark to come with our camera so that I could take pictures with all of them. As it turned out, they all wanted pictures with each brigade, then all together, and some even with Mark in them, for no other reason than that he was my husband. Most of them had never even met him. He good-naturedly snapped and posed for all of the requested shots. I felt grateful, and told him so. He smiled sadly at me.

Once all of the brigades were present, I called the meeting to order. We were about an hour behind schedule, running on "*Hora Nica*". I made a joke about it as we started the meeting and many of the brigades guffawed with genuine affection. They had taught me to relax and differentiate when I wanted something to start out in their *colonias* – "*Hora Nica*" or "*Hora Gringa*" – "*Nica* Time" or "*Gringa* Time".

The agenda I had created was simple; I wanted each of the brigades to present what they had accomplished in our time together, then say what they still hoped to accomplish in the coming year. Counting on the presence of the NECOG staff, I was hoping to apply a subtle form of public pressure for them to feel obligated to continue what we had worked so hard to begin. As we started, Lennon and Eduardo were there, but Juan Carlos was noticeably absent. Without him, the other two would go back and say whatever they wanted. I tried to think of a way to delay.

I decided to do introductions. Many of the brigade members didn't know each other. They lived in separate *colonias* and gathered infrequently for NECOG meetings, if ever. Since I had recruited a number of them, many had never even attended a NECOG meeting. I asked them to go around the room and say their names, *colonia*, and if they had something specific they'd like to get out of today's meeting.

The first person to stand was Carlos – the leader of the brigade from Carabas where I had spent a lot of time. He was one of my fiercest protectors and had been one of the most outraged when I announced that I had to leave. Carlos was also a bit mischievous and had a sparkle in his eye. As he stood, he pulled a folded piece of paper from his pocket. After he had introduced himself, he began unfolding the piece of paper. The other members of his brigade looked at each other and stood as well.

"Well, what we had hoped to get out of today's meeting was to publicly let Juan Carlos and the rest of the NECOG staff know what we in Carabas think of Elenita, our *gringita fea*," he smiled and paused, winking at me as a ripple of warm chuckling ran through the room. "And what we think of what they have done that facilitated her leaving us." He paused again, looking up at me before quickly looking down at his piece of paper and continuing. With that, he began to read a letter of praise and recommendation written on behalf of the entire brigade in Carabas.

As he read it, I could hardly believe what I was hearing. Tears stung my eyes and I was overwhelmed with humility as this barely-literate man struggled to read this letter for all to hear. When he had finished, he looked up, tears glistening in his own eyes, and spoke again.

"It was my hope that Don Juan Carlos would be here today to hear, in addition to this thanks and praise, that we are most disappointed that

Elena will be leaving us." His eyes dried up and took on a hard look. "We feel that her situation has been inappropriately judged, and that no consideration for the very important work we've done here together has been given. We in Carabas are angry with NECOG and disappointed in Don Juan Carlos. Thank you." With that, he sat down. At first there was silence, then someone began to applaud. Quickly the room was filled with the sound of applause, which overwhelmed me even more than the letter had. I sat watching it all, not sure how to react.

One after another, representatives from each brigade stood and gave a similar rendition to what Carlos had done. Each brigade had written a letter, each had appointed someone to speak for the group, and each time the members of the brigade stood together as their letters were read. Juan Carlos came in sometime during this presentation, which lasted over an hour, and listened quietly. His normal bluster and fidgety manner that endeared him to many who lived in the campo disappeared as he heard what was being said.

At the end of it, I stood before Juan Carlos had the chance. I took a deep breath and tried to focus on the trees beyond the outdoor building where we were gathered so as to keep my composure. It didn't entirely work.

"Well, I'm absolutely humbled by your kind words. I can't begin to describe to you how much they mean to me." My voice cracked and I took another deep breath. Shouts of encouragement came quickly from my brigades to continue. "Our time together has meant more to me than I can tell you. It was you who taught me to speak Spanish and respect your culture through patience, kindness and generosity. I have learned at least as much from you, if not more, than you claim to have learned from me," I laughed. "And in times when all we had to work with was each other," I paused momentarily and shot a look over at Juan Carlos, "you have always made me so proud."

My voice finally broke and I put my hand up to my face. The emotions washing over me were so intense that I had to sit down. The pain at leaving them and leaving this life was more than I could bear, but listening to their letters had also awakened in me some important realizations about how deeply we had impacted each other's lives – so much more so than I had originally understood. I wanted to say so much more to them but didn't have the words. I sat numbly listening to their applause and watching as they got to their feet, many of them crying, too. Finally I rose, limped off the platform and into their embraces.

The rest of the meeting was something of a blur. We took a break, and people hugging me and wishing me well while stuffing their letters into my hands quickly surrounded me. I moved through it like a zombie. I was on overload.

Juan Carlos spoke at some point, acknowledging the sadness and anger that had been expressed at my departure, and even claiming to share it. The brigade members were too polite (except for a few) to do anything but listen, faces set in hard, stony looks that reflected their anger. The few who did more than look on in anger made comments to their neighbors loud enough for Juan Carlos to hear but not loud enough to disrupt the meeting. He chose to ignore them. There was polite applause when he was done.

Each of the Social Promoters, Lennon and Eduardo, took a turn speaking briefly as well. Each one quietly promised to support the continuing work of the brigades, and neither made any comment about my departure or me. They were not met with the same hostility as Juan Carlos, but received the same cold, polite applause from most.

The meeting had been scheduled for two hours, and by the time everyone had lunch, which the NECOG Women's Pastoral Committee had prepared for us, and said their goodbyes, it was late in the afternoon. I finally had to just walk away – I could not take the prolonged farewells.

My knee was aching but much better than it had been that morning. The next day was to be our last full one in Santo Domingo, so I had to return home to finish packing. Mark had packed most of the house up, leaving my stuff untouched. There was a clear line of separation it seemed. I moved through the few rooms, wondering how I could pack a year of memories into my steamer trunk.

Joaquin, Mireya and a few other friends came by to visit and offer assistance. Mark was out with the teachers he'd worked with, having a farewell dinner to which I had been invited but declined to go. In light of his help with the pictures earlier that day, I felt a little guilty for saying no, but was glad for the extra time with my friends.

We had planned one more night out on the town together of dancing and drinking, so I put on my new red dress and white sandals, wrapped my knee in an ace bandage and swallowed an extra aspirin. When Joaquin arrived to collect me, I felt like I looked better than I ever had. He seemed to agree, judging by his enthusiastic greeting.

We walked slowly over to Mireya's house, meeting Mark along the way and inviting him to come along. She wanted to take some pictures of us all together one more time. He didn't look happy about it, but agreed to come. Joaquin respectfully did not hold my hand but instead frequently took my elbow to make sure I wouldn't do further damage to my knee. Mark noticed I was limping a little and asked what had happened. He shook his head and looked worried when I told him. I wondered again what was going to happen to us when we returned home to the States. I decided to push those thoughts out of my head for the time being – I wanted to focus instead on my remaining time with Joaquin and Mireya.

Chapter 55

Juan Carlos's truck pulled up in front of our house before the sun was up. We had a long trip to Managua in front of us. Joaquin and Mireya were walking down the street towards us as we loaded our trunks and bags into the back of the truck. They threw their own bags in and helped us manage ours. No one spoke more than required.

I walked back into the house, empty except for the double bed, which would be going to Mireya after we left. I did not try to hold back my tears and sadness as I looked around. Walking down the stairs and into the kitchen, it dawned on me that Flea had not come home for the last couple of days. I needed to say goodbye to him. I started calling him, softly at first, then more desperately as he didn't emerge. I was sobbing and could barely pucker my lips to kiss the air, my usual way of calling him aside from his name. Finally Joaquin came up behind me and gently took my shoulders.

"Come on, *amor*, we have to go," he said softly, his own voice breaking.

"But I have to say goodbye to Flea!" I sobbed at him. "You don't understand! That cat is like my baby! I can't leave without seeing him!" I broke free and continued calling him.

Mark came over to me and spoke to me softly in English. "Ellen, we have to go. We can't wait any longer. I'm sure Flea knew we were leaving and didn't want to say goodbye. I'm sure the neighbors will take good care of him for you. Come on, we have to go." He tugged at my arm. I allowed him to pull me up into the pick up truck where I was consumed with grief. It was incredibly painful to watch as we pulled away from the house, but I couldn't bear not to, for fear that Flea would emerge and I would miss it. The pain was unbearable. I felt like someone was ripping my soul out.

We turned the corner onto the sleeping main street, and I buried my head in my hands, sobs racking my body. There were hands on my shoulders and back trying to comfort me, but I could not help feeling as if a big part of me had just died.

1/98

Dear Esther,

Thank you for your note the other day. I am also sorry that we could not connect by phone. Since our return from

Nicaragua, we have been very busy - preparing for Ellen's return to "the nest", as well as clearing away all of the holiday trappings that we left behind the day after Christmas! I read over the draft letter and feel it does a pretty good job of asking for both gratitude and breathing space for Ellen and Mark. I just have a couple of comments to add.

First of all, I think it will be a great show of support for both of them to have some members of the Partnership Committee on hand at the airport on Thursday. HOWEVER, please allow us parents to greet them at the gate and then join you in the baggage claim area. This will not be a happy nor triumphant homecoming for them. Ellen especially is extremely distraught over her need for closure and leave-taking in such a short time span. Please respect her need for comfort and privacy at this time.

We are inviting Mark's parents to follow us home, have a brief supper with us, gather up some of Mark's warm clothing, and then head back to their home. Due to the problems between Ellen and Mark, Ellen asked that you not plan to try a group dinner at this time. I do not know what your plans are, but these are her wishes at this time.

I spoke to Ellen last night. They left Santo Domingo at 5:30 a.m. yesterday, arriving in Managua about 1 p.m. After refreshing themselves, they attended the meeting with Juan Carlos, Ana, and Jane Sims. They then collapsed at the Johnsons'. Mark has a miserable cold and Ellen thinks she may have a parasite (she hoped to get to a doctor today). It will be all they (at least Ellen) can do to get through the next few days.

Please drop me a line to let me know that this arrived.

Thank you,

Charlotte Patnaude

Chapter 56

The streets were still dark in the pre-dawn hours as we put our trunks and other bags into the back of the taxi. Mireya and Joaquin helped us both, though the distance between Mark and the rest of us was palpable. No one spoke as we climbed into the taxi, Mark in the front and me with Mireya and Joaquin on either side of me into the back. Each held one of my hands tightly, and Joaquin had his other arm wrapped protectively around my shoulders. I leaned into him, looking over at Mireya, as we rode in silence. I was filled with an unbearable ache that threatened to make me physically ill at any moment.

The sun was starting to come up as we arrived at the airport. Early morning was the busiest departure time for all International flights, and the terminal was already crowded. As the cab driver unloaded all of the bags onto the curb, Mark pulled out some money. Glancing coldly over at me, he said in English so the others present wouldn't understand, "Think you can disentangle yourself there long enough to help pay for this cab?"

I reached into my pocket, too consumed with my own emotions to play his games that morning. "Whatever", I managed with a weak smile at him as I handed some money to the driver.

We moved inside of the terminal and checked in. I cringed as the travel agent at the counter referred to us as Mr. and Mrs. Hendricks. Mark made no comment.

Having checked in our luggage, we returned to the waiting area where Joaquin and Mireya had stayed watching the carry on items. Mark wandered off to the side somewhere as I folded myself into Joaquin's arms, Mireya holding one of my hands once again.

"I'm not sure I can do this. I'm not sure I can make myself walk through that doorway and go get on that plane over there", I said in Spanish with tears starting to roll down my cheeks. The unbearable ache in my chest was giving way to panic.

"*Amor*, you have to", said Joaquin gently, sadness in his eyes. "As much as I want you to stay right now, you have to go back to the States and get things straightened out there. Then you come on back to us."

Mireya had begun to cry silently as the first tears fell down my cheeks. Now with a sob she pulled me to her fiercely. "Joaquin is right, sweetheart. You have to go. But promise me again that you'll come back. Promise me again that you won't forget us."

I let out a short laugh that sounded more like a snort through my tears, causing all three of us to use the excuse to laugh. "How could I possibly forget the two of you, even if I wanted to?" I asked incredulously.

There were so many things I wanted to say to them both about how much they had each changed my life. But the words died on my lips. Everything I thought of sounded corny in my head. I felt emotionally spent.

So we made small talk and stupid jokes while the three of us stood around together. Every now and then, Mireya or I would get overwhelmed and start crying again. This went on for the next hour until the flight was announced, first in Spanish, then in English.

"Continental international flight 743 with non-stop service to Houston, Texas will now begin boarding through gate number 3", said the mechanical voice over the loud speaker.

I was again filled with an overwhelming sense of panic. How could I leave? What was I going back for? How was I going to wake up tomorrow without Joaquin and Mireya to walk through another day with me? I began to sob into Joaquin's chest.

"I can't do it! I can't do it!" I whimpered, clinging to him.

"*Amor*, you must", he choked out. "Don't make this worse than it is. You have your dignity back. Now go walk through that door acting like it. Don't leave me like this. Pull yourself together, *mi gringita fea vieja*."

That made me laugh, in spite of myself – he'd called me his "little old, ugly American girl". With one final, fierce embrace with each of them, I took a deep breath, closed my eyes, let it out, opened my eyes, put my chin in the air set with a determined jaw, and focused on putting one foot in front of the other towards the gate through which Mark had already long passed.

Epilogue

Mark and Ellen were divorced shortly after their return to the States. Through counseling, they realized how incompatible they were from the beginning, and the divorce was a mutual and amicable decision.

Mark went on to achieve success in many areas of his life, including having a family of his own. Like everyone else in this story, he has grown and changed tremendously over the years since the moment in time captured here. He and Ellen remain amicable.

Mireya went on to open her own small eatery in the central market place. She is a proud grandmother to Estelita's three children, and is healthy and happy. She and Ellen keep in close contact to present day, and Ellen has visited her many times.

Joaquin has fathered two children, one of whom was conceived during his affair with Ellen.

Lennon fathered a child with one of Ellen's Ecological Brigade members. The child was conceived during his affair with Ellen. The Brigade member, like Ellen, had no idea at the time that she was not the only one with whom he was having an affair.

Juan Carlos is currently a City Council member in Santo Domingo, and continues to wield influence with large numbers of people.

Ellen is happy and healthy. The story of her life after this year in Nicaragua is complicated and too much to write here. Look for her blogs online.

Acknowledgments

To Cecil Hickman – without you, this book may not have ever come into existence. Your patience, stamina, persistence, coaching, tough love and unfailing belief in me made it all possible. You are a true friend, and a fabulous editor.

To my parents – throughout my life, you have shown me nothing but constant support and unwavering belief in my ability to do whatever I set my mind to doing. I know I haven't always appreciated it, but I do now. Thank you for standing by me through all of the ups and downs. And thank you for loving me, even when I needed to plow ahead and make mistakes that you could see coming a mile away.

To the MOMS Club of Waterford North – your friendships, encouragement, and persistent but gentle "nagging" to get this thing done helped me to see it through to the finish line! You are a fabulous group of women from whom I continue to draw strength, courage and love. Oh, and the editorial help was great, too!!!

To Argerie Vasilakes and Terri Erwin – my first readers! You saved this book from being one of self-flagellation. You helped me to find my focus, and to help me decide what story I really wanted to tell. You are two wonderful, beautiful friends, even with all of those miles that keep us apart.

To Shannan Heaman and Bonnie Mead – thank you for your honesty, editorial assistance, and caring input. You were instrumental in helping me put the book into this, it's final form, and made me realize that some things go better left unsaid.

To Bonnie Palmer – you will transform this lengthy document into something beautiful to look at. Your friendship has always meant a lot to me, and I am humbled by your generosity and creative gifts.

To Mireya – *Mamita, vos sos una mujer fuerte como nadie mas que he conocido en mi vida. Nuestras almas son ajuntadas para siempre. Gracias por ser.*

To Danielle – for giving me the final push, and courage, that I needed to hold my head high, keep my spirit calm, and release this.

To all the random people, friends and strangers alike, who encouraged me along the way; who said, "I want a copy!"; and who reassured me that it was an important story to tell – thank you, thank you, thank you.

5309514R0

Made in the USA
Charleston, SC
26 May 2010